Catching the Light

Praise for Catching the Light

Susan Sinnott's novel, Catching the Light*, captures, with wonderful precision, the inner lives of two of the most vivid, richly-realized characters you're likely to come across in a long while. This novel is full of adversity and heartbreak, art and redemption, fear and bravery, and ultimately, love in all its fine shadings, tones, and colours.*

–Lisa Moore, bestselling, award-winning author of *Flannery* and *Caught*

Susan Sinnott's Catching the Light *exhibits the same high level of artistry sought after by her protagonist, Cathy. Perceptive, psychologically intricate, wise, and beautifully written, the book is memorable, above all, for its truth and how it catches the poetry and complexity of everyday life.*

–Ed Kavanagh, author of *The Confessions of Nipper Moony* and *Strays*

Catching the Light *is a novel about perception…a lofty theme grounded in authentic detail, like the grey and unpredictable weather, bologna sandwiches and Cheezies, a small town's proclivity for gossip and solace, and whether Red Rose really makes the best cup of tea.*

–St. John's Telegram

Catching the Light

Susan Sinnott

Vagrant is an imprint of Nimbus Publishing Limited
3660 Strawberry Hill Street, Halifax, NS, B3K 5A9
(902) 455-4286 nimbus.ca

Printed and bound in Canada

NB1282

This story is a work of fiction. Names, characters, incidents, and places, including organizations and institutions, either are the product of the author's imagination or are used fictitiously.

Cover image: *Here and Now*, 40 x 48, oil on canvas, © Katharine Burns, katharineburns.com
Design: Jenn Embree

Library and Archives Canada Cataloguing in Publication

Sinnott, Susan, author
Catching the Light / Susan Sinnott.
Issued in print and electronic formats.
ISBN 978-1-77108-596-0 (softcover).--ISBN 978-1-77108-597-7 (HTML)
I. Title.

PS8637.I635C38 2018 C813'.6 C2017-907957-3
C2017-907958-1

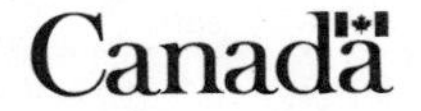

Nimbus Publishing acknowledges the financial support for its publishing activities from the Government of Canada through the Canada Book Fund (CBF) and the Canada Council for the Arts, and from the Province of Nova Scotia. We are pleased to work in partnership with the Province of Nova Scotia to develop and promote our creative industries for the benefit of all Nova Scotians.

To John R.

Prologue

✦

They held the memorial at the Sheppards's church—the one with the red roof on the north side of the harbour. People poured in from everywhere, converging on the scraped and salted car park, heads down into the wind, swivelling necks to greet each other. A whole year. Imagine.

Parking was a challenge once the lot was filled. Some drivers dropped off their passengers first then had to scurry round people to catch up. Latecomers rammed two wheels up snowbanks and wondered if they would get out again. Inside, the shuffling continued well past the appointed hour as the seats filled and the aisles filled and still people were squeezing in at the back.

The school choir was growing restless. Cathy Russell, in the fourth row of the congregation, pulled a pad out of a red quilted bag and sketched the nearest choir members—just a few quick lines but she captured the leg-crossing and sideways looks, the nudges. Then she turned a page and drew the one immobile figure, Hutch Parsons, perhaps because he embodied the real mood in the church. He seemed to be looking beyond the walls to some faraway place, remembering.

The doctor's wife was too far back to see the choir but she would still hear them sing. She was wiping her eyes after Hutch's solo. His voice was pure and mellow and powerful. "Abide with Me." The sound seemed to rise and expand, drawing the tears out of those pale faces, pulling the sorrow up out of the church, up into the clean cold air, and away.

PART ONE

"I could paint the mountains the way they look,
but it isn't how I see them."

—JUSTIN BECKETT, ARTIST

On the Edge

*

June 1995

It was the F word that did it. Fail.

She couldn't tell them. Couldn't tell her parents that Mrs. Elliot asked her to stay behind after class, got up and closed the door. Have a seat, Cathy. And Cathy knew what was coming but couldn't stop it—she'd failed her exams. Last year's teacher just said she hadn't passed, which sounded nicer.

Mrs. Elliot pulled a chair up close. Cathy hunched down over the table between them, traced a groove with her finger—dug with a compass point maybe and filled in with ballpoint. She could feel crumbs from an eraser and pushed them into a pile, swept them onto the floor with the side of her hand. Kids were shouting outside, somebody yelling at Parsons—Cathy's old class.

"Don't you agree, Cathy?"

Cathy took a quick breath and coughed on a bit of chalk dust. She looked up. "Yes, Mrs. Elliot."

The chalk hung in the air, lay like snow on the teacher's green sweater, all down the arm she'd used to clean the board. It had gone into lines in the bend of her elbow. Cathy could paint that. She tried to fix the picture in her head: four long lines spreading out from the front and two short—

"So we have to think what's best for next year."

She didn't want to hear about next year. Mrs. Elliot was going to tell her she'd have to do grade seven again. *Again.* Couldn't bear it. She'd still be in junior high, a mile taller than the rest, kids all calling her Lighthouse, saying how's the weather up there. No hiding being two years older. No hiding being dumb.

She'd been counting the days, minutes, to the end of school, to when she could be at her pictures all day. No more homework with red lines all over, no more saying *don't know* in front of everybody. No being left 'til last when they picked teams—*Cathy's on your side. No, she's not, she's on yours.*

Life stretched out thin and grey and she couldn't see past the greyness. If only she could drop out—and do what? She was no good for anything or anybody. The one thing she could do, wanted to do, was paint. But she needed someone to show her, needed proper paints and boards or canvas or whatever, and she'd never have money for all that, and you couldn't buy them round here anyway. So she was stuck going round and round and—

"Cathy."

Mrs. Elliot was holding out an envelope, saying it would all be sorted out next September. Cathy didn't want to touch that envelope, whatever was inside it. The teacher stood, patting her shoulder, and Cathy went on sitting like a lump.

"Off you go now or you'll miss the bus. And give that to your parents, soon as you get home."

Cathy missed the bus on purpose. She cut behind buildings, out of sight as much as she could, but she had to use the bridge across the Tickle, and Main Road was the only place to walk in some spots so she pulled up her hood, disappearing inside. What was in that letter? Was it even worse than doing grade seven again? What could be worse? The question gnawed at her all the way home.

The road was bending away from the shore past Aunt Joanie's house. Cathy pulled the edges of her hood together so she could only see the pavement in front—head down up the hill and round the bend, fast. Her aunts didn't care that she was dumb, didn't notice. They just thought she was weird because she never played with other kids, didn't Join In. She was A Problem. *It's not healthy being at those pictures all the time. Not normal.*

The sky looked how she felt: grey and dull and saggy. It just sat on your head and squeezed the juice out of everything. Nothing moved down in Mariners Cove, on the wharves or on the water. Even the gulls looked bored. The tears started up again, drying in the wind, so by the time she had walked the six kilometres home to Mariners Head her face had stiffened in stripes. *Can't stay back; won't stay back.* She hid the envelope in a drawer under her paint things.

It was Mom's card night so supper was a rush job, macaroni and cheese, none of the usual questions. Cathy scrunched down and pushed food round her plate, but Mom was flapping about so she didn't notice.

When Cathy said she was going to bed her dad stared at her over the top of his newspaper like he was checking the ocean for signs. Anything wrong? No. She only just made it out of the room before her eyes filled up again. She hated this crying stuff—never used to cry. And in bed with the covers over her head it all got worse and worse. What was she going to do?

And in the hour before dawn, she decided.

+

The sky was a thick purple, a new day with its eyes still closed. Nothing stirred in the houses scattered across Mariners Head until, in the last house up the hill, a door opened. Someone came out, easing it shut with both hands—someone used to the wind having its way with doors. The girl stood for a while, leaning her forehead against the surface, smoothing it with her palms. One finger followed the grooves round the brass knocker her mother polished to perfection every week; the knocker nobody used because they preferred to *hallooo* and walk in.

She pushed herself off and strode away and by the time she reached the road, the day had lightened through indigo to a glorious cobalt blue you could almost see through, almost sail through. At least that was how Cathy usually saw it, though she could never tell you in words, but today she was blind.

She walked with a long-legged swing, unhurried but effective, accustomed to roots and rocks, to being on foot. She picked up the pace where the track met the road, stomped almost, elbows jabbing behind and hands clenched. *Can't stay back. Won't stay back.* She pushed off her hood despite the east wind that sliced and flayed. Cathy was walking up the road to the Mariners Point Light where she went to be alone. To paint. To escape. She usually carried a bag with her paint things but not this time.

She slowed down, arms no longer pumping, legs losing their rhythm. Now every step took effort. She stopped for a while, eyes closed, then started up again in a dragging way. As the sky turned a gold-tinged pink she arrived at the cliffs beyond the lighthouse and looked down into the black depths of ocean eighty feet below.

This was the line between here and there. No landwash, no vague intertidal zone, no undecided. She stood at the edge, a mass of instincts and yearnings and despair, while the dawn painted itself in around her, shade by delicate shade.

A big hairy dog licked her hand and when she jerked and yanked her hand away it barked and sat back with its tongue flapping and all those teeth. Cathy looked round for a stick or something to shoo it away but the new doctor's wife was coming through the spruce, calling to it. Cathy moved back where it was darker, into the trees.

Mrs. Brooks grabbed the dog's collar and stood rubbing its head. "Sorry if he scared you. It's all a big act. He'd only hurt a fly if he sat on it by mistake." She smiled at Cathy, then the smile kind of straightened out and she stared a bit. Maybe seen the tears. Cathy turned away.

Mrs. Brooks half sat on a rock but before she even reached it she was asking questions. Was that where Cathy used to live, that house up there by the lighthouse? Mmm. Did she miss living there? Mmm. Why did they move? And she just sat there waiting for answers. Stayed and stayed. She moved to another rock but she never took her eyes off Cathy.

"They automated the light," Cathy said, scuffing up a bit of peat with one foot. "Said they didn't need a keeper living up here no more."

"I suppose a modern light needs less looking after," Mrs. Brooks said.

"It still needs someone to clear off the snow and ice all the time so you can see it and those new lights don't shine as far as the old ones. And you could put your ear on the new foghorn and it wouldn't even rattle the wax. The old one would take your head off." Cathy had turned towards Mrs. Brooks. "And what happens when the light breaks down? *Oh, it won't break down*, they said. Ha! Broke down three times last winter, always in storms when it was needed most."

Cathy kicked up a few fir cones with her toe and the dog rushed over and pounced on them, shoving its nose through piles of brown needles and moss, then sneezing.

"But don't ships all have that new GPS now?"

"That's what the Coast Guard said. But that boat with engine trouble last fall didn't, with three men aboard. Those two duck hunters didn't. And seamen still want a light they can rely on for backup."

Mrs. Brooks didn't say anything but she was leaning forward, listening. Cathy jabbed her toe at a root. That was the Coast Guard for you. She might have failed her exams all by herself but the Coast Guard had spoiled everything else. Mariners Point Light was her home. They'd lived here always—four generations of Russells. Until last year when she turned thirteen. Until the Coast Guard made them leave.

"They gave Dad a new office but you couldn't even see the ocean. What good's that to a keeper? He quit. Now he's doing biology in St. John's so he's gone altogether, 'cept in the holidays." She had kicked all the dirt off the root so it was starting to shine white along the top. Her voice sank. "First they took my home, then they took my dad."

"How sad."

Cathy shrugged. "Dad was expecting it. Bought the Stuckless place on the Head when the old lady died. It was falling down but it was away from the other houses with a nice bit of land. Spent three years fixing it up. *He* was ready."

The dog came back from wherever covered in mud and rested its drippy chin on Mrs. Brooks's knee. Then it nudged her elbow with its nose, harder and harder until she scratched its foolish ears. But she never took her eyes off Cathy.

"Dad says it's no use regretting. Move on." There was a long pause then she muttered, mostly to herself, "All right for him. He's smart."

Cathy wrapped her arms round herself and stared at her feet. She wished Mrs. Brooks would look away, go away, because she could feel the tears in her chest building and building and any minute now she was going to shame herself and.... A big sob burst out. Couldn't stop it. And she felt arms go round her. She started to push them off but her own arms were trapped, and another sob burst out. The dog was jumping up at them, barking, and making them stagger.

Then Mrs. Brooks was giving Cathy a tissue and telling her to sit on her rock while she leaned on a spiky-looking spruce growing next to it and she was going to get her jacket all sticky from the sap.

"What's wrong, Cathy?" Mrs. Brooks was looking at her, waiting, and after a bit she said, "Tell me. You'll feel better." And she went right on waiting.

"Failed my exams." Cathy blew her nose so hard her ears popped. The pressure disappeared, that pressure in her head and in her chest. She could breathe.

"Oh, I'm so sorry. I remember when I failed math. I was about your age and I didn't want anyone to know, didn't want my parents to see my report card, didn't want to go home even. It felt like the biggest disaster ever."

Cathy nodded. She could feel Mrs. Brooks looking at her but she kept her eyes down and Mrs. Brooks said, "I don't know what I thought my parents would do, but they just said, 'Oh dear, we'll have to do something about this.' So they started helping whenever I was stuck. And I did math homework first instead of leaving it to the last minute." She paused, then said, "I never in my life got a good mark in math but I didn't fail again."

A beam of sunlight slid through a break in the trees. First sun for days. Cathy reached her foot out so the light bent up over her sneaker.

"Don't have much trouble with math." She hiccupped and her eyes prickled again. "It's English and science and social studies...." And all of a sudden the words burst out of her: "Can't even read the questions." She couldn't stop those hiccuppy sobs. She stood up. "Can't even read the stupid questions." Her voice squeaked on that last word and she swallowed hard.

Mrs. Brooks was coming toward her again but Cathy couldn't handle another hug so she turned and began walking up and down, and the only sounds were from the wind and the ocean and her feet rustling through winter's leavings.

She slowed down after a while and stood very still in front of Mrs. Brooks. She looked straight at her. "I can't read."

Mrs. Brooks nodded slowly, then smiled. A warm, friendly smile. "Maybe we can do something about that," and she patted Cathy's arm. Then she looked away for the first time, tried to scrape the moss off another rock, and sat on it. "Not one flat rock anywhere," she said with a laugh. "And this one is probably full of creepy-crawlies with bad habits." She put a hand under her bum on the low side of the rock, levelled herself up. "Has anyone tried to help you read, one on one?"

"What?"

"Just you and a teacher—one you and one teacher," Mrs. Brooks said.

"Oh. No."

Mrs. Brooks went on asking stuff about school and books and what she'd done and not done, on and on.

Partly to stop the questions Cathy said, "Can you help me? Please?"

Mrs. Brooks said she would try but Cathy needed to ask her parents first. She asked about next year and Cathy said she couldn't remember what the teacher said because she hadn't heard half of it. And when she said she hadn't told Mom and Dad that she'd failed, and about the teacher's letter, Mrs. Brooks almost jumped off that rock.

"Oh, Cathy, I know how hard it is—I felt the same way. But your parents will want to know. They'll want to help. And they'll be so hurt if you don't tell them. Why don't you tell them now?" She offered Cathy a ride home but Cathy wanted to walk, wanted to give herself time. But she promised to give her parents the letter.

In the Middle

✶

The teacher was wedging the main entrance open and some of the girls were taking their time, like it was any old day. Hutch didn't mess about: he flew out those doors and down the steps with a big *whoop*. Two steps at a time, three at the bottom. He was in the air before he noticed the puddle. He tried to jackknife himself beyond it, but didn't quite make it. Muddy water sprayed over the nearest girl and she yelled "Hutch Parsons!" in an I'll-get-you kind of voice. He looked over his shoulder—Phyllis Barnes. He hollered a sorry but didn't slow down.

The guys were shouting, "Wait up, Hutch!" and "Where you going, Hutch?" He called back, "Bald Head!" and they clattered into the yellow school bus behind him.

He was wearing his old jean jacket because it was the easiest way to carry it, but it was wide open to the wind. His backpack hung heavy on his shoulders, bulging with binders, loose-leaf, exercise books, the dregs from his locker, and oddments that always showed up on the last day of school when the grade nines brought round the boxes of lost and found. In an outside pocket was his report card. It would be the same old same old: straight As except for English, which might be a C or a B minus. Grammar was such a pain in the ass. There'd be comments about *not using his potential* and *occasional disruptive behaviour* and *could use his leadership qualities in more constructive ways*. He'd open it later.

As they reached Bald Head he could hear the screech of Jack's father's sawmill even over the roar from the bus. The screech died down as they piled out, and there was a wooden clatter as Mr. Sheppard dropped a finished four-by-four on the stack.

"Boys."

Jack called out, "Got a B plus in math, Dad," and the two of them got into the back-slapping bit while the rest dropped their bags inside the shed door. Hutch hauled off his jacket. He breathed in deep through his nose, smelling the wet spruce on the hill, new-cut lumber, and fresh sawdust. There was always sawdust round the mill, squeezed into every crack, clumped in corners. It got in the grooves in your sneakers and stuck to your laces and socks.

The boys raced each other up the track next to the gully, letting loose all their done-with-grade-eight steam. They ran flat-out lower down and slower and slower up the long steep curve until they were doubled over, gasping. Hutch and Andy made it the furthest. Hutch had a stitch in his side, sweat running down inside his shirt, and his legs burned. But it felt great. He was so sick of being folded up at a desk, half dead. Sometimes he would ask to go to the bathroom just to stretch his legs. Then he would walk fast up and down the corridor, run on the spot, do jumping jacks. He'd sneak out the door for a breath of fresh air when there was nobody around.

Hutch stretched up tall, spread his arms wide, and the wind knifed through him, chilling the sweat. He didn't care. He could feel his blood pumping into the furthest corners. The cold air scraped in and out of his lungs, scouring out the stale stuff. All the guys had caught up now saying wow and doing high-fives and they did the last lap at a walk. Next time he'd run all the way up.

Above the trees from the scrubby top of the hill you could see all around, even though visibility wasn't the best today. Over there they'd go trouting—and there, and there. Clouds hid the start of it, but over on the left was his favourite trail round the cliffs. Out of sight the other way was Uncle Em's pond, where Hutch and his dad had taken Hutch's boat last weekend; a sea kayak he'd built all by himself over the winter: *Dolphin.* They would put it in the water to test it. Maybe tomorrow. There was the harbour, and beyond that the bay, with all the ins and outs and sunkers and little islands with places to stop for a picnic and places to avoid because of the current. They'd check out every inch, maybe right out past the last buoy and along the coast on a good day. Couldn't wait.

Hutch chose a flattish bit and flopped down on the weedy, stony slope and lay back, looking up into all that space. Freedom. All summer. He watched a gull bank and glide.

Yesssssss.

The Letter

✶

When she left Mrs. Brooks, Cathy walked home the other way, more out of sight. The track dove through the woods down the steps and sometimes she stopped and stared out through the trees. A leaf in front of her nose suddenly popped open. Didn't know they could change so fast. Her dad made videos of those nature things—flowers growing and opening. They were a bit jerky but she had always thought that was because of pieces of film being joined together, thought flowers just kind of unrolled and stood up straight.

This leaf was a bud, all sticky on the outside, with the sticky stuff keeping everything tucked in. Then something popped and now it was like a little hand. Still hadn't opened all its fingers but it was a leaf now, not a bud. It must have built up such a need to grow that it just burst through the glue in one big jerk. Cathy reached for her drawing stuff but it wasn't there. Frig.

✶

She gave her father the letter while they were still at breakfast and he read it out loud. It said she'd failed, that she couldn't read. He stopped and there was not a sound in the house. When Cathy sneaked a look, her mom and dad were staring at each other, not at her. Her father looked…well, the same way he looked when he saw the weather outside and knew for sure his hunting trip was off. And her mother's chin was wobbling and she jumped up and gave Cathy such a big hug that the chair creaked.

"Never mind, my love," she said. "It doesn't matter."

And the hug was wonderful and Cathy felt comforted, but it did matter. It did.

Dad shouldn't have been surprised. He knew she'd failed last year. And Cathy always had to ask him the names in his bird books, although maybe he just thought it was the Latin—she'd never made herself tell him she couldn't read any of it. If he'd said, *Cathy, can you read?* she'd have told him, but he never did.

Cathy stared at her knees, rubbed at a mark on her jeans. Now the letter was going to say she was the dumbest kid in the school. Dad leaned over and put his hand on her shoulder and said they'd work on this over the summer. Oh, god. Should she tell them about Mrs. Brooks? But her throat was too tight to say anything.

He started reading again and there was a load of stuff about children learning at their own pace and having special help when needed—yeah, right—but at least it made it sound as if there were other kids like Cathy. And something about schools in small communities, but they would do what they could when Cathy moved to grade eight in September.

Grade Eight. September.

Cathy stopped breathing. Then she let out a big yell and leaped up so her chair fell over and her mother said *eek* and her father said *shit, Cathy*, and he never said shit. She ran out of the house and charged up the track and back down again because she couldn't keep still. She'd be in grade eight and Mrs. Brooks was going to help and look what she nearly did. Look what she nearly *did.*

Come From Away

*

The doorbell rang a hundred times that first day. Sarah Brooks kept saying don't take off your shoes but they all did, and piles of footwear and jackets mounted in the porch because she still hadn't found the box with the coat hangers. It was mostly the housewives, all looking much older than Sarah's thirty-three years except for two with toddlers in tow. And one brought a garrulous old man for an outing—grandfather or uncle or neighbour. He had trouble with his top teeth so now and then a guillotine would drop down and chop off a sentence.

Sarah would never sort out who was who. This is my aunt on my mother's side. I'm married to her husband's cousin. Not Browne with an e now, they're over on the west coast.

Names were so different here: not the familiar Eastern European names of Saskatchewan, but Powell and Parsons and White and all those red-headed Sheppards who flickered through the crowd at a barbecue the following week like a fire run amok. Stephanie Sheppard waltzed high-piled dishes round unpredictable elbows, pointing out her son Jack who stood with a group of youths. Not that he needed much pointing with those transparent eyebrows and electric orange hair.

May Parsons's son, Hutch, was in the middle of that group with Jack. Less noticeable at first: brown hair, brown eyes, medium everything. But as he turned towards her, Sarah saw the animation in his face, the one-sided grin that widened and narrowed constantly like an electronic line measuring energy, ending in a pothole in his left cheek. Paul Wilson, next to him, was handsomer, a real Viking, but she'd bet Hutch would cause more trouble in the henhouse.

Now and then there would be a wave of laughter from outside, the kind of big-hearted laugh that made you join in even if you hadn't heard the joke. Eugene, they said. That was Eugene. Next one up in age from Jack. Six Sheppard brothers and only one girl! Yes, the Hills have all the girls. You met Cathy up at the lighthouse? Her mother's a Hill.

They all introduced Sarah as the doctor's wife and maybe that was natural. At least teaching Cathy would give her another role. It would be easier when she was a mom. A mom would fit in. Everyone was so welcoming here, with doors wide open from Day One, but the space they made for you inside was a Mariners Cove shape.

Step One

*

Cathy told her parents about Mrs. Brooks the day after they saw the letter—at least Cathy said about her wanting to come over for a chat. Her mom was pleased. She'd been upset with Cathy that other time, back when the doctor first arrived.

That had been the Victoria Day long weekend, and Cathy was out at her pictures on the rock face behind the house. She liked to start early because of the light, and because the wind picked up in the afternoon. Mid-morning Mr. and Mrs. Brooks parked their Bronco on the hill near the track and walked off, must have been all round Mariners Head. When they came back they stood looking her way, then walked up the track and asked if they could look at her paintings, asked had she done the pictures up at the lighthouse too. They both said how great they were, especially the people pictures.

When Cathy wandered into the kitchen her mother was lifting pies out of the oven, hands in those big green oven mitts with black cat faces.

"Was that the new doctor and his wife you were talking to?" her mother said. "You should have invited them in." There was a pause and Mom looked at Cathy as if she was waiting for something. "So what did they say?"

The warm fruit-and-pastry smell was making Cathy's mouth water. The pies looked pleasingly plump, as Mom liked to say, only she was more than plump now—too many pies. They wore off-the-shoulder frills like that dress of her cousin Annie's, and one pie looked end-of-winter pale. Missed it with the egg white.

"Cathy? Answer me."

"Liked my paintings."

"Is that all you talked about?"

Yes. Well, the woman said their names. Brooks. Cathy couldn't remember the rest.

Mom sighed.

+

Wednesday, Mom knew all about them. She'd been down to see the new doctor. Not that Mom was sick, she just liked an outing. She always went to old Dr. Powell on Wednesdays, before he had that stroke.

"He's Dr. Timothy James Brooks. Nice. Big and quiet. Nice smile. And he listens, doesn't rush you out."

She rattled around in the cupboard for her mixing bowl and grumbled about not being able to reach things because she was so short. Ten times this week. Hundred times this month. "And his wife's name's Sarah. Came in for a few minutes. Little scrap of a thing with wrists like wishbones. She'll be gone over the cliffs in a good blow. And all that dark hair."

"Beautiful hair," Cathy said. "Black, but not dead black. Loads of life in that hair. Love to paint it. Colours in the black: blues and reds, even green."

"Oh, Cathy," said Mom and sighed again.

They all sighed like that, 'specially her teacher. Like the day of that big thunderstorm when Cathy was watching the clouds—beautiful, how the light through that crack in the cloud split into lines and spread out. Strong to travel all that way, but could be gone in a blink. The lines spread out like the sounds Mom's best glasses made when you dinged them with a spoon, each sound a bit different, so if you dinged them quickly enough they all rang together like a…like a tune. Each line of light had its own voice. One line touched a spiderweb wobbling in the corner of the window and lit it. Now, *that* she could paint—or try to, anyway. She wished she could paint the out-of-this-world light. Was there a way to do it? Did someone out there know? Could—

"Cathy."

It was Mrs. Elliot standing over her. "Cathy, I'm going to move you away from the window because it's too much…you'll never learn if you don't listen."

Mrs. Elliot sighed. Cathy dragged her stuff over to the empty chair under the blackboard, flopped down, and stretched her legs out in the aisle.

"And tuck your legs under the table please, out of the way." Another Mrs. Elliot sigh.

They all did it: the teachers, her mom, the aunts—the Big Sigh. Like part of her name, Cathy-Sigh-Russell.

+

Cathy saw Mrs. Brooks arriving but kept out of the way until Dad showed up—hung around the kitchen door. She could hear her saying *what a lovely house* and Mom telling her about how Dad had to knock it down, all but the chimney, and start over.

"Poor old Mrs. Stuckless lived here with the place fallin' down round her. The family tried to help but she wouldn't let anyone in with a hammer. Said leave her alone, she'd be gone by next week. Said it for years."

Mom brought out her partridgeberry muffins, said she bet they didn't have these in Saskatchewan. The cat got interested then, all lined up towards the plate, ready for a quick snatch but looking off to the side just to fool you. Didn't fool Mom. Mom swatted her down off the chair some fast and the cat screeched, then got huffy, and took her time leaving with that stiff walk, tail up, nose in the air. Cathy's pencil fingers twitched. Better not.

Then Dad came in and parked his great boots next to Mrs. Brooks's tiny things by the door. One big gulp and they'd have them gone. Cathy wanted to draw the boots with their tongues hanging out, lining themselves up like the cat, but Mom called out, "Cathy. Where are you?" So she had to go in and be polite.

Mom kept right on talking and the rest of them just sat there. Did Sarah like old Doctor Powell's place? Such a nice big house to have children in and she'd always thought that old maple out the back was a great spot for a swing and there weren't as many children around now as there used to be but Mariners Cove was better than a lot of outports where there was nobody under fifty. Any other time Cathy would have switched off, only she was waiting for Mrs. Brooks to say something. Waiting and waiting.

Finally, Mom stopped for a drink of tea and Mrs. Brooks said, "When I bumped into Cathy the other day we got talking about school and studying and reading and things." Mrs. Brooks was looking from Dad to Mom and back again. Dad sat up straighter. "I said practicing reading might make schoolwork easier and Cathy asked if I'd help her. And I said I would. I hope you don't mind. In fact I've come to ask your permission to coach her over the summer."

Dad went all stiff like the cat and Cathy held her breath. He looked over at her mom but she was staring down at her hands, turning her rings round and round, then he looked at Cathy.

"Would you like that?"

Cathy nodded. Dad kept looking at her as if he really wanted to make sure, but she couldn't make any words come out so she nodded again, harder.

"I'll be around more this summer so I could help?" Dad said.

Oh, god. He was upset she hadn't asked him.

"I know I wasn't around much last summer, what with trying to finish the house and moving and starting at Memorial. This summer will be easier."

"Dad would be real good. He used to…" Mom's voice trailed off and the rings were flying round now and she was scrunched down smaller in the chair and Dad was looking over at her, all worried.

"I don't want to interfere," Mrs. Brooks said. "I'm sure you'd be a lot better than me at this. And I studied English, not education. I only agreed to try to help because I have loads of time on my hands and…well, Cathy is so talented and I'd love to help if I could."

"What do you think, Cathy?" That was Dad.

"Both." Cathy looked and looked at her dad, trying to make him understand how much she wanted this. "I want both of you to help. Please?"

Dad nodded and got a bit less stiff. He turned to Mrs. Brooks again and said, "And what would you charge for this?"

"Oh, my goodness." Mrs. Brooks went red in the face and her hands came up as if someone had thrown something. "Nothing at all. I don't want…. Just something worthwhile to do."

"Just thought I should ask," Dad said. "It's very kind of you."

Mom got up and passed the muffins round again and the plate was shaking and they all slid sideways. Mrs. Brooks took one and said how delicious they were and she would love the recipe and Mom got even more fidgety and said she didn't have one and you just added a bit of this and that but you needed two cups of berries. They were no good if you were stingy with the berries.

Mrs. Brooks said they must have had a lot of *whatever* to pack up when they moved out of the lighthouse. She and Tim had had such a lot in their little apartment in Toronto. She couldn't imagine the amount you must *whatever* in a whole house after a hundred years or so.

"You should see the boxes of charts and books Mel has. Eighty or more." Mom sounded more like herself, though she was still twiddling with her rings. Then they kept talking about those old logs and big dusty books, Dad starting to say something about sea stories like *Moby-Dick* and *Treasure Island.*

Mom said, "Oh, Mel used to..." all excited, then stopped. And there was a little gap in the talk.

"Want to get everything onto shelves in that back room." Dad said and went on and on about those shelves and it was not like Dad to talk so much.

Things were back to normal by the time Mrs. Brooks left, though Dad put his arm round Mom after and said it was okay. Everything would be okay. And Mom said she had a headache and needed a cup of tea.

Jumpin's, it was Cathy who needed the cup of tea.

+

So lessons started and Cathy sat on her bed sounding out her list of words for the week over and over, writing them down in lowercase letters and reading them back to herself. Mom would come and shut the bedroom door.

Once, Cathy started reading aloud at the kitchen table, a bit of *Ramona the Brave* she'd been having trouble with that now she could read okay. She thought Mom would be pleased. Mom was cooking but she turned everything off and just left it all half done and walked off down into Mariners Cove all without saying a word.

Another time Dad told her not to say *Sarah says* anymore because it was getting on Mom's nerves. So she didn't. She really didn't. But her mom still went up in smoke when Cathy told her she was putting too much salt in the stew—started banging cupboard doors as she put things away.

"This is how I make my stew." *Thump.* "This is how my mother makes her stew." *Thump.* "This is how Dad likes it and I like it and everybody else likes it." Plates banging together—and Mom got mad when you did that because it chipped them. "And I'm not changing the amount of salt I use just because Mrs. Clever Brooks doesn't do it like that."

Cathy started to explain it was just that she'd seen the tiny amount Sarah put in hers and asked her about it, but Dad shook his head at her over his newspaper so she stopped.

+

Mom had a funny look on her face the day Sarah came to the house to see how she cooked her fish and brewis, like when somebody says the temperature is going up to seventeen degrees but you know it'll never happen because the wind is steady in the east. Sarah had asked her for the recipe—told Mom Cathy had praised her fish and brewis to the ceiling, so Sarah wanted to try her hand at it. Mom didn't have a recipe, said just come and see.

"Cathy. Go paint."

That was her mom when Sarah arrived. Cathy wasn't even allowed to stay in the house so she never knew how it went, didn't see Sarah leave. But Mom had a different look on her face afterwards—the same look she'd had after she sold that leaf rug to some tourist who was all gushy about how clever Mom was with her fingers, how artistic.

Mom told Dad she gave Sarah some of that good salt cod Em Parsons had given him. Hoped he didn't mind. Said someone had given Sarah a recipe for salt cod and bananas. Imagine. Bananas! Must've been a mainlander.

Mom wasn't as upset about Cathy's lessons after that.

Starting Point

✶

Cathy was a challenge, no question. Sarah called her teacher friends for tips. Motivation wasn't an issue here but what if there was a learning disability she wasn't equipped to handle? Sarah talked with the friend in psychology about how the brain decodes the written word, and fervently hoped Cathy's problems were nothing more than being left behind in school.

How could a girl who saw so much, learn so little? Sarah wondered about hearing loss but Cathy said her mother had asked Dr. Powell to test her hearing back in grade six and it was perfect. Yes. Most of us displayed selective hearing now and then, but Cathy seemed to have grown a soundproof shell.

Yet she noticed such visual detail in the world around her. On their rambles through Mariners Cove, Cathy always had her pencil out. She would draw anything—a strip of plastic trapped between rocks, barnacles under a wharf, waves just being wavy. Ocean-sized talent.

"Let's talk about them instead," Sarah said. "Tell me what you see when you draw."

But Cathy had no words for what she saw.

So one rainy morning Sarah plonked herself and Cathy down on her chesterfield in front of a painting by an artist from home in Regina. It was all movement and colour and she asked Cathy to describe it. For minutes she listened to the two of them breathing, which was encouraging in its way, but finally Sarah said, "So what is it?"

"A market."

"What else?"

One shrug. Two shrugs.

"Is it around here?"

No. Sarah asked how Cathy knew. The colours were all wrong. And the fruit was different, on those tables. And the clothes. Beards. Bare feet. Sandals. Yes. It was Tunis in North Africa, and there followed a session with an atlas and a Sarah Brooks monologue, a Condensed History of Tunis. Any questions? No.

"So what strikes you most about that picture?"

"Noise."

"Really! Oh, I agree with you but I thought you'd say colours."

Cathy said yes, noise and colours, and Sarah said tell her more about the noise. It was shouting all piled up, like school only louder. And the wheels on that cart. And hens. And that donkey braying. One big racket.

"So tell me about the colours," Sarah said.

They were straight-out-of-the-tube colours. Thick, strong, and in your face. Not mixed. Edges real clear. Different from home. Everything home was in-between colours, running into each other, thin and smudgy. Cathy had been leaning forwards more and more but now she looked round at Sarah. "I'd like to paint in Tunis."

Art had kept the world out, but perhaps art could let the world back in.

Step Two

*

Her first lessons were nearly all reading. Cathy said she didn't need writing as well but Sarah said of course she did. It was reading the other way round. How could she start passing exams if she couldn't write down what she knew?

Sarah gave her a hardcover notebook and said start writing a journal. Cathy picked it up and put it down a few times. So many empty pages. There was no help from an all-white page, not even a few words to start you off: *complete this sentence....* The book didn't even want to stay open. Cathy had to stretch it out, flattening the pages so they creased along the binding. She gripped the pencil, wound her legs round each other, and hunched down over the first page.

MUNDY MONING

Sarah said don't worry about grammar or spelling for now. Just try to put your thoughts down in straight lines. But Cathy's thoughts floated round in lumps. She gripped her pencil tighter. She could write about that art book Sarah had given her—a discard from Gander Library.

I LIK SARAS BK

Mostly Cathy just looked at the pictures but she did try the two-colour thing—a lighter crayon for the lit-up parts and a darker one for the shade. She used yellow and brown and drew bowls and shiny stuff round the house. She'd tried changing the source of light but her mom got upset when Cathy moved the lamps. Had to be careful not to stretch cords across places because Mom walked through one last week and the lamp fell over and broke the shade.

That was two sides filled. Cathy put her head in her hands, dug her nails into her scalp to let the steam out, then looked sideways at the clock by her bed. Thirty minutes was enough.

+

She was early at Sarah's so Cathy sat cross-legged on the picnic table and read over those two journal pages. Then the dog was circling the table, barking, and Sarah came out.

"May I have a look?"

May I. Nobody said that round here. Can I. Let's have a look.

"Wonderful, Cathy. Some great thoughts. Now, how about breaking them up into bite-sized pieces—a period maybe here and here? Easier to read. And lowercase letters, please." The phone rang and Sarah said sorry, she was expecting a long-distance call.

Cathy closed the journal and drew that big maple on its front cover. The cover was a creamy beige colour with a cloth feel to it, like the book was still in its underwear. She studied the shape of the tree, how the branches came off, how the whole tree bent left above the roof where the wind caught it. She was doing the twigs when Sarah came out.

"That was my sister," she said. "She has exciting news—she's expecting a baby." Sarah had a funny look on her face, kind of pulled in. Her voice was all bright and cheerful but her face wasn't. "And only married in the fall."

How could she draw that? Cathy tried to see what had changed—the mouth mainly, only Sarah turned away before Cathy could fix it in her head and when she turned back again she was wearing a wedding-picture smile.

+

Sarah laid a little notebook on the picnic table and a big dark red book like a Bible with gold letters on the front. She said she wasn't too concerned about spelling but maybe they could look up one or two words in the dictionary each session and they'd start a list of words Cathy had trouble with in her journal, like *journal* and *thought.*

She pushed the book over and waited and Cathy stared at it, not touching it, and the silence went on and on so in the end she had to say she didn't know how to use a dictionary.

The next few days she was saying the alphabet to herself over and over, faster and faster, because the words Sarah made her look up all had a ton of letters.

~~Ogust~~ August 22 1995

Tht 2 color stuf is grt fr trees aftr its ~~raned~~ rained.

It would be even better when the snow came and the snow stuck to one side and blew off the other. Every twig would show up. But Cathy wanted to show the mood of the tree, not just a copy with every hair in place. Mood was one of those words they had talked about.

Mood: noun: *a temporary state of mind.*

She hated it when the dictionary used a bunch more words she didn't know and she had to look them up too. She ended up with so many fingers marking so many places that she ran out of fingers. Her father's dictionary was big and heavy and sometimes her fingers came out feeling nish.

Sarah dusnt no the ~~wurd~~ word nish. She shud luk it up in the dictionary.

Mood: noun: *a temporary state of mind.*

Temporary: she knew that one. Like jobs that didn't last.

State: noun. Cathy thought state meant mess because her mom always said, "Look at the state you're in: your hair, your room, your sneakers." But state just meant how things were. So *mood* was a temporary *state* of mind like feeling great or feeling down. But that didn't work for a tree.

Cathy stopped and wiggled her fingers. She was trying to write lightly but she pressed even harder for lowercase letters and it took longer.

More studying meant less time to paint but if it meant she'd be able to paint better in the future, Cathy didn't care. If she could start passing exams maybe she could get a job one day, have money to buy paints, pay for art lessons.

Mostly Cathy skimmed through the writing in Sarah's art book, but she liked the look of "Gesture Drawings" so she forced herself through that part, looked up enough words to get the idea. It was like walking through woods with no path: some words were so matted together you had to go round or start chopping.

Just a few quick lines and those gesture drawings could show where the weight went down to the base and the direction of movement. Cathy drew Mom's cat, Missy, stretched up tall because she was checking out a bird on the window ledge so she was only sitting on a small bit of bum. The bird flew away and the cat sank back and you could see the weight spread out, more bum touching the ground. Cathy drew her again. The cat started licking her feet. Trust the cat to act like she didn't care.

Gesture drawings were great for moving targets, like baseball players and figure skaters on TV. Hockey players moved too fast. She went down by White's store and drew everyone who came by, leaning against the clapboard near the door, bending one knee up so her foot was flat on the concrete below, then resting the pad on her knee. Nobody took any notice until Ma Tucker wanted to see and got upset.

"Well, I know I'm big, Cathy, but you've made me look like a house."

"I'm just showing where the weight goes. I'm not trying—"

"Don't you talk to me about weight! That's ignorance that is. Pure ignorance." And Cathy's mother knew all about it by lunchtime.

+

August 25 1995

Mood: noun: *the atmosphere or overall tone of something.* Sarah was surprised Cathy knew the word atmosphere. Jumpins, you didn't grow up in a lighthouse without knowing about atmosphere. Sarah said people could make atmospheres too and Cathy said yes, some guys were big atmospheric disturbances like that smartass, Hutch Parsons.

She'd sketched him and his crowd in their kayaks last week but she had to draw fast before they got too far away. Usually that was where she liked Parsons—far away and going farther. Funny, she drew most of the kayakers in two gestures: one for the person and one for the boat. But with Parsons she drew everything in one gesture. Maybe it was because most of them looked like they were just sitting in boats, separate from them. Parsons looked like part of his, like he'd grown out of its bones.

August 26 1995

Mood: noun: *the atmosphere or overall tone of something.*

Tone: noun.

There was a load of stuff about tone but most of it was no good for trees. Voice blah blah, music blah blah. Sarah said don't get sidetracked by the blah-blahs until you need them. Sidetracked was something to do with trains going the wrong way. Where was she?

Tone: noun: *the general character of something.*

Yes. The *mood* of the tree was the general character of the tree. Cathy wanted to draw the snarl in that bark's face that looked like it wanted to grab you, and those soft branches on the larch that looked like they wanted to give you a hug.

+

Sometimes they walked miles during lessons, talking. Sarah said getting used to hearing words and using them in conversation helped reading too. Often Cathy was so tired after those walks she had to lie down and close her eyes—not leg-tired; brain-tired. Sarah said yes, think of it as a marathon. Her brain had to cover miles of thinking as fast as it could because the rest of the class was way up ahead. But she'd catch up. She said Cathy hadn't shown any signs of this *whatever* where your brain was screwed up—couldn't see letters in the right order or something. Cathy hadn't realized there was such a thing.

So as they walked they talked about Mariners Cove and people and boats and weather and things on the radio. And why did Sarah not have a better name for Dog? Well, he was a stray, too old to learn new tricks. They'd tried—all kinds of literary names like Huckleberry and Oliver and Ishmael. Sarah wrote them down for her afterwards. And Ulysses, which was Dr. Brooks's favourite because he could abbreviate it to Hey U. But their big hairy mutt only ever answered to "Dog."

Sarah asked questions about everything. One day it was the names of birds.

"Cormorant," said Cathy.

"Whole sentence please."

"That is a cormorant."

"What do you know about them?"

Well, they were big and they sat low in the water and you could pick them out when they flew in a V because their V was so messy. Great in the water. No good in the air.

"What's it doing?

"Drying its wings. It is drying its wings. Must've went diving for fish."

"It must have *gone* diving for fish."

"Dad says *went* diving." They walked out of sight of the cormorant.

"I expect when he's writing an exam he'll put *must have gone diving*."

The Gang

✶

As they rounded the point in their kayaks, the boys saw three cormorants take off, struggling to get airborne and looking as if they'd crash any minute. There were people on the shore behind: Sarah Brooks and the Lighthouse.

"Joined at the hip these days," Jack said. His boat was just ahead of Hutch's. "See them together everywhere."

"Look like a bat and a ball," said Hutch and the guys cracked up. "And she is kind of batty—the Lighthouse, I mean."

"Don't let Jenny hear you say that." Jack glanced back at him. "Cathy's in her class now and Jenny looks after her. She'd have your head."

"So what else is new. Your sister's always having my head for something."

"And you're always innocent of course." That was Paul on his other side, paddling with Bud.

Jenny Sheppard was off doing something with her mother that day so she wasn't behind Jack in Dad's old double kayak as usual. Andy was there instead. So it was an all-guy group today, which wasn't usual either. There was often a girl or two wanting to come with them, which was fun although it slowed them down, and Hutch preferred it when he could paddle all-out, all of the time. Jenny never slowed them down.

He urged *Dolph* ahead now, pulling hard to outstrip the others, and a song welled up from deep inside—nothing particular, just berm-berm-berm—but it fit the rhythm of the ocean, the mood of the day.

But he couldn't maintain the burst and his arms were screaming and the others caught up, telling him he was a show-off, and he had no breath left for a comeback.

It was their last chance for the core crowd to kayak together before Paul and Bud went back to St. John's on Labour Day. Bud Powell was a year older than the rest and going into grade ten, changing schools. Hutch never really thought of him as a townie because his parents were from here and he and Bud had played together all the time as toddlers. But Bud's father taught at the university so they'd lived in St. John's forever during the school year.

Paul was different. He was a real townie, but he was okay in spite of that. His parents taught in the History Department with Dr. Powell and had started coming to Mariners Cove with them years ago. Bought a place from one of Hutch's uncles. Paul played soccer with them and was on an all-star hockey team in town—he was a good guy.

They paddled round the last buoy and headed back, Hutch's strokes growing more and more ragged. A gull glided ahead of them with just a dip of the wings now and then to keep it on course. Hutch would hit the weights all this winter to build himself up for the next season. He wanted to be as smooth as that gull.

Step Three

✦

Sarah said let's work on listening, the other side of conversation. She had this recording of two people talking and they listened for five minutes then Sarah said she'd be the interviewer asking the questions and Cathy would be the interviewee answering. Let's see how much they could remember. Never mind if she didn't understand some of the words. She could guess. They'd go back to them later.

"But we're just testing memory, not listening," Cathy said.

"How can we remember what people say if we don't hear it first?"

And that was it. Cathy didn't listen to Mrs. Elliot because she kept talking about things they'd done before which she hadn't listened to, so this new bit didn't make sense. And she didn't listen to her mother because Mom always went the long way round. And she didn't listen to her cousins because they just talked about stupid stuff like clothes and boys.

August 31 1995

Sarah says jus bcos im not intrested in what sumbodys torking about dusnt ~~meen~~ mean I dont have to lisen its part of shairing giv and tak

"If you want people to listen when you talk about painting," Sarah said, "it's only fair that you listen to them talking about clothes or what they did on Saturday night."

"But I don't want to talk about painting. Nobody ever understands. Nobody cares."

"Do you think you're the only person in the world who likes pictures?"

"You and Paul Wilson maybe. But you're different and Paul..." Cathy turned away. Kids asked to look at her pictures and said "wow" and stuff, but Paul was the only one who really *saw* them the way Cathy saw them. And he took real art classes in St. John's and was even thinking of going to art school after grade twelve. She'd love to talk pictures with Paul but—in her dreams. Mostly he just said hello. But she didn't say any of that to Sarah.

+

Sarah started asking for a look at Cathy's sketches whenever she finished a pad.

"Why don't you draw your mother?" she said one time. "You have four marvellous pictures of your father here and none of your mom."

The first reason that popped up was that Mom was such a fidget and she always wanted to see what Cathy was doing before she'd done it. It drove Cathy crazy. But it was more than that: Mom was a little ball of doing, of bustle. She was a voice Cathy didn't listen to, a pair of hands in the kitchen.

"Not sure I can draw her."

"Just draw what you see, like you always do."

So Cathy drew her mother's hands: in the dishpan, hooking a rug, peeling potatoes. She drew her back-on, stirring something on the stove, and side-on, reaching into the washing machine.

Once she drew her aunts playing Auction from a photograph: Aunt Maisie and Aunt Joan like squashy pillows; Aunt Elsie, showing her gums when she laughed and waving her cards around; Aunt Gert with her mouth turned down and her chest stuck out so Cathy went back and stuck a helmet on her and armour like a Roman soldier from some Bible picture she remembered. Aunt Dot with her cards almost touching her nose because she'd forgotten her glasses again. But nothing of Mom.

Now and then Mom talked about needing glasses but she never did anything about it. Said she didn't have trouble seeing cards or cross-stitch. It was the newspaper she complained about the most, *all that small print*, and she was always asking Dad or Dot to read things out. She said reading by yourself wasn't neighbourly, that it was more friendly with two people—two people thinking about the same thing. And anyway, how could she hold a newspaper when she always had her hands full?

+

Dad had Cathy reading to him from newspapers sometimes and from the easy parts of his bird books. He said his other books would have to wait a while. All through his time at Memorial, he took her on day trips when he was home for the summers. He'd asked her in the past and she'd always said no, couldn't drag those old paint cans with her—marine paint, masonry paint, latex, auto paint, rust proofing—any outside paint or stain left in her dad's shed. She still used those for rocks and walls but now she used fancy tubes or oil pastels on paper when she had them, crayons sometimes, pencils when she'd run out. When supplies were really low, the pencil stubs got so short she had to dig her fingernails in to steady them the way the old guys made a cage of their fingers round a cigarette. Every gift was picture stuff. The aunts said it was never a problem shopping for Cathy. A packet of crayons was nothing compared to the brand-name clothes their daughters wanted.

Cathy loved being dug in somewhere with no people for miles, watching the change in the light as the sun moved across the sky, how it changed colours and brought out the yellow in things. She saw how it lit the near side of every leaf, every wrinkle and whisker, making a tiny shadow on the far side, like a mini landscape. When the sun went behind a cloud and the light went out, the leaf went flat.

It was great watching the wildlife and picking out birdcalls. She tried counting the different mosses but it was too hard after five or six—the differences were small and it was no good sticking a bit in a baggie because by the time she got it home to look it up it had shrivelled into something different. Grasses were beautiful swaying in the wind, but they turned drab after you picked them.

Drab: adjective: *lacking brightness or interest; dull and dreary.*

After their first day trip, Cathy began packing her small dictionary because Dad used new words and made her work them out. He was as bad as Sarah for that. Said he was using different words *deliberately* so she'd be *familiar* with them. Didn't talk like that other days. Maybe he'd read all those fat books in the back room.

She listed the mosses in her little notebook and Dad made her read them back to him and seemed pleased when she could remember which bit of moss went with which name. Said Mom had had trouble with that. And Cathy wanted to ask what he meant but Dad saw something over in the trees and was getting his camera ready and saying hush, so she never did.

A rabbit. That was a rabbit—a snowshoe hare, Dad called it. It bounded between two clumps of trees, back legs going past the front ones, muscles all bunched up then stretched out, rippling with life. Rippling was Dad's word. She knew what it meant but it was only when she saw a hare in action that she could see how well it fit something that wasn't water.

Later she saw one Dad had snared, hanging up by its back feet, dead. No ripple. The muscles just sagged down; elastic that would never go tight again. Dad said paint that, she could still copy the way the fur lay, the shape of the bones. But it was missing the spark. It was *drab* without the spark; the aliveness was what she wanted to paint, that *something* inside that said, "wheee, I'm me!"

And when she said that to Dad, in fits and starts because she wasn't sure of the words, he put his arm round her shoulders and said yes, he knew just what she meant. And it was so nice to have someone say they knew what she meant in that way, as if she'd said something special, something clever, that she felt tears in the back of her throat but she didn't let them up.

+

After Cathy started lessons with Sarah, Mom didn't mind hearing her saying a Dad word in the house and explaining what it meant—like when Cathy said it was a drab day—but she didn't want to hear Sarah words.

"Well, Cathy, I'm pleasingly plump all the time and that's how I like it. I don't want to be 'plump' on Mondays and 'chubby' on Tuesday and 'well-padded' the rest of the week and anyway that sounds like a chesterfield and I don't like you talking about me to Sarah Brooks like that and—"

"We weren't talking about you, we were talking about *words.* I just said pleasingly plump because you say it all the time."

"Well, I say it to you and Dad but I wouldn't say it to her so don't talk to her about things I say."

"Well, okay."

"Now don't get snippy with me. And don't go scowling. You'll get wrinkles."

And the timer went off and Mom gave a little squawk and said the gravy was going lumpy and go away, leave me alone when I'm cooking.

+

On Labour Day Dad went back to Memorial for his second year and he wouldn't be back until mid-term break. When Cathy's own school year started, Sarah cut back their lessons to three or four times a week after school, and said she would give Cathy a ride home afterwards.

Cathy walked into her very first grade eight class early, head up and ready to start. She sat at the front because Sarah had said there would be fewer distractions at the front. Mrs. Elliot was their homeroom teacher again this year and she smiled right at Cathy and said it was nice to see her back. It was not just the everyday smile she gave to the whole class and her eyebrows didn't go up in that fed-up way they sometimes did when she looked at Cathy and she didn't sigh once. It made Cathy feel like she was getting somewhere, even before she'd started. And after a month or so, Mrs. Elliot said how much better her schoolwork was and to keep it up.

If she stared at her desk all the time it was easier to keep her mind on listening. Only in science class, Mr. Roberts said look at him when he was speaking and his moustache had something stuck in it and by the end of class it had worked its way down to the bottom of the bristles and was hanging there and Cathy just kept waiting for it to drop. She only heard half of what he said and had to ask Jenny Sheppard what he'd given them for homework. They had a giggle over a moustache being a funny place to keep leftovers. Sarah had said pick someone nice to ask stuff if she had a problem and Jenny was the nicest. But it didn't happen often, now. Her listening muscles were getting stronger all the time.

Summer

*

Hutch was heading over to the soccer field at the school for a scratch game, three days after the end of grade nine, when he saw Mrs. Brooks and Cathy Russell meeting up with Dr. Brooks at the bottom of their road. Nice woman, Sarah Brooks. Nice couple. They came for supper sometimes with Mom and Dad and once last year they'd asked Hutch to show them his boat. He'd taken them down to the shed and they'd asked about the kind of wood and said how important it must be to avoid knots and how long did the planks have to soak before they'd bend the right amount. Sensible questions. Dr. Brooks had done river kayaking in Ontario. Later they bought a double from Dad and Hutch would often see them paddling round the harbour at sunset.

Tim Brooks was Hutch's official doctor—he was everybody's doctor—but Hutch was healthy as a horse and never needed him. When Hutch needed attention it was straight to emergency in Gander Hospital, Do Not Pass Go: a broken arm falling off the shed roof, a broken nose from someone's elbow in basketball, a broken collarbone wrestling Jed Batton—wrestling was the polite name for it, anyway; Batton had been waiting there too, looking even worse.

Today there was a brisk northwesterly blowing and it was picking up to gale force now so kayaking was probably out for more than just one day. It would blow the ball off course too, but if you waited for the wind to go away around here you might as well stay in bed. Hutch stopped and stared out at the ocean, willing the wind to blow itself out, and Cathy Russell walked past him.

She looked at him from the corner of her eye and grunted, "'Lo."

"Hi, Cathy."

She had the same old bag over the same old shoulder with that everlasting sketch pad sticking out and school books, even in summer. And that was the arm she used for painting walls and barns and anything else that was flat and couldn't run away. It was a wonder her whole right arm wasn't twice the size of the other one.

Hutch grabbed his ball cap as a gust took it. He remembered a windy day just like this back in grade two or three, when Cathy Russell was still in his class. Her scribbler had gone flying across the schoolyard and he'd chased after it, jumped on it, put it right side out, and given it back. In the process he'd noticed lots of red X marks and not many ticks and no gold stars at all. His own scribbler was always thick with stars and until then he'd thought that was normal. And now she was down a grade, just finished grade eight, and still having trouble. Homework in summer. What a life. Hutch set off again. He had a game to go to.

Full Steam Ahead

*

Grade eight was a struggle and sometimes Cathy thought her brain might boil over. At first it took almost twenty minutes to focus on her homework and stop her thoughts zigzagging from wondering what Mom was cooking, to how to tackle some painting problem, to the fog rolling up the ocean. But over the weeks it took her less and less time to zero in on the page in front of her until sometimes she could do it straight away.

Cathy came home with her report card on the last day of grade eight with mostly borderline marks but the only subject she'd failed outright was English, and Sarah said they'd really work hard on the set books next year.

Mrs. Elliot said Cathy was reading at about a grade seven level now, although she was still slow. The report card hardly mentioned her writing, which took so much more effort, just that her spelling needed work. Reading was getting easier but writing had all those extra steps of thinking what to put and making words *legible* (though she couldn't say what ledges had to do with anything) and capitals and commas and whether it was there or their. Mom always complained about the standard shift in Dad's truck, said Aunt Dot's automatic gears were so much easier. Cathy thought writing was a lot like reading with a stick shift.

Earlier that day, Mrs. Elliot said how well Cathy had done—right there in class, in front of everybody, said she'd caught up so much in just one year. Jenny Sheppard came over after, put her hand on Cathy's arm, and said, "Good for you. That'll show 'em." The rest of Jenny's crowd smiled at her too, saying yes and wasn't she doing great.

"Yeah," Jed Batton yelled from the door, "pretty soon she'll be able to write her own name. Loser."

The girls all muttered and glared at him but Cathy never minded Batton. He was like that with everybody. But Joan White was right behind him, looking at her feet. Joan failed things too—not as much as Cathy—but she was starting to skip class, starting to "forget" her homework more often, wasn't hanging around with the girls as much. Cathy knew what that felt like.

She caught up with Joan in the hallway and said, "I'm only doing better because Sarah's helping. She might help you if you asked."

"What for?"

"Well...so you could pass things. Graduate maybe. Get a job."

"What job?"

"Well, there might be a job somewhere bigger."

"My sister Eva graduated. Good grades. Went to St. John's. Only jobs she could get were minimum wage and they'd only give her a few shifts 'cause they didn't want to pay her benefits."

"Well...it's a start?"

"Worked funny hours so the buses had stopped running. Had to walk. Couldn't afford a taxi. Girl she knew was attacked walking home on that same street so Eva quit. Moved in with my aunt 'til she could find something else and now Aunt Madge is breathing down her neck all the time. Eva says she might as well be home."

"Oh."

Silence.

"Is she all right?" Cathy asked. Joan stared at her. "The other girl. The one who got attacked?"

"Looks all right on the outside."

"Oh."

Joan pushed open the bathroom door and looked over her shoulder at Cathy.

"Don't care if I ever graduate. Don't give a shit."

Cathy stood outside the door with her mouth open, couldn't think of a thing to say. Poor Eva. Poor girl who was attacked. Cathy walked off quickly before Joan came back out. On her way home she thought Poor Joan. Then she started worrying about herself too. Would she ever get a job? How much did art classes cost? Grey fear rolled over her again.

No way. She was learning more, passing things. She didn't have that brain thingy. One step at a time like Sarah said. She marched up the long hill faster than usual.

+

Cathy couldn't wait for Mom and Dad to see her report card but when she bounced into the kitchen, Dad was gone and Mom didn't know when he'd be back. Her mother insisted on waiting for him. Cathy said they could go through it twice, couldn't they?

"Well, why don't I just sit here and you read it to me, because my eyes hurt." Mom sat back in her chair and put a hand over her eyes and it made Cathy think of Jed Batton when he told the teacher the dog had eaten his homework. What a pile.

"Oh, come off it, Mom. There's nothing wrong with your eyes."

Her mother's chin crinkled up like she was trying not to cry and the hand stayed over her eyes and after a bit she got up and went into her bedroom and closed the door.

So when Cathy heard the truck arriving she was outside before the engine stopped.

"Dad. Can Mom…? Can she…? Does Mom really have a problem with her eyes?"

And Dad stood by the truck holding the door, looking at nothing in particular. Then he swung it ever so slowly to the side of the truck and leaned on it and there was that big click as everything slid home.

"Have you asked Mom?"

"I just asked her to read my report card. She says her eyes hurt. They weren't hurting five minutes ago when she was mending your shirt. And she always asks you to read stuff for her." This was far harder than Cathy expected when she'd first rushed out and there were long spaces between thoughts. "She can read numbers, no trouble. You give her columns of figures to add up because she's so fast."

"Betty's faster than anybody with figures. Works out percentages in her head like nobody else. Better than a calculator. Fahrenheit to Centigrade, miles to kilometres—all in jig time."

"But she never looks at the newspaper, or books." Silence. "And she doesn't.... She doesn't like to read stuff with words." Cathy waited a moment and took a deep breath. "Dad, can Mom read?"

Dad stood still—still like a bird when there's a cat around. Mom flapped about doing stuff when she was upset. Dad went still as a stone.

"Why don't you ask her if she has a bit of trouble reading the same way you have?" He looked at her then. "And Cathy, ask her *exactly* that. Do you understand?"

And Cathy did understand. She did. "Can't you tell me?"

He shook his head. "I promised."

They went inside and Mom still hadn't come out of the bedroom so Dad knocked and said it was him and went in and stayed for ages. Cathy walked up and down practicing what she was going to say, over and over, and wondered whether she should give her mom a hug, or look at the floor or something while she asked, and she got more and more nervous the longer she waited. But in the end she didn't have to say anything.

They came out of the bedroom, Mom first, and her eyes were red. She sat in a chair facing Cathy and Dad stood next to her with a hand on her shoulder.

"Dad says you've been asking about my eyes." Cathy opened her mouth but her mother didn't wait. "I've always had trouble with reading." She took a big breath. "Much worse than you, although I hid it better. And I was able to leave school early and go work in the fish plant like a lot of girls round here so I could hide it later on, too. Mostly. Dot knew. Mel knew." And Mom gave Dad such a beautiful smile and put her hand over his, the hand that was still on her shoulder. Then she looked at Cathy. "But there's no fish plant for you. Nothing for any of you."

Not just closed but all the machinery taken out and sent somewhere. Head Off. Gutted. Mom sounded so sad but Cathy didn't mind a bit, couldn't think of anything worse than working all her life in a fish plant, but she didn't say so.

"...didn't want you to know about all that. Felt stupid. Wanted to help you with reading so much and I couldn't, and then some total stranger walks in off the street and does what I should be doing." Her eyes filled up and Cathy hugged her and Dad hugged them both, and little snags of hurt feelings surfaced and swirled and passed on: should have, tried, wouldn't listen, so sorry, no I'm sorry.

And Cathy handed the report card to her dad to read out loud but he said no, you can read it to us from now on, Cathy. So she did. And afterwards they discussed it, piece by piece, and Mom and Dad both said how well Cathy was doing ten times each and how proud they were and Dad said next time they were in Gander they'd have lunch at the Albatross to celebrate.

Change of View

✶

Cathy had asked her father about her mother's reading difficulties: were they really that much worse than Cathy's? And he said yes, definitely. So she asked Sarah more about that brain mix-up thing, dyslexia, and afterwards Dad said yes, Betty had all those problems. So how did Mom cover it up better than Cathy had? Dad said he wasn't getting into that, better ask her mom.

Mom said she could read symbols easy enough and there were symbols on road signs and clothes and detergents and all kinds of household things. "And Mel and Dot helped with the reading and writing parts of homework. I listened real careful to the teachers so I could join in class discussions, said things over and over in my head so I'd remember. Then I was just as good as everyone else at classwork."

Mom really had made the best of it, hadn't let anything stop her, didn't get left behind. Most people still didn't know she couldn't read. Cathy opened her mouth to say all that but her mom was back to moaning over how Cathy never listened to her, only ever listened to Sarah Brooks. Here we go again. Cathy switched off, walked out of the kitchen, out of the house. Out.

She brooded over all that. Why hadn't Mom explained all this to Cathy years ago? Why did she have to learn about it from Sarah? She should have learned from her own mother.

"Dad, how did you find out Mom couldn't read?" Dad was sitting opposite Cathy at the table and her mom was at the counter.

"I worked it out. We were in the same class and I noticed Betty didn't even have her book out half the time, and didn't write things down. I was always aware of what your mom did. Then one day after class I just asked her straight out and offered to help."

"Why didn't you ask me?"

"I should have. I'm sorry."

Her mother turned away from the counter, not noticing gravy dripping off the spoon onto the floor and said in a very quiet voice, "Why didn't you tell us, Cathy?"

"I did, at the end of grade seven. The second one."

"No, you didn't. Because it's hard. Dad read it out of Mrs. Elliot's letter."

"Well, okay. But you never asked. You could have been helping me all this time, could have told me about listening and remembering—"

"Good heavens, Cathy, I've been trying to tell you for years, over and over, but you never heard a word I said. You never want to hear what I say."

"If you'd told me you couldn't read I'd have understood." Cathy's voice was rising. "I'd have listened then."

Mom turned back to the counter and put the spoon down. "I tried to tell you once. It was just after we moved here and you kept saying how you missed the lighthouse and how it was easy for me because I liked being nearer my sisters. And I said it had been hard when I first moved out to the light, just as it had been hard for me not being able to read." Mom's voice was real soft and Cathy had to strain to hear. "I was terrified," her mother said. "It was the first time I'd told anyone right out. And I waited and waited for you to say something, holding my breath."

She looked at Cathy then and Cathy said, "I don't remember any of this, Mom."

"No. Because you weren't listening. Know what you said in the end? You said, *well, anyway, Mom, what's for supper*?"

Cathy couldn't move. Her heart banged extra hard but the rest of her was frozen. Mom and Dad were both looking at her with their mouths all tight and Cathy couldn't think of anything to say except sorry, a million times sorry. Finally she unfroze enough to get up and hug her mom and say sorry out loud. And ages later she said how hard she was working at listening and she'd never do anything like that again.

August 24 1996

Done reading Superfudge by Judy Blume. Read every word. Just a litel kids book but 192 pages in chapters. Funny. Laffing made it easier to keep going. Start Fudge-a-mania nex. Grad 9 in 10 days.

On the Move

✶

June. First week of summer vacation and all finished with grade ten. It was only twelve degrees and blustery but Hutch couldn't wait to get out on the water. Usually Dad wouldn't let them go out with less than three boats, said he didn't trust the weather, but he let them go in the end.

"...only because you three are strong paddlers and only this end of the harbour." His father looked them each in the eye: Hutch, Andy, and Jack. The boys were scuffing their feet and saying "yes sir," and "yes, Mr. Parsons."

Then Dad looked straight at Hutch. "That means not past the red buoy, Hutch." Dad brought the kayaks down to the launch in his pickup: *Dolphin*, and one double. "Remember what I told you."

The boats bucked a bit near the wharves where the water going out got in a shoving match with the water coming in. Then Hutch was free, riding the swells, feeling the water through the paddle, turning *Dolph* into the waves. He clipped the top of one wave with his paddle and the wind blew icy spray in his face but even that felt good. He heard Jack in the back of the other boat yell, "Hey! Watch it!" at Andy too, and Hutch laughed.

He reached ahead, dug deep, and raced straight out, still laughing, with a damp wind in his face, salt on his tongue, gull screams in his ears, and a grey-green world leaping all around him. There was nothing in the universe as good as this.

They'd been paddling for an hour when the wind changed from chilling Hutch's ear to freezing his cheek. It must have veered a few points and fast. It smelled less of harbour now and more of deep ocean, fresh and clean, and there were whitecaps with threads of spray unwinding off the tops. They had to paddle harder to stay on course so they headed back and by the time they reached the slipway the light had changed, taking the colour out of everything.

Hutch carried his boat over his head and he could feel the gusts pushing, letting up, then pushing again. His wrists strained as *Dolph* tried to twist out of his grip and he had his work cut out to keep her straight as he walked up to the truck. They loaded the double first, checking it was secure. A car drove by with Phyllis Barnes's face in the rear window and Hutch watched until the car disappeared.

Jack said, "Like her, do ya?"

Hutch leered at him and Andy sniggered. They went back to the ramp for *Dolph*, Jack to one end and Hutch to the other. Jack nodded at someone on the road and said hi. Hutch glanced round but it was only Cathy Russell, striding away down Main Road, the wind flattening her clothes against her back.

"Like her do ya?" Hutch called into the wind, grinning at Jack.

"Just being polite," said Jack. "Should try it sometime."

"To Lighthouse?" Hutch was still shouting. Andy sniggered again and muttered something about Cathy needing a keeper.

"Yeah," said Hutch, "they forgot to turn on the light in that one."

"Keep it down, Hutch," Jack said, frowning at him. "She'll hear you."

"Too much wind."

"Hear you in Bonavista."

Jack must have ratted on him because Jenny called him a mean bastard the day after. She was like litmus paper—turned red if you did anything she didn't like. Hutch did a lot of things Jenny didn't like.

It turned out to be a good summer for girls, though, that summer after grade ten. He dated Jane Butt and Maggie Abbott and oh-my-god, Phyllis Barnes.

There were more high-wind days than usual that year. When Dad said the wind was too risky for kayaking, Hutch and Jack would work on the shack the guys were building in the woods from scraps, or they would pester Jack's brother, Eugene, for a ride in the back of his old Silverado. When he had any gas. When it was working. Hutch spent more time under it, passing stuff, than riding in it. But Eugene was a laugh and didn't act the big brother with them and never minded Jack and Hutch hanging around. So there was always plenty to do, but nothing beat being out on the water.

The first time he'd rolled a kayak was in their second summer of paddling, all the gang on Uncle Em's pond. Hutch's dad and Hutch's brother, Brian, had done kayaking safety courses so they could take tourists out on the bay. They practiced on the pond then taught the gang. That roll was harder than it looked: you could get fooled up when you were upside down and push the wrong way, then your lungs started taking on water. You needed strong trunk muscles too, for that flick of the hips that brought the boat right side up, but Hutch never had trouble with that part. Paul bought little clips to stop the water going up his nose—always had the fancy stuff.

They practiced the roll, both directions. That summer, Hutch could roll every time with his regular paddle, two or three times with a shorter paddle, even once with just his arms. He was the only one strong enough to do it with just arms. Dad said it was good to be able to do it with no paddle in case it got knocked out of your hands on a rock or something.

And at the end of that summer, Hutch had the run of his life: a white-water run on the Gander River. And it was the best. The Best. Jack couldn't come, but apart from that, Hutch would remember it always as being perfect: Bud, Paul, and Hutch and their three fathers all in rented river kayaks. If there were flies they didn't bite, if there was wind it blew the right way, and the sun never stopped shining. The campsites were flat, their cook fires lit on the first try, and the food was endless.

River sounds were different from ocean sounds: like an orchestra with less bass. Hutch would lie in his sleeping bag, listening, and fall asleep trying to figure out why. The river sounded more pure, more light and bubbly, even the big waterfalls. The ocean had all that weight of rock and mineral in it. The river talked, chatty some places, shouting in others. The ocean didn't bother to talk—it was all roar.

Hutch did a roll in a real choppy patch, twice, and it was easy. A wave tipped him sideways and he just rolled with it and came up the other side and kept paddling. Felt natural. But he could see why you needed helmets on the river—some of those rocks were wicked.

He slept like a rock too. It was the portages that were tiring more than the paddling, but it was the sort of tired he loved. Satisfying: like coming off the ice dripping with sweat after a real tough game, or finally seeing the top of the bus in the distance after a long tramp with cadets, or like playing soccer on a full field with half the team missing.

Hutch dreamed of doing it again the next summer but Bud was heading to Memorial that fall. He had a summer job lined up, and could only come to Mariners Cove for a week. Paul's family had visitors all the time and anyway Paul was always off somewhere with Jenny, doing boring stuff like peeling buckets of potatoes for the family dinner. The gang still kayaked when they could, and Hutch helped Dad take tourists out when there was a big group but wouldn't it be great if....

Maybe after grade twelve.

Paparazzi

Cathy passed all her exams at the end of grade nine and not one borderline mark. She was passing everything these days and if she was stuck with something she'd ask a teacher and they always helped. None of them made her feel stupid for asking. Joan White was skipping more and more classes. She showed up for the exams but walked out halfway through. All year, she had nodded at Cathy, said hi, but never stopped to talk. If Cathy started to say something Joan would shake her head and walk away.

Cathy was almost done grade ten when her father graduated in the spring of 1998. He had a job for the summer in Labrador, right in the interior. He flew there by helicopter from Goose Bay and lived in a tent and had to watch out for bears and got isolation pay—which was funny because Dad loved being isolated.

He bought a new digital camera in St. John's for the trip, for the work he was doing. He gave Cathy his old one and showed her how to use it and they practiced with it before he left. Cathy started taking photographs sometimes for people pictures because it was quicker—everyone moved around so much. Some guys had told her where to shove her sketches. Now they said things like, "Here comes the paparazzi," and "Look what they did to Princess Diana." But most kids just grinned or pulled faces at the camera. Jed Batton did a moon. Sarah said Cathy really should ask people's permission first, but they'd all be gone if she did that. Anyway, people wouldn't grab an expensive camera out of her hands the way Parsons had grabbed her sketchbook that time.

That had been the first week of summer vacation. Paul Wilson had been going out with Jenny Sheppard for a whole year and Cathy's insides still got in a knot when she saw how they looked at each other. And she could understand. Jenny was so pretty—not as tiny as Sarah but small and dainty and Sarah said what glorious hair she had and that was the right word. It was like a sunset: long and smooth and shining red-gold. And everyone liked Jenny. She was friendly and always helped Cathy when she asked and never laughed at her or said unkind things about her or about anybody. If Cathy had been asked to pick out a girlfriend for Paul it would have been Jenny. But she so, so wished it could have been her.

So Cathy drew a lot of pictures of Paul instead. Didn't paint any because you couldn't hide paintings, but she had half a book full of sketches of him—one of her good sketchbooks with the thick paper that didn't wrinkle. Sarah had picked up a whole bunch, cheap, at that new Price Club place in St. John's.

And that was the book Hutch Parsons had yanked out of her hand and taken off with, waving it above his head, laughing. He slid into his kayak and pushed off. Some of the others were already on the water and they all pulled their boats together to have a look and Paul and Jenny were there in a double and Cathy didn't know what to do. There wasn't anything she could do.

She wanted to kill Parsons, run away, curl up in a ball and howl. But she just stood there. Then Jenny had the book and Parsons was holding his hand out saying "hey!" and Jenny was backing out her and Paul's kayak, saying something in an angry voice which Cathy couldn't hear. She and Paul paddled back to shore, Paul with his head ducked down.

Jenny laid the sketchbook on the dock a few feet away and called, "A few splashes on it. Better dry it off quick." She smiled and waved to Cathy and they turned the boat and paddled out again.

+

Cathy tried not to think about it but it kept going round and round in her head, how Parsons had shamed her in front of Paul and Jenny and the other guys. She was slow getting to sleep that night because of it, woke up thinking about it. Bit by bit she got used to the idea of the guys knowing how she felt about Paul—half the girls in Mariners Cove felt the same way. She'd see that crowd around and they behaved how they always did, said hi, or not. Nothing much she could do but carry on.

But her anger at Parsons grew. She never wasted time planning revenge, but when the opportunity arose she didn't think twice.

It was one of those iffy August days. There was a system off the coast and the forecasters didn't know whether it would come close enough to cause trouble on land or pass them by. It was one of those things you lived with when you stuck this far out into the ocean. They had a bit of time before it hit, so Cathy was down on the dock early to finish some sketches. She'd finish them indoors if the weather bottomed out.

The Parsons crowd had the same idea.

"Not beyond the first buoy and come straight in at the least sign," Mr. Parsons shouted from the dock, just behind her. Then he left.

The guys lifted their kayaks down the ramp and climbed in. Parsons was floating just below Cathy, close to the dock and looking out at the horizon, like he was trying to read its mind. Cathy slid her paint things out of the way and scooted to the very edge of the dock. She stretched one leg down and down until her toes reached the side of the stern of the kayak. Then she pushed down hard.

The nose of the boat bounced up and a bit sideways. Parsons went back and his arms shot up, and his paddle flicked round and caught Cathy on the ankle. She jerked and her rear end slid off the edge of the dock, and down she went on top of everything.

She hit the boat and the water at the same time. Freezing. Water up her nose, hair over her face, yucky oily taste. Roaring in her ears, gurgling. Something smacked her on the arm, hard, and then on the head. Something solid and orange pushed her down, down—through every shade of green with grit in it. Then she was kicking herself up and gulping air and grabbing one of those tires tied to the side of the dock as buffers.

A face appeared in front of her, coughing and spluttering, and with more fury in it than any system.

"You did that on purpose!" More coughing. "If you've hurt my boat I'll kill you. Fucking idiot."

"Your boat for my sketchbook."

"I didn't hurt your fucking sketchbook."

"And I didn't hurt your stupid boat. Why don't you go find it."

Cathy turned her back on him and started pulling herself along the dock towards the shore. After a few pulls she could feel slimy rocks under her feet. They rolled as she put her weight on them, so she had to keep pulling herself along the dock, trying to find solid footing.

When she could stand up, the water came up to her knees and she turned to look, pulling her hair back off her face with both hands. Paul and Jenny had Parsons's boat, upside down, keeping it from bumping the dock, Jack was trying to reach one of those little yellow waterproof bags, and Andy had the paddle.

Paul was calling out that the boat looked okay, no damage that he could see, and Parsons was up on the ramp, saying bring it over. Always giving orders. And he had a life jacket on, which would cut the wind. That wind was a knife going through Cathy. She turned to scramble up the beach. Not your soft Florida sand, this. Lumps—big and hard and grey, like old scrambled egg. Someone should have mashed it more. Then she remembered her art stuff and had to shiver her way down the dock and gather it up, trying not to drip on anything. At least Parsons hadn't noticed—too busy with that stupid boat.

Cathy walked over to Sarah's house, praying she was home, holding the sketchbook away from her wet clothes. Dr. Brooks opened the door.

"Cathy. Good god. What happened?"

"Fell in."

"Come in, come in. You must be frozen." He called out for Sarah, turned back to Cathy, and said, "I'll make you a hot drink."

Cathy stood and pooled on the porch floor until Sarah rushed out with towels and exclamations and sent her into the bathroom for a hot shower. She brought dry clothes belonging to Dr. Brooks: a green T-shirt, a sweatshirt with *Roughriders* on the front, and shorts the colour of government envelopes. They reached her knees and then the waist dropped halfway down her hips even though she fastened the belt on the very last hole, so Sarah found some string. She gave Cathy woolly socks but said she'd have to manage with her own sneakers, although she stuffed them with paper to soak up the worst of the wetness. Then Dr. Brooks had steaming hot chocolate on the table and it was perfect.

When she heard the full tale Sarah said she wished someone had taken a video of it all. It would qualify for *America's Funniest Home Videos.*

+

Cathy started to see there was more to photography than just recording a moment. This could be art too. So at the beginning of grade eleven she joined the school photography club. It had only started in grade eight after someone donated a camera and equipment to the school and Mr. Roberts said he'd teach anybody who was interested. He was like Dad—always out at dawn looking for birds. Dad's old camera was a Canon AE-1 and it had a zoom lens and a wide-angle lens as well as the ordinary one. He'd had it forever but Mr. Roberts said it was a great camera. Cameras the other kids had didn't do the things Cathy's did and most of them just shared the school camera or used Mr. Roberts's own.

Now and then he took the club on a field trip. One day, down on the wharf by the Mariners Cove fish plant, they were sizing up boats, on the shore and on the water, but Cathy noticed that old bike belonging to the school caretaker, Obadiah Jenkins. Kids called him OJ and Obi-Wan but he only ever answered to Mr. Jenkins.

His bike was leaning against the concrete wall, all ruler-straight lines with sharp shadows, and perfect circles with all those spokes. What was the plural of radius? Imagine geometry being useful! Cathy chose black-and-white mode and moved the bike wheels to make the angles tighter where the shadows met the ground, tilted the handlebars more.

She took a whole roll of pictures. When Mr. Roberts taught them about prints she made a print of the best one and he showed her how to frame it. They entered it in a provincial competition and it won first place. Cathy got a certificate in the mail and a free pass to a photography show, which she couldn't go to because it was in St. John's.

She gave Mr. Jenkins a signed copy of the photograph. Sarah had said she should practice her signature first so Cathy worked on all kinds of swoops and swirls with the tail of the Y and the last stroke of the R.

"Doesn't feel right," she said to Sarah. "Maybe when I'm a real artist."

"Well, I think you're an artist already. But whatever you're comfortable with."

"A signature's like a little portrait of yourself and I'm Cathy Russell: straight up, no frills."

And Sarah laughed and said, "Go for it."

So Cathy signed the photograph on the back with her usual round, careful letters and Mr. Jenkins said he had a frame he could use and he'd put it up on his kitchen wall.

Sarah gave Cathy a stiff folder to put the photo and the certificate in, said this was a good time to start getting a portfolio ready for art school.

Portfolio: noun: *a set of pieces of creative work intended to demonstrate a person's ability.*

Cathy kept looking at the folder, running her hands over it, smelling the cardboard smell of it.

Little Pigs

✶

Mom tucked Cathy up in her room with Tylenol, a hot lemon drink, and some "man-sized" tissues. Said there was a nice pile of books by the bed, and the dictionary. But Cathy's head hurt so much she just lay back and closed her eyes.

Scuffles at the front door. It was the aunts arriving for Tuesday Night Cards.

"Oh, that wind."

"Move in a bit, let's get the door shut."

"Had to dig out gloves and hats and it's not even November month!"

"—be okay when I get my hands on a hot cup of tea."

The draft made Cathy sneeze and blow and cough and blow. She hauled the covers up round her ears. Downstairs, they'd reached the tea ceremony.

"Ah, Tetley. Maisie just had Red Rose last time, ran out of the good stuff."

"Once in ten years! Anyway Red Rose is good, my guys like it best."

"Where's my mug?" That was Aunt Gert.

"That mug with the flowers broke," said Mom. "But there's another china one the same, right there, only it has a Santa Claus on it."

Aunt Gert *humphed* about the Santa Claus, saying how did the flower one break.

"It just broke," said Mom. It broke when Cathy was reaching behind her to put it on the table without taking her eyes off her book. She thought she'd reached far enough but she hadn't. First thing Mom said was, "Aunt Gert will have a fit."

"You put that tea bag right in." Aunt Elsie's voice. "You know Joanie just likes her tea bag waved over the cup twice. Abracadabra. She'll never drink that."

"Yes I will. Anything hot on a night like this. Just fish it out quick."

"Mugs don't break by themselves," Aunt Gert was saying. "Did Cathy break it?"

"Mugs wear out same as everything else. Sometimes the handle just falls off in the wash. Give it up, Gert."

Yay, Mom. GertRude. Sometimes Cathy wished she had a sister but mostly she didn't. Never one like Aunt Gert, anyway. Someone like Jenny Sheppard, maybe.

Then Aunt Maisie was saying something about hating carpenter bugs and where had that come from this time of year and Aunt Dot said it was in the birch junks and Mom was saying I'll do it, I'll do it, and they all started laughing and joking about Betty to the rescue again.

"Remember that piece of cardboard next to the kitchen window?"

"—out of a package of pantyhose!"

"Nobody was allowed to touch it. Little Betty's Bug Carrier."

Aunt Gert said, "Better than picking them up in her fingers like that rain beetle that fell apart when she put it out by the kitchen door. Remember? Cried all day because it didn't say thank you and run off and play."

"Did not."

And Aunt Dot said how about those kittens old Albert had in a sack, and Elsie said, "Oh, but the baby crow was the best."

"Oh, my god, yes. Every crow on the east coast lined up on the roof and the barn and jammed side-by-side on the wires—"

"—screeching at us: 'leave our baby alone!' Real Alfred Hitchcock. Thought we were all killed."

Then Mom's voice, dignified: "When you're finished..."

Game time. Chairs being moved and that solid *thunk* of the end of a pack of cards being banged on the table to even up the edges. Slapping-them-down noises.

"Go easy, you're bending the cards."

Silence. Mutters. Creaks and bumps. A busy silence.

"What did you do that for?"

"Well, I thought..."

"My lord. Your deal."

Then it started all over again.

Cathy blew her nose, blew and blew until her ears popped. She aimed the used tissues at the garbage but mostly missed. Then she lay still with her eyes closed. It was a different world with no eyes. You could hear the house breathing, hear rattles you'd never noticed. Not that there were many here, not like the house up at the light. Dad had done a real good job building this house. But a night like this made the trees rattle, the rocks creak. It made the ocean boom close in and roar further out.

"...Sarah Brooks."

Cathy opened her eyes.

"Little pigs have big ears." That was Mom.

The voices went real quiet but Cathy could still hear Aunt Joanie in her Big-News voice speaking low. Cathy rolled out of bed, wrapped the comforter round her shoulders, and trailed it to the door. She pulled it open a few more inches—slow, slow—and stuck out an ear.

"...Jessie Rowsell's cousin...married that townie...Holyrood...one of those giant Ford trucks." Aunt Joanie's voice was coming and going—leaning in and back, maybe, or turning her head. "...Grace Hospital...old nurse's residence. There they were...both of them, Doctor and Missus... that clinic. Her with tears down her face and him with his arm round her."

Oh god. What was going on?

"What clinic?"

"Oh, come on, Else—that fertility place."

"You mean where they do test-tube babies?" Aunt Elsie sounded shocked. "Didn't know...in this province."

"...a nice bit but..." Joanie said. "...Halifax for the rest."

"Bet you don't get that on Medicare." Dot's big laugh.

"Don't agree with it." That was Aunt Gert, loud over the others. Of course it was Aunt Gert. "If The Good Lord intended them to have a baby they'd have had one the proper way."

"Poor thing," said Aunt Maisie. "When I think how often...*Time and Tide*...must have got her drove."

"...just last week: 'That tree will fall down before you gets a swing in it.'"

Someone was on her feet—for a bathroom break, maybe. Cathy eased the door shut and climbed back into bed, knocked the pile of books as she climbed in so the top ones slid off, standing *Harry Potter* on his head. She didn't have time to get the comforter straightened away before the door opened. Mom came in and Cathy tried to look half asleep.

"Need anything?"

"No thanks."

+

Cathy remembered back at the beginning, that first summer, when she spent hours at Sarah's house or going for walks with her. Cathy had said thank you and sorry for taking up so much of your time. And Sarah had said something about her having to take her turn when she had ten children, but for now it wasn't an issue.

Issue: noun: *an important topic or problem.*

It was also something legal to do with children of one's own. Did Sarah know that? Of course she did. Sarah knew everything about words—just not how to have a baby, how to have an issue.

Cathy lay in her bed, unaware of the comforter lumped round her legs or her sore throat or the wind thumping. Sarah had said things about starting a family here in Mariners Cove, Cathy just hadn't taken much notice. She tried to remember. Early on Sarah had said things like that but not in a long while. And she'd been doing all this running up and down to St. John's in all weathers, staying over a couple of nights each time, Dr. Brooks driving in to join her. Cathy had asked her about that. Sarah had said she didn't mind the drive except sometimes when it was foggy in the isthmus. Said about those stupid trucks scaring her, crossing the centre line like that, and Sarah would grip the wheel and wonder if there was a pile-up ahead and what was off to the side if she had to go round—a cliff up or a cliff down.

"Yes, but why are you going so often?"

And Sarah would say stuff about a few meetings and then get into a story about something funny that happened when she had dinner with

Mr. and Mrs. Wilson, or how pretty it was just past Clarenville with those little white communities in the cliffs like flowers tucked behind ears. Cathy should paint houses in the cliffs round here like that. And Cathy thought about trying, only she didn't know what magnolias looked like. Sidetracked. Cathy had been sidetracked. But now they'd been seen, so the whole coast would know.

+

Another Tuesday a month or so later, Dad had the radio on CBC listening to more stuff about that Monica Lewinsky person. Then they were advertising a series of health talks and there was one about infertility. Mom was going to Aunt Joanie's for cards when it came on and Dad was doing a lot of banging in the back room, so Cathy listened.

She missed the beginning about Intrauterine Insemination because Dad kept coming in for things, but the next part was on In Vitro Fertilization and how they only went on to IVF if the first bit hadn't worked. What a lot of bother. You had your insides checked out and blood pressure taken a million times and blood tests and needles and pills—Sarah must really miss her coffee and red wine—and more tests and adjusting the drugs and piles of ultrasounds, and you had to go to a special clinic all the time, which would be annoying even if you lived next door but Sarah had a four-hour drive each way.

There was a little bit about the sex part, which Cathy didn't want to hear, but it sounded like you didn't just mix it up in a test tube—they had to get together a lot and try things out so you couldn't have one person in St. John's and one in Mariners Cove.

And it could go on for months, going in for ultrasounds on certain days. And what if there was a snowstorm and you couldn't get there that day? Must have to start over. And it cost—god, did they really say *thousands*? Dad was making such a racket, hammering. And the chances of success were not great. People must really *really* want a baby to go through all that and pay all that with such a small chance of it working.

And for Sarah, it hadn't.

On Course

*

Hutch chewed the end of his pen as he sat balancing the chair on its back legs at the kitchen table. On the table was the application for the Marine Institute, all filled out. He'd be off to the post office with it in a minute before the folks came back. He'd tell them after it was done. He figured he'd get the theory at the institute and write his fishing master certificates—right up to first class if he could. He'd get the practical experience in between with Uncle Em.

Everyone kept saying no, don't do it, the bottom was out of the fishing industry. The fishermen were all tight in the face and grim round the mouth saying, "Forget it b'y," and his mom saying, "Do something less dangerous—you've got the brains to do anything." He could understand Mom because her brother's boat had been lost before Hutch was born.

But. He wanted to be out on the water.

Brian's friend Chris had come to stay for a few days. He'd been in Africa working as a geologist, Tanzania and Kenya, and he was going to South America soon. He worked outside a lot, not stuck behind a desk all day. Now that was an exciting life. Chris had stories about everything and money in his pocket. He'd talked Hutch into considering a geology degree and the family had been pushing it ever since. He'd even filled out the application for Memorial last month.

But. He wanted to go to sea.

His family was always trying to discourage him, and only let him out once with Uncle Em last summer. Dad said Em had sunk a lot of money into his longliner adapting it for shrimp, said he'd need some real good catches to make it worth it. Hutch had been out fishing for herring but never for shrimp. And by the summer of '98 the cod were long gone.

+

So the summer just past, Hutch had sailed with his uncle to Shrimp Fishing Area Six. Uncle Em let Hutch watch the sonar in the wheelhouse so he was there when they spotted shrimp. He watched the guys lower that big ramp at the back to let out the net. It had doors on the sides to keep it open, weights on the bottom line to keep it down, floats on the top line to keep it up, and that gate inside the net to siphon off the bycatch. He liked the way they worked together, didn't get in each other's way. And when the net came up, what a catch! An orange flood of cold water shrimp, millions of them. Hutch helped with the bagging and the throwing of those thirty-pound bags down into the hold, where another guy heaved them into the pens along with shovels full of crushed ice.

He loved sleeping on-board. The rumble and throb of the engine went right through his bones when he was lying down, although there was always that smell of diesel and fish. He was used to ocean and wind noises, but here you were right inside them: the creaks and groans, the *hissss* of water being pushed aside by the hull. He could feel each climb up a wave and the slide down the other side, the surge and the pause, the bang when they hit a deeper trough. Things he hardly noticed in daytime with everything going on.

The next morning was grey with a much bigger sea and more white-caps—everything restless and twitchy. Hutch had to stand with his feet farther apart to steady himself as he worked, one foot turned out so he could balance himself in more directions. His grandfather always walked that way from having his foot turned out for so many years.

Hutch pulled his mind back to land, back to the here and now. He dropped the front legs of his chair to the floor with a *thump* and stood up. He'd made up his mind. He was going on the boats.

The Game

*

It didn't get better than this. The crowd was lifting off its feet, shouting, the horn gave a blast, and the organ played one of those hockey tunes you only hear in rinks. *Da da da daa, da daaaa.*

Jack's cousin, Gus, had been called up from the East Coast League to play a game in the American Hockey League with the Leafs farm team, and everyone was in full-on support mode. It was a rush to get ready before the game. Not that Hutch did much other than root around in the cupboards for Gramps's old Newfoundland flag until his mom growled about the mess. Mr. and Mrs. Sheppard did all the work: the block of tickets at the stadium in St. John's and transport to and from Mariners Cove. There were too many people for one bus so they met up with a crowd from over Gander way—where Gus was from—to share a second one.

Jenny had made a banner with *Go Gus Go* in blue letters on white, which looked great. She was good at that stuff. And here they all were, jumping up and down: Paul and Bud on Jenny's other side, Hutch between Jack and Eugene, all that carroty Sheppard hair sticking out from under a sea of blue Leafs caps, and Gus on the ice with his big orange beard.

The first period was a bit slow but the game picked up in the second with a goal each and a bunch of shots on net and a couple of nice little fights. Then Gus got an assist with three minutes to go in the second period and the crowd went crazy.

The PA announced the goal: "And an assist by Gus Sheppard."

Hutch and the Sheppards were cheering fit to burst, and Hutch was jumping up and down, fizzing with energy, giving off sparks. One of their own was down there on the ice and people were yelling his name. The roar bounced off walls and circled and crashed back over them like breakers. And it mattered, that goal. Their team won three to two in overtime.

It was different watching a game on television with replays from every angle so you could see just who did what. Hutch saw Gus deking two players and making the pass across the goal, but he couldn't see the winger flick it in—just saw the puck hit the back of the net as the red light flashed. They put it all together afterwards, on the bus.

Dad always said you saw more of the game on TV, so he hadn't come. But at the game itself you were right in it, the vibrations rattling your teeth, the noise exploding in your head. You smelled winter melting off people's jackets, wet wool, dust from old concrete, hot dogs and aftershave. You were part of the crowd when it roared to its feet at that perfect moment.

They came out of the stadium around eleven into a messy mix of snow, sleet, and freezing rain.

"St. John's," Eugene scoffed. "Even the weather doesn't know its ass from a hole in the ground."

No use griping about it, that was Hutch's philosophy. Ignore it.

But if you live on the eastern edge of everything with your face in the North Atlantic and a four-hour drive after the big game, you can never ignore the weather.

+

The first bus was full and pulling out as Hutch wandered across the parking lot with the Sheppards. After they'd shouted goodbye and banged on the side of the bus and caused a nice bit of havoc, they piled into the second one. They took over the back three rows and saved the back corner seat for Jenny, who stayed outside saying goodbye to Paul until the very last minute. The driver had to rev the engine before she climbed up the steps. She turned at the top, ducked down to look back, and called, "Seven weeks 'til Easter."

There were replays everywhere.

"—definitely high sticking."

"Should have..."

"Did you see?"

Jack dug a bologna sandwich out of his backpack, a bit squashed. He gave half to Hutch and they shared Hutch's Cheezies. Then Hutch said Jack's hands matched his hair now and Jack yelled, "redhead joke!" and rubbed his cheesy hands into Hutch's face. Eugene leaned over the top of the seat from behind and grabbed Hutch's ball cap, mussed up his hair, and rammed the cap back down, laughing his big boom of a laugh. There were chuckles all down the aisle, people craning round to see, murmurs of "There goes Eugene." And it was comfortable tucked away on the bus—friendly—but black as your heart outside.

After an hour or two there was a change of topic here and there, to gossip and plans for next week. Fathers closed eyes. Mr. Sheppard snored in front of Hutch and Mrs. Sheppard leaned across the aisle to chat to her friend. Eugene and the rest were singing some old Beatles songs in back with Jenny adding top notes in a jokey kind of soprano. Hutch joined in now and then, yelling, "Love, love me do!"

Jack went up front for a minute and Hutch tucked himself into the corner, half seat and half side of the bus. He leaned his head against the window, shoving the hood of his jacket between him and the cold glass. His legs were stretched out diagonally, feet under the seat in front on Jack's side, one foot snarled in the straps of Jack's backpack—

Smash. Breath knocked out of him. Falling. Flickering. Black.

Goal Change

✶

The weather had been spring-like the previous weekend on the west coast around Corner Brook. One of those freak occasions that happen sometimes in early February around Groundhog Day. Sarah said she and Tim were going over to Corner Brook for "meetings" and would Cathy like a ride out. There was a visiting exhibition she might like to see at the Grenfell Campus of Memorial, which housed the art school she had been dreaming about. The art exhibit was showcasing work by a well-known portrait painter from NSCAD—the Nova Scotia College of Art and Design—in Halifax. They left right after school on Friday and Mom arranged for Cathy to stay with some cousins.

✶

That Saturday, Cathy stood in front of each portrait, examining it inch by inch—close up and farther away—searching for clues as to how the paint had been used. Sometimes she could work out a technique and the reason for it, sometimes she couldn't. She went round all the exhibits then started again. Kept going back to her least favourites to find out what was missing, and the best ones to see what made them best. Maybe it wasn't a matter of technique; maybe it was how each picture made you feel.

Cathy only left when the caretaker started saying, "Miss...excuse me, Miss?" Said he was locking up. Then she realized she ached from all that standing and was a bit lightheaded from skipping lunch and supper.

Sarah and Tim went with her on Sunday to the public lecture Madame Papineau—the artist from the exhibition—gave on portrait painting and Cathy didn't miss a single word, not a breath taken, not a wave of the hand. This woman would know the answer to all Cathy's questions. She knew. Cathy hung around afterwards, waiting for the crowd around Madame to thin, waiting until last so she wouldn't be rushed. Finally, there was Madame, looking at her.

"I need you to teach me," Cathy blurted. "What do I have to do?"

Madame seemed to be waiting for more.

"Please," Cathy said. "What do I have to do to be your student?"

Madame stood up a bit straighter then and her eyes drilled right into Cathy. "You must apply to NSCAD, in 'alifax. Talk to your teachers." She walked away, then stopped and looked back, said there was always a waiting list for her classes, no guarantee she would get in. "What is your name?"

Madame Papineau had asked Cathy her name. Madame knew her name. It changed everything. Cathy wanted to go to NSCAD. Yes, Grenfell was probably wonderful but Madame was at NSCAD. Cathy remembered nothing about the trip home, her head full of painting and plans. She would still apply to Grenfell, but also to NSCAD. Now she would need two portfolios.

"Everything will be more expensive: tuition, transport, accommodation," Dad said when she told her parents. And they needed a new truck.

Mom was shrinking down into her chair, into her clothes. "It's farther away," she said. "You won't have the money to come home for the short breaks. Or the time. Won't have the money for anything. It's bad enough Mel being away all summer but at least he's earning. And he didn't have any choice." Mom wasn't even twiddling now. "And what do you get at the end?"

"A bachelor of fine arts," said Cathy. Same as Grenfell.

The argument went on all year. Sarah kept out of it, except she was already in it.

"If Sarah Brooks hadn't taken you to that exhibition you'd be happy enough with Grenfell," said Mom. "Remember when the only thought in your head was to go to art school? Remember when you didn't think you'd ever get there? Now all of a sudden Grenfell isn't good enough."

Even Dad nodded at that.

"It's not that I don't want Grenfell," said Cathy. "Grenfell would be great. It's that I want Madame to teach me." Over and over, round and round. And Mom just banged about saying first it was Sarah this and Sarah that and now it was Madame.

Out of the Blue

*

Twelve holes across. Twelve holes the other way. One-hundred-and-forty-four holes in each tile. Ten tiles over to the wall make 1,440. Seven tiles to the fluorescent light make—8, carry 2—10,080 holes. A woman was looking down at him, her face coming, going, coming back. It steadied. Mom? No, but she had the same stop-messing-around-and-listen expression.

"Glad you're awake, Hutch."

A nurse. It took a while for the information to sink in—like a dry sponge that floats on the water for a bit before it starts getting wet. An accident. The bus....

Bus?

Gone off the road on a bend. Bad visibility. Ice buildup. Crashed rear-end-first down a bank. He tried to get his tongue to work, to ask questions. Hutch had the worst injuries, the nurse said, but a lot of folks had broken bones or concussions, or soft-tissue injuries—whatever those were. Someone had a punctured lung from a broken rib, and Jane Butt's father had a small heart attack. Didn't know they came in sizes.

He began to remember pieces—singing and eating Cheezies—but nothing about the crash itself. He started to notice his body in a muffled kind of way, everything stiff. Too stiff to move. He tried turning his head to see his mom better and his side hurt all the way down. He turned back and noticed the lights shining in his eyes, making his head ache. His mouth tasted like he hadn't brushed his teeth for a month. He started to take a deep breath to ask where everybody was and knives stabbed through his ribs, so he took a little breath and kept his voice small. Mom said folks hurt the least were taken to Clarenville or Gander but they'd brought Hutch straight to town.

"What about Jack?"

"He's got a minor concussion and a broken arm. Gone to Gander."

"And Eugene? And Jenny?"

Mom looked at Dad. "Not sure where they were taken," said Mom. "Weren't brought into town."

His parents kept getting into a huddle with whatever nurse walked in the door, muttering so he couldn't hear. "Just checking," they said when he asked. "Just making sure everything's being done." He wondered about that but it was too much effort to keep after them to see what they were hiding.

And anyway, what about him? What about Hutch Parsons? This was going to mess up every-frigging-thing. Just when he'd applied to the Marine Institute. He'd miss a pile of school and this was grade twelve. This would affect his grades. It mattered this time. Why hadn't that bus driver been more careful? Why had they set off at all if the roads were so bad? It's February, b'y. The other bus made it. Not fair.

+

There was a meeting. They wheeled his bed with all those tubes and stuff into a tiny space off Intensive Care. They were slow and careful but something bumped and he felt the bump go all through him. Felt like he'd just jumped down onto concrete. Hutch tried to move his legs a bit to ease them but it only made it worse.

Mom and Dad came in and smiled at him, but their eyes were scary. There was a tall guy in a white coat with a hawk face and bushy old-man eyebrows, a younger doc wearing a name tag, Somebody MacPherson, and the nurse who was around all the time with the singsong voice. Then a grey-haired lady with brown folders under her arm and glasses. Never seen her before.

The singsong nurse introduced everybody. Said she was the charge nurse. Hawk-face was the orthopaedic guy and his name had *ov* and *evsky* in it like hockey names all strung together. The young one was his resident.

The nurse's voice was nice but distracting—Hutch kept listening to her voice, not her words. Not from around here. Welsh, she told him afterwards. The grey-haired woman was a social worker.

The nurse looked at his mom and dad and him, each in turn, and talked about the accident and his injuries. Chatty. Said something about his rib cage, something thoracic crushed. Crushed didn't sound good. Couldn't get too excited because it all sounded so far away, nothing to do with him. Stable spine. Discs, nerve roots…pressure. Inflammation. Swelling going down nicely. Wait and see. Lost some blood, under control, lucky the paramedics got to him in time.

Holy shit.

"And I'll let Dr. …evsky explain about the legs."

Hawk-face looked straight at Hutch. Nice that he was talking to him, but hard to be stared at like that. Just him. That guy standing and him stuck flat on his back like something in science class with a pin through it. What was he saying? The right leg had been sorted out. The left leg: "bone fragments…tissue loss…vascular surgeon…."

A whoosh of fear scorched through Hutch, white hot.

"Limb salvage…."

Like a frigging ship wreck.

"…best we can hope for." Not. Minimal. Unable. None. Eventually. "Best outcome, the most functional outcome, would be to remove the severely damaged leg below the knee and—"

"No. No!" Hutch was yelling in spite of his stitches. "No way you're cutting off my leg! Never."

Dad said, "My boy," and Mom said, "Hutch, Hutch," and Hawk-face kept on explaining and Hutch kept on yelling. Didn't care about the risk and all the surgeries, didn't care how good prosthetics were these days. He wanted his own leg. It was his fucking *leg*. He heard the doc saying, "Just think about it and we'll talk later."

But Hutch wasn't changing his mind. No way.

+

They moved him into a general ward. There were people in other beds but he couldn't see them. Dr. MacPherson, the resident, was around a bit.

Said he'd been to Mariners Cove once, paddled in with a group from Memorial back when he was doing his undergrad.

"In sea kayaks?" Hutch was interested then and told the doc maybe he was with the group Dad saw. "Dad had a good look at a bunch of kayaks that visited one day, then he took a paddle in one and built one himself. Still has it. It's called *May* after my mom."

He said how the Parsons had always built their own boats for the inshore fishery but there was no market for them now, so his dad had turned to kayaks instead. Sold about fifty. Hutch even told the doc about *Dolph* because he seemed an okay guy. He didn't say about kayaks being made of fibreglass these days, made by the dozen in factories on the mainland. So the arse was out of that industry as well. The legs.

+

Hutch went right on refusing an amputation. And everyone had a go at him: Dr. MacPherson, his family, the nurses…the frigging mailman was probably on his way. Dad said he was thinking with his gut not his head.

Mom said, "They're treating you like an adult, Hutch, giving you a choice."

"What choice? When I choose everyone yells at me and tells me I'm choosing wrong."

Mom came nearer the bed, loomed over him. "Patients your age usually go to the children's hospital. You only ended up here because the ICU was full. But you're still a child—"

"I'm *not* a frigging child!" The roar made his ribs stab and he broke off. Dad shifted in his chair, told him to watch his tongue, and Mom glared at Dad for a change.

"I know it's hard, Hutch." There were tears in her eyes. "But you have to look facts in the face. You'll walk better, look better, have less side effects…if you have an amputation."

Hutch clamped his teeth together to keep his thoughts in, and keep himself from shaking. His heart was pounding like he'd just run up Bald Head. As if. Mom put her hand on his, gave it a squeeze, and moved away before he had time to fling it off.

"We'll be back tomorrow. If you want us."

He tried to yell that he didn't but he couldn't breathe, couldn't speak.

Dad stood up, chewing his lip. "We want what's best for you, Hutch," he said after a bit. "You know that." He nodded. "If it was someone else in this spot what would you tell them?" He gripped Hutch's shoulder for a moment then they were gone.

Hutch closed his eyes. Now he was alone—alone except for being picked at by some nurse or other, and the man in the next bed with the beige screens who he still hadn't seen, and the beeps and buzzers, smells, trolleys rattling, and the loudspeaker paging Dr. Murphy for the thousandth time. He'd never minded being alone. Always plenty to do, places to go. This was different. Felt like he wanted to hide but someone had moved the trees.

Everything was sliding away, out of control. Stuff was being done to him all the time—stuff he'd always done himself. Taken for granted. Even washing, for god's sake. He'd tried to grab the face cloth out of the aide's hand, but he'd twisted his rib cage and given himself a real jolt.

Without the amputation one leg would be way shorter than the other, would need more surgeries, and he might end up with the leg off anyway if infection set in. Might be in and out of hospital for years. With an amputation and a prosthesis, he could be functional within months and look almost normal. Get on with life.

Or so they said.

But an amputation was so...forever.

+

Hutch asked Dr. MacPherson when he'd be able to play hockey and the guy didn't look straight at him like he usually did, just said something about it being early days. Well, residents didn't know everything. God, he and Jack had really been working at it. The coach had put them on the same line because they were a good combination: Jack for speed and Hutch for power.

Power. He had no power now, over anything. Well, he could fill out that menu card and choose his breakfast. Yeah, right. Prunes or grapefruit. The only real choice he had now was about the leg, and he wanted to tell them all to shove off.

A nurse said Hutch was lucky to be so fit and muscular, but when Hutch checked out his arms he noticed how flabby his biceps had gone, how they'd shrunk. That nurse didn't know what muscular was. And his shoulders had shrivelled away to nothing—his big kayaking shoulders. Frigging vanished. Months to build them up and they were gone in a few days. He couldn't believe it, kept checking. Gone.

Dr. MacPherson wanted to look at the leg. He asked if Hutch had seen it yet, said it was time. If he couldn't see it lying down they'd find a mirror. The nurse was ages coming up with a mirror. *Don't let her find one. Don't let her.* The doc had opened up the splint or whatever was down there and peeled away all that padding.

"Look at it, Hutch." No. Not looking. "Open your eyes Hutch." No. Can't. Not looking. No. "You need to look at this Hutch. Open your eyes."

Fuck. Holy fuck.

+

The aide was bellowing in his ear, "Never ate your lunch b'y."

Hutch looked at him, blank, and buddy lifted the cover off a plate near Hutch's nose. "Liver," said the aide. It looked like a piece of bark curled up at the edges with a mushy scoop of mashed potatoes and some dead carrots.

"Not hungry," Hutch said. "Thanks."

He hadn't even noticed the food being brought and that little plastic thing for pills was empty, so the nurse must've done her rounds too. It was ages before Dr. MacPherson came back.

"If I don't have the amputation, what would you have to do to turn that," he jabbed his chin toward the splint, "into a leg?"

The doc stood looking at Hutch, then said he needed pictures to explain. He came back later with this big book. Like a geography textbook—*Grant's Atlas of Anatomy*. He leaned it on the table, tilting it so Hutch could see. "This is what the lower leg looks like inside, the layers. See these bones, joints, these muscles…."

"So that's like a lever," said Hutch, after a bit.

The doc nodded. "Exactly."

"And the muscle that would move the lever should be down there but mine's gone?" He waited for the nod. "And you'd need to glue all those bits together before you could stick it back on again?" Yes. "And it wouldn't work anyway because the wiring's gone?" More nods. Hutch stared at the diagrams, reached up and flicked a page. "You do plumbing too?"

Dr. MacPherson smiled. Waited.

Hutch's throat closed up and his mouth felt like wrinkled cardboard. How would he manage on a trawler? In a storm? He'd manage. Somehow he'd manage. But he'd have to change stuff. It meant letting go of hockey and hiking, even chasing a ball around the schoolyard. He'd walk like an old man. And girls. God, don't think about girls. He could practically hear his Mom: *Nice girls won't care.* Yes, but the other kind was more fun.

He tried to speak but had to clear his throat and start again. He took a tight breath and forced the words out; they came out in a bellow, like when his voice was breaking.

"Better take it off then."

+

Mom and Dad smiled when they came back, hugged him, and said they were proud of him. Said he'd just needed time to think it through.

"So now you can stop whispering to all the nurses." Hutch's grin felt a bit stiff.

They both stood there like lumps with that scary look back in their eyes.

"What?" He looked from one to the other. "*What*?"

Nobody spoke.

"Tell me."

"Eugene and Jenny," Mom said. Stopped. "The back of the bus." She was whispering. "It went through the ice into a pond."

Dad put his arm round her shoulders. "They were both killed, Hutch. They're gone."

Hutch lay there. The facts seeped into the edges of him but his insides had frozen solid. Eugene and Jenny? Couldn't be. Now and then something tiny would float up: Jenny splashing him with her paddle, Eugene's big front teeth. After a time he turned his head away and pulled the sheet up over his face.

Surprise

*

Cathy dropped by, which was something she never did. Sarah wouldn't mind—always said she liked unexpected visitors. But Sarah paused for a second when she opened the door, didn't open it wide straight away, and the smile was just a bit slow arriving. She said she was sorting out some mail and the kitchen was up to your eyes.

"Sorry. Can I just wait here for half an hour until Mom's ready?" Cathy said. "Won't get in your way and I'm soaked." Sarah said of course, switched on the coffee pot and started shuffling papers into a pile. Cathy pulled out a chair and an envelope caught her eye. She'd seen that logo before.

"Mount Allison University," she said, surprised. "That's where Mary Pratt went." She remembered reading about her in one of those art books of Sarah's. Colours swam up before her: reflections off glass bowls, the shine on aluminum foil, the way the light shone through a jar of fruit jelly—translucent, Sarah called it. "I've tried painting a jar of Mom's partridgeberry jam the way Mary Pratt does it but I can't."

"That's why you're going to go to art school."

The rain was really rattling on the windows now, leaving those little smudges that said some of it was sleet. Cathy's jacket was steaming softly where Sarah had hung it in the corner by the radiator and a wet-laundry smell was trying to smother the smell of fresh coffee.

Sarah set a blue-and-white-striped mug in front of Cathy. "Don't burn yourself."

She came back with the milk. Those mugs each held a pint, easy. Cathy had drawn a cartoon once, of Sarah trying to climb out of one. The sketch hung on their fridge for ages. Then Dr. Brooks said it was starting to show its age so he put it away in an album to save it, saying it was better than a photograph.

Now Sarah was putting a bowl of nuts between them. All the papers and stuff were gone. That envelope. Cathy looked around and there was a pile of papers on the counter with a blank sheet on top. She looked at Sarah, trying to read her face. It looked closed up. Mustn't ask. Was it about art school? Was it about babies? Mind your own business, Cathy Russell. Her eyes crept back to the pile.

"Have some nuts."

"Thank you."

Cathy took a handful and one bounced onto the table and rolled off. Dog scrabbled to his feet and went hunting then stood by Cathy's elbow, staring at the bowl, first with the left eye, hauling that eyebrow up in folds, then with the right. Nothing sneaky or sideways about dogs. Not like Mom's cat.

They talked about Dog for a few minutes and took tiny hot sips from their mugs. Sarah spread her hands flat on the table, fingers straight, and sat staring at them, then she looked up and said, "I've been applying for jobs. That's why there was an envelope from Mount Allison."

"You're leaving." Cathy's mug jerked and coffee slopped out onto her hand. The world turned dark: black and white, grey, brown, sepia. "When?"

"Oh, you'll be gone long before me." Sarah fetched a tissue and held it out. Cathy just looked at it. "To dry your hand," Sarah said. "I've been applying for jobs but there's a lot of competition. No luck so far. I knew it would be like this—that's why I've started already."

The fridge gave a little bang and a shake and Dog flopped down on the floor again.

"Don't you like it here?"

"Of course I do. But I need something to do, Cathy, especially after you're gone." They drank another inch of coffee. "Please don't tell anybody. It's not a good time to be talking about this when everyone's so upset about the crash. I'd started before it happened."

Cathy nodded.

"And I don't want people asking about it all the time. It's a slow process, chasing academic jobs. Might take years."

"But you've got a doctorate."

Sarah's eyebrows twitched. "So have lots of other people. And other people didn't go off to a little Newfoundland outport for four years. Other people taught in universities or got some sort of experience to put on their resumé." She laughed, but it wasn't the kind of laugh that meant you were enjoying yourself, and said, "Resumé: summary: nothing at all."

"But you've taught me for four years. You got me from grade seven to grade eleven. Doesn't that count?"

Sarah looked at Cathy and smiled her own real smile. "It's a wonderful achievement as far as I'm concerned. Worth everything." This was more like Sarah. "I have so enjoyed teaching you. And learning—you've taught me a lot too, you know."

"But can't you put that on your resumé?"

"Oh, I have. But it doesn't carry as much weight as a regular job." Sarah finished off her coffee, gathered up the empty mugs. "But I haven't given up. There may be a job out there for someone with practical experience in literacy problems and I'll just—"

Was that what Cathy was? A literacy problem? Does that mean…?

"What exactly did you say? About me?" Sarah turned and looked at her, mouth open. "On the summary," Cathy said. "The resumé."

Sarah looked like she was thinking. "Just that I taught someone for four years whose level of literacy was not sufficient to keep up in school and who had therefore failed grade seven. And at the end of those four years that person was passing everything—and I put in a few grades as examples—and was about to graduate from grade eleven, and was determined, moreover, to continue with post-secondary education."

Moreover. Move over, moreover.

"You didn't mention my name?" No. "Or the name of the school?" No. "Or about art school?" No, nothing personal at all.

"Did you say I was illiterate?"

"No. You were never illiterate. That means you can't read or write anything."

Like Mom. But she had that brain thing where the letters get all fooled up. Dyslexia. It was something in your body, like diabetes or arthritis. Nothing to be ashamed of. Cathy's kind of illiteracy was more that you were lazy or a bit dumb and just couldn't keep up. Cathy took a big breath, "Can you be a little bit illiterate?"

Sarah said she never used that word. Cathy asked if other people did and she said, well, yes, some people. And did they say you could be a little bit illiterate? Sarah didn't answer and her lips were all pressed together so Cathy said it was all right, she didn't have to answer, Cathy would look it up.

"Well," Sarah said, and sighed. Sarah didn't usually do the sigh thing. "Some textbooks refer to functional illiteracy—some reading and writing but not enough to function in the workplace or daily life."

Like school. So Cathy had been functionally illiterate back when they first met? There was a long silence, then Sarah said it was an expression she never used and didn't like. Some people just liked putting labels on things. But would some people say Cathy had been functionally illiterate? Perhaps, but it had only been for a very short time. Cathy had come a long way since then and was definitely going a lot further.

She, Cathy, had been Functionally Illiterate.

+

Funny how having a label made such a difference. It meant she was in textbooks. It meant there were enough other people with the same problem to make it important enough to *be* in textbooks, which should have been comforting but wasn't. It just made it official.

It was like having a criminal record. Jed Batton's uncle had always been a bad lot. Everyone knew that. Mom said you just don't put temptation in his way. But then he ended up in court in Gander and was found guilty. So now he had a record. Now he'd have trouble getting a job—not that he'd ever try. Now he was a criminal, so they wouldn't let him into the States—not that he'd want to go.

It was like the time Aunt Maisie had that awful cough. Once she started coughing she couldn't stop and she'd be almost choking and going red in the face. Made noises like when you're drinking from a straw and there's nothing left at the bottom. The aunts just said oh dear, poor Maisie, and carried on. Except for Aunt Gert, who said it was ruining card night. Then old Dr. Powell told Maisie it was bronchitis. And the aunts changed their tune:

"Oh my, Maisie. Go home and go to bed. Should be looking after yourself better."

"Make Reg cook supper for once. Do him good."

"I'll pick up groceries for you. Just tell me what you want."

Aunt Maisie kept saying she didn't feel any different from yesterday but nobody listened.

Relearning

✦

Hutch's eyes were open. If they'd shone a light in, his pupils would have contracted and dilated obediently, but he was not at home. The room was a blind white square and he was a blind white shape inside it. For two days the trolleys went on rattling, the fluorescent light near his bed kept up that high F-sharp hum, and Dr. Murphy was still the most wanted man in the hospital. It was all white noise to Hutch.

The amputation was just a shadow in the background while his mind flickered through reruns of Jenny and Eugene, of life Before. He was aware of being transferred to stretchers and wheeled along hallways for scans and X-rays and to the operating room, but nothing felt as real as those reruns.

✦

Bright light on his eyelids. The sun warm on his arms and the gentle lift and fall of swells under his boat. The best gift ever: back in grade eight when his parents gave him material to build a kayak of his own—if he promised to work harder at school. And Hutch promised. Do anything.

He triple measured every piece and fussed over each step. He hung over the soaking wood strips, smoothed every tiny roughness to perfection, breathed in that wood-and-resin smell. Dad checked stuff but Hutch wouldn't let him help. This was His Boat. He stencilled her name on the side in bright green: *Dolphin.* And he did put a bit of effort into his homework now and then. He only pipped off a few times.

And over those next summers he got more of a feel for the ocean, for the pull of the tide, for wind direction and dampness in the air. He watched for changes in visibility and the clearness of edges, knew where he'd be less sheltered from the wind and where sunkers could cause waves. He learned everything about his boat. They moved together, him and *Dolph.*

+

His leg was gone. Hutch couldn't see the stump because it was all wrapped up but he could see what was missing: his foot, his shin. And he could still feel it, all crunched up and really hurting, how it was after the crash. Now that wasn't fair. When he told the docs about that they upped his pain meds. Something about reducing pain memory. He was never quite awake after that.

He thought maybe Paul had been leaning over him once except he looked awful. Never seen him like that. Looked like he was on something heavy, only Paul wouldn't, ever. Never did join in when the guys had something special. Jenny would give him hell. He could never see why Paul was so wound up in Jenny. Pretty, for sure, but bossy. Bossed all her brothers. They never seemed to mind—just laughed—maybe because she was the youngest and the only girl. But she treated Hutch the same way and he didn't like it. Didn't have a sister. Didn't want one. And whenever he broke up with someone Jenny always took the girl's side, especially after Jane Butt.

"...Hutch? *Hutch.*" A nurse was looking down at him.

Jenny.

Eugene.

The leg.

It was like hearing it fresh every time.

As soon as his stitches were out they transferred him. Hutch asked about the other leg, why that burning pain was still there, but the docs just said give it time.

+

He was moved to rehab. It was just fifteen minutes away by ambulance but it seemed to put him back in the real world. He was in a four-bed room by a big window and he could see sky and the top halves of trees. Almost like home only not many evergreens, and it was April so they were mostly twiggy black lines with crows in them.

This old guy, William, had a bed at the other end of the window. He was in a wheelchair. Must have had a stroke because his right arm was floppy. When Hutch asked him how long he'd been there, the good half of his face screwed up but he just drooled and the only word that came out was "shit." He looked embarrassed and held up four fingers of his good hand.

"Four days?" Hutch said.

William shook his head.

"Four weeks?"

Big nod.

There was something Hutch liked about William's face. It was gentle, like Dad's.

"Well, at least you can see trees," Hutch said to him. "But they're a poor lot compared to Mariners Cove. We've got thick spruce and fir at home, right down to the water in some places." William looked interested, nodding his head and smiling right-handed.

Hutch got into the habit of yakking away to William, not waiting for replies.

"Mom always expects me to do something bad—she's saying no before I've even thought of it sometimes." Then he gave a sly grin and added, "But mostly I've thought of it."

William chuckled and did a thumbs-up with his good hand.

"Dad just gives you a look but you know he means business. Whatever you're plotting, forget it." Wouldn't it be nice if the family walked in the door right now. "And my brother, Brian, he's a whiz with computers. Does computer repairs, in Gander mostly. Stays at Lori's, his girlfriend's. Seven years older than me but he's never treated me like a kid, ever. Great brother."

One day Hutch said, "Put your smile and my smile together and we'd have a whole one between us."

William laughed and laughed.

+

He worked his ass off in rehab. Maybe he overdid it sometimes—he just wanted to get better fast—but overdoing put him back every time, so he learned the hard way about "slow and steady."

He was up in a wheelchair now for half-hour stretches. He'd never thought about the effort it took to do the simplest thing from a wheelchair. And how slow life was when elevator doors stayed open for minutes at every floor. Then he heard Eugene's voice saying, "Just get on with it, b'y." Sounded so real, it gave him a start.

It was a relief to be up and doing. His folks had given him a Game Boy, which he loved, but lying flat and holding it up hurt after a bit and his back killed him when he sat for long. Couldn't concentrate. Listening to his music was great in small doses—Eminem, Red Hot Chili Peppers, AC/DC—but it was better as an accompaniment, not the main attraction, and some were kayaking songs, like "Slim Shady." He tried not to think about how to balance his kayak, now all that weight of leg was gone, that he would miss exams, wouldn't graduate.

He tweaked his headphones and turned up "Gangsta's Paradise."

+

"And how are we this morning?" said a singsong kindergarten voice.

"We are single," Hutch said, sticking out his arm for blood work. How old did she think he was?

The guy in the next bed looked not much older than Hutch but the screens were round him half the day and he spent hours on a stretcher in the lounge. He'd broken his neck in a Ski-Doo accident, been thrown off and hit a tree. Guy was paralyzed and had a head injury. Words came out chewed; he sounded like a recording played at the wrong speed.

"Shoot me," Hutch said to Bud on one of his Friday-night visits. "If I'm ever like that, please shoot me."

Eugene and Jenny would agree with that. Wouldn't they?

Bud's visit was a bright spot in the week. He talked about his classes at Memorial and girls and the NHL and sometimes he brought stuff to study and it was just friendly having him sitting there next to him.

Hutch liked the staff although one of the aides wasn't as friendly as the rest, didn't pay much attention. One time she put a folded blanket down on his good leg. He didn't say anything first, but it was right where it had been pinned in surgery and it was still tender. After a few minutes the weight was making it uncomfortable so Hutch asked her to move it, but she rushed out of the room right then as if she'd just remembered something.

He called after her, "You forgot your blanket," but she didn't come back.

Hutch couldn't reach it lying down and when he tried to kick it off he got a sharp pain in his back and that awful burning pain shot down his leg. He just started yelling.

"Come and take this frigging blanket off me! You don't fucking listen! You deaf or what?"

He kept right on yelling until some woman with a clipboard rushed in and he was pointing at the blanket and sputtering because by then he couldn't get the words out and the pain was on bust and he was so mad he didn't know what he was saying. By this time the nursing supervisor and a security guy and the clipboard lady were all telling him to calm down and the cause of the trouble was nowhere in sight. Fucking vanished.

A social worker came and talked to him. No, he wasn't going to make a formal complaint. No, he wasn't going to sign any incident form. He just wanted that woman to stay away from him. And most of the time she did.

+

He drifted off to sleep one afternoon and when he woke, there was a guy he didn't know standing by his bed. Not staff. Old. No, not that old, but he had those deep grooves going from nose to mouth that make a face look worn out, worried. He just stood there without saying anything.

"Hi," said Hutch.

"You don't remember me." The man pressed his lips together for a second, making those grooves deeper. "I was the driver." He was looking right at Hutch, like he was waiting to see his reaction.

Jesus, this was the guy who caused it all. Walking around free while he was stuck in bed. While Jenny and Eugene...Jesus.

The guy looked away, nodding. "I'm sorry," he said. "Nothing I can do except say I'm sorry." He started to walk away.

Hutch called out, "No. Wait."

The man half turned towards him and said, "Wish I'd died myself instead of those kids, instead of what happened to you."

Then he walked away and Hutch never saw him again.

Chance

✵

Somebody was sitting in Cathy's spot on the wharf. It was Jane Butt, all huddled down, blowing her nose. Cathy slowed and almost kept walking, but then turned onto the wharf and sat cross-legged next to her, fidgeting from side to side until she was comfortable. Jane glanced over once then looked back down at her knees, huddling down even more.

"You must miss Jenny some lot," Cathy said. "You were her best friend."

"Yes."

After a minute or so Cathy said, "They used to start from here sometimes, in the kayaks."

"Yes." Jane looked out over the water. "I've been picturing them all going off paddling together, calling out and laughing. Jenny was always laughing." Gulls were riding the swells—the experts, being cool. "Mom says I shouldn't come here, shouldn't keep poking at it. The hole."

"Yes, but you can't help poking at it."

They sat in silence, so still a gull landed on the edge of the wharf in front of them with something dangling from its beak. It stood tossing the loose end up and gulping, tossing and gulping, until it was all gone.

"She was the only person who always spoke to me," said Cathy. Jane looked at her and frowned, shook her head a bit. "Well, you did too," Cathy said. "But it was always Jenny said hello first."

"That's because you didn't answer when *I* said it—if I spoke first or was on my own. You ignored me. I gave up trying ages ago." Jane pulled away a bit.

Cathy was put out. Never did that.

"Don't remember you saying hello first. Ever." She had a little tussle with herself. "Sorry. If I did that. Must have not heard." It came out a bit gruff but at least it came out.

Jane just shrugged and after a bit she said, "So why did you hear Jenny and not me? My voice is just as loud. Louder." She sounded annoyed.

Cathy tried to think back. She pictured Jenny last summer on a day just like this. She'd appeared out of nowhere carrying her paddle, put a hand on Cathy's arm and said, "Hiya Cathykins," in that bouncy way she had. And once, in class last winter, she'd put her hand on Cathy's shoulder as she passed between desks and whispered, "Don't mind her, Cathy." She could feel the hand now. Couldn't remember who'd been mean that time—there was always someone. Although people had been nicer mostly since she'd started catching up in school. Or was it because she listened more? Answered people? She began picturing other times when Jenny had greeted her and there was always that touch.

"Her hand." Cathy turned to Jane, her voice excited. "Every time Jenny spoke to me she put her hand on my arm first, got my attention. Never thought of it before." She could feel a big smile on her face.

Jane was staring at her. "You serious? D'you mean to say you need a punch in the arm to make you know someone's standing right in front of you?"

Cathy's smile slipped. "Maybe. Don't always see what's in front of me when I'm thinking about stuff."

She turned away and watched the gull hopping and flapping its way down the wharf.

"You really do have your head in the clouds, don't you?" Jane's voice had lost that sharpness but she still didn't sound too sure. "And here I thought you saw things better than the rest of us, being an artist and everything."

Cathy was good at noticing. She was excellent at noticing. Just not all the time.

"Pity we didn't know this years ago," said Jane. The gull was pecking at something further along the wharf now, looking for dessert maybe. "Now that I know, I'll give you a slap upside the head every time I see you."

Jane's smile was the tiniest ever. Cathy leaned across and put an arm round her for a second, gave her a little squeeze.

+

A week later Jane grabbed her by the arm and yelled, "Hi!" Made her jump. Cathy was walking away from Sarah's house where they had been working on "goals and objectives" for her art school applications. She needed two portfolios now, which meant a lot of pictures, but they both looked great—*impressive* Sarah called them—some actual sketches and small paintings with photographs of some of her bigger pictures. Cathy would take everything to school in September. Sarah said she'd help with the forms.

"Cathy? We're just going to The Café. Come with us."

There were two other girls with Jane, both from Cathy's class, and Cathy was feeling so excited and hopeful about her portfolio that she said yes without thinking, then paused. "But I don't have any money on me."

They all stopped and looked at her.

"You don't need..."

"But..."

"Have you never been to The Café?" said Rose Tucker. They were still staring at her and Cathy's *no* was very small because this was telling them she was weird more than anything.

"Jenny invited me but I never went."

"Well," said Jane, and there was a kind of group sigh and they all started moving again and Cathy had to hurry to catch up. "You know how the place started...? Ricky Abbott was getting into stuff—"

"—Chris Abbott's brother, the one out in Alberta—"

"—back in grade seven—"

"—and his Dad said there was nowhere for kids to hang out."

"Turned the shed behind his auto body shop into a hangout."

"He's got machines for Coke and chips and stuff but you don't have to buy anything if you don't want to."

They all clomped in and grabbed chairs. Cathy's cousin Annie was over by the pool table and she yelled "Cathy!" like she hadn't seen her in months and some of the guys looked round, a bit surprised, but nodded to her before they went back to their conversation.

Over the next year Cathy went down to The Café now and then, just when she knew Jane and the girls would be there. Sometimes when she was out and around, the girls banged her on the arm with a big yell and a laugh and she started to notice them coming and not to need the signal anymore, but she didn't let on.

Rocks and Shoals

*

Early on, Hutch went down to Prosthetics to be measured for his new leg. He was surprised how soon they made him put pressure on his stump to mould it into a good shape. He spent hours in the gym too, stretching, strengthening, "re-educating."

His first day down there he met a guy called Bruce from Conception Bay South. Bruce had lost a leg in a motorcycle accident. He was a few years older than Hutch and was a good laugh but he kept talking about his girlfriend—they were getting married. It reminded Hutch of Paul and Jenny, and gave him a knot in his stomach. Nobody heard anything from Paul these days.

Paul's parents came once. They said now Paul's only thought was to get away, out of Newfoundland. He had applied for art school in Halifax and he always had his nose in his books, making sure his grades were good enough.

"But at least he's doing that now," said his mom. "Not just staring at nothing. At least he's eating again."

He'd started running three times a week too, always by himself. He avoided everything else, everybody. They hoped Hutch would understand. Well, he didn't really. But then Hutch liked having people around, didn't want to be left alone with his thoughts.

He checked out the people jogging round Quidi Vidi Lake once, from a window of the high-rise joined to his building, Southcott Hall, where the nursing students went, but it was too far away to see faces. Yes, jogging would be good. Pound, pound all the way round. Good to stretch the legs, feel the power. Never fancied running until he couldn't.

+

William always had visitors, mostly suits with posh voices. The men brought books and grapes and the women brought flowers. His sister came most days and always had a cheerful word for Hutch. Now and then there was a real stunner in a fancy outfit with spiky heels and jewellery. Hutch couldn't keep his eyes off her at first. Someone said she was William's wife but she was years—decades—younger.

She took no notice of Hutch, and never looked at William either. She looked at her hands, the ceiling, out the window, anywhere but at William, while he looked up at her like a dog waiting for a pat. But Hutch saw her study William once when he was watching the nurse with the meds trolley. She pruned up her face then, like she saw a worm in the salad, as if all she saw were the grey roots and the droopy lip and the sticky something down the front of his sweater. Hutch wanted to smack her then.

Mom and Dad came when they could, phoned every night. Dad and Brian arrived one day when Hutch was by the bed in his wheelchair.

"Where's Mom?"

"School stuff."

They chit-chatted with William for a few minutes but then William left and they had the room to themselves. Their smiles disappeared and their faces closed up, and Hutch didn't like the way they dragged up chairs and plonked themselves down, looking at the floor.

"So how was the drive in?"

No answer. Dad looked straight at Hutch.

"We came to make a suggestion," he said. "You won't like it but we want you to think about it."

Hutch stiffened up and was saying *no* before Dad even opened his mouth. But Dad started in anyway—said it in a rush, like he'd said it in his head a bunch of times already.

"We think you should start thinking about your future in case you can't go on the boats."

"I'm going on the boats."

"The Marine Institute requires a medical."

"I'm going to walk out of here ready for anything. And I'm going to pass the medical and I'm going on the boats." Hutch folded his arms tight.

"But just in case...."

Something churned in Hutch's stomach, something nasty down in the mud. "I'm going to sea."

Brian looked up then, said Hutch should consider computer studies. He was a natural. And Hutch managed a laugh, kind of, and said he thought his brother would have been pushing geology. Brian shuffled around a bit and said he'd been emailing Chris, who was in Brazil now, and maybe Hutch wouldn't be able to handle the physical end of geology either—out in the field.

"You'd be great at computer studies." Brian's voice seemed loud, pressing in on him. "You have that kind of brain."

There was nothing in the world except that churning and Brian's voice. It was an effort to pull his thoughts together, find his own voice.

"Just like the games." It came out in a growl. "Not spending my life in front of a computer."

"You spend hours on my computer. You're a natural."

"That's playing."

"This would be playing *and* you'd get paid for it."

"I'm going to sea."

Hutch backed out his chair and wheeled himself through the door fast, banged into the door frame and effed at it in spite of his father and effed his way down the corridor and effed at the slow elevator.

They didn't follow. Hutch wheeled himself up and down every corridor on the ground floor, miles of them, head down, scanning the ground from the edge of his eyeballs, feeling them strain, seeing feet getting out of his way in a hurry, hearing a woman calling his name once, ignoring it. He found an empty corner and stopped, facing in, and blew his nose. The churning was still there. Worse. He wondered if he was going to lose his lunch. Yes, that's all it was. Something wrong with his lunch. But they'd just given it a shape, made it more solid. He blew his nose again. What if he couldn't.

Change of Scene

*

Sarah and Tim drove into St. John's to take Hutch out, and to treat him to a good meal. Old Josh Parsons, Hutch's grandfather, was not able to live alone since his stroke and May Parsons was overwhelmed with organizing his discharge from hospital and his removal to their house: wheelchair access, nursing care....

"Hutch will just have to manage for now," May said. So Sarah suggested she and Tim take him out for a day that weekend. It was a shock to see Hutch in a wheelchair, but he manoeuvred it like a pro round their new Jeep, asking about gas mileage and how the Jeep took corners. Hutch chatted and smiled as easily as ever but there were changes in his face—not the contours but the expression. There was a holding back, a wait-and-see. That headlong dive into the next moment was gone.

They went to a steak house with an elevator. Hutch ordered the prime rib, the same as Tim, and watching him enjoy his dinner was worth a foggy journey. He ate it with his eyes first, smiling, examining each item in turn then moving things slightly with his fork so he could see underneath. Then he turned the plate round to get the best route in and paused for a second, considering.

Sarah remembered a lunch at May's house last summer when May had complained, *food never touches the sides.* She'd told Hutch to try chewing before he swallowed. *Slow down. There's another day to live.* Hutch just shovelled everything in at top speed and tore out of the house with his mouth full.

Now he cut a small piece of beef and laid it in his mouth softly, the way a wine taster would, slid it round inside with his eyes half closed. He chewed gently, seemed to be coaxing the meat apart and spreading the pieces round every taste bud. Then he chose another morsel and started all over again. It was a long, slow meal.

"Well, Hutch," said Tim, when they were finished. "I see you left nothing standing."

Hutch just nodded and said, "That. Was. Good."

And then when the waitress came with the bill and asked how they liked the meal, he smiled and said, "Just like home."

Further Education

*

Bruce was discharged and he marched up and down the hallway in his going-home clothes and you wouldn't know he was missing a leg. Hutch was glad when he was gone. They used to practice walking together and Bruce would say, "Come on, slowpoke. Get yer ass in gear!"

At first Hutch would try to keep up, but he had to take longer strides to be faster and it tweaked his back. Then he'd be on the edge of losing his balance because his hips weren't too steady. It made him land hard on his right foot and he'd feel a crunch in his back; burning pain would shoot down his leg and it would be there for the rest of the day. Hutch tried to explain to Bruce about his back and his weak muscles, but Bruce interrupted and said he'd lost more leg than Hutch and look at Terry Fox.

"Think positive, b'y," he'd say in that talking-down-to-you way. "Think positive."

"Think I'm not trying?" Hutch had shot back one time. "Think I want to hobble around like an old man? Jesus, I'm a hockey player."

It was no good explaining to this guy. Bruce worked in an insurance office so his amputation wouldn't affect his job much, and his idea of sport was a darts league. Said he'd have to change his stance a bit but he'd still be able to play. He'd have to give up on motorbikes, though, and he'd made that out to be a big deal.

"Gotta take it like a man, Hutch," he said.

But later Bruce's fiancée said he'd been planning to give up his bike since before the accident because she hated them and said they'd be no good once they had children. It made Hutch so effing mad. He wanted to yell and punch things. Didn't know what to do with himself sometimes. When he'd got boiled up at home, which wasn't often, he kicked a ball around or threw rocks in the water or hiked through the woods. He'd been able to work it off. If he tried that now he'd fall flat on his face.

Hutch worried about his weak muscles. He worked and worked at them but just couldn't get them back to normal. But it was the pain that pulled him up short more than anything.

There was another scan and a consult with Hawk-face. Too much play in the left sacro-iliac joint...pain on weight-bearing...some instability... nerve roots in his back...loss of strength could improve over time. Joint pain, nerve pain.... He'd see Hutch in the Orthopaedic Clinic for follow-up after he was discharged.

Hutch had a bad back. Jesus, old men had bad backs not him, just turned eighteen. With his bad back and crappy balance, how would he manage on a wet deck, an icy deck—a deck on the ocean that tilted and corkscrewed?

He'd wait and see how things went. In a few months.

+

Mrs. Powell Senior lived near the Rehab Centre and once Hutch could handle two hours in his wheelchair, he was invited every Sunday for lunch along with Bud. Bud said Paul was invited too but he never came.

The house had wide doors and a ramp, left from when Dr. Powell had been in a wheelchair, so Hutch wheeled himself over every weekend. The house sat on a hill with a view of the lake and they watched the action on the water while they ate. Mrs. Powell said the rowers were out at all hours practicing for the regatta but it didn't seem to bother the wildlife. Hutch scoffed at her idea of wildlife.

"Townie ducks. They've got an easy time of it—people throwing food at them all day and no risk from hunters." He would not think about the rowing.

And here comes the Royal St. John's Regatta. You would hear the loudspeakers from the lake all over the building. There would be back-to-back races all day, people talking about teams and times, and whether the whole affair should have been postponed until the next day because of the wind.

Hutch prepared himself for Regatta Day by persuading people to bring him a beer or two. He used up every cent he had, even though some of them said, "Nah, keep your money." Most people assumed he was of legal drinking age, if they thought of it at all. For them it was just a matter of breaking the *No Alcohol on the Premises* rule.

"It's Regatta Day for god's sake. Give the poor guy a beer."

Hutch collected eleven bottles, and he drank the first two with breakfast. At least he waited until he had food inside him. William had gone to live with his sister and wasn't there to give Hutch the eyeball—just an empty white bed, waiting for the next poor slob.

He skipped his rehab appointments and just wheeled himself up and down the hallway all Regatta Day. Each time he came back to his bed he pulled out a bottle from his locker and took a few swigs. Two more bottles with lunch.

He slowed down in the afternoon and there must have been a smell of alcohol because the aide ransacked his locker and took it all. Hutch had expected that and had hidden two bottles in the cleaning closet. But then a nurse saw him getting one and there was a tussle and she called security and things got a bit fuzzy after that.

The next day he was told he'd thrown up all over the place and the cleaning staff was in revolt.

"And you kept everyone awake singing that awful rap song."

"...one in the morning..."

"...every other word the F word."

He had no end of tongue-lashings. He was warned he would be discharged if it happened again. Did he know they'd have to report him to the police for underage drinking? Hutch just sat there and let it roll over him. But it was one of his worst days, and not just because of the hangover; he'd probably yanked every nerve he owned.

"And you know alcohol isn't a good painkiller."

Well, not the day after it wasn't.

+

Nine months passed before Hutch was discharged. The pain and instability held him back, but he managed to walk over to Mrs. Powell's for his last Sunday lunch and even managed the steps. And he did not take that frigging cane. They kept pushing the cane all the time *for safety.* "Not all the time. Just for uneven surfaces or ice or for hills and steps."

His mother bought him one that folded so he could carry it around out of sight, *so it's there if you need it.*

Brian and Lori drove in to take him home. It was the first time he'd seen them since they got engaged. The staff advised him not to wear his leg for the long drive but Hutch wanted to be able to walk into the house like a normal guy so he wore it anyway. By the time they pulled into the lane his stump was sore and everything ached, but he was too excited to care.

The minute they stopped, the door opened and light poured out. The family was pulling on boots and calling out. The dog was winding round his legs, bumping into him, his mom was giving him a hug like she hadn't seen him for months, Gramps was calling from the kitchen, and Dad was in there somewhere patting his shoulder. Hutch had a tight hold of Brian's arm because he couldn't see where he was putting his feet and stones were tipping them every which way and throwing him off balance.

But it was so good. So good to be home.

The Aunts

*

"How's Stephanie Sheppard doing?" Aunt Dot asked.

"No change," said Aunt Maisie. "Still staring into space. Doesn't eat. They say Dr. Brooks is trying to get her in to see someone in Mental Health but there's a year's waiting list."

"That's shocking. She could be…you need the help when you need it."

"And young Hutch Parsons," said Aunt Gert. "My, oh my. How are they going to keep him on the farm? He'd applied to Memorial, you know. Wanted to do geology. But you can't go tramping around mines and oil wells on one leg."

"Or volcanoes. That show the other night had geologists on volcanoes."

"Too bad," said Aunt Gert. "Him and volcanoes would have got on great together."

"Gert! That's mean, Gert. That poor young man."

Then there was more talk about this person with the frozen shoulder or that one with the bad neck or the wicked headaches, all from the accident. Every family had a victim of some sort. Even Cathy's cousin Annie was having nightmares because she had been at the back of the other bus—the same seat where Jenny had been sitting.

Cathy left the aunts to their first picnic of the summer, headed down the steep road to the little wharf next to the Mariners Head fish plant. The building looked like it was remembering a time when it had a life—it seemed to sag, though if you looked closely everything was still at right angles.

But Cathy would draw it with a sag. Weeds poked up through the pavement and litter snagged up against walls, which were stained and rusty looking near the ground. Three old-timer gulls sat on the edge of the roof, facing the ocean. Used to be flocks of them. Cathy sat on the wharf, her back toward the building.

It was true, what the aunts said. The bus crash had changed the whole town, especially Jenny's family. Why did it have to be Jenny? Why, out of that whole bus, out of all of Mariners Cove, did it have to be Jenny? And they said Josh Parsons had that stroke when he heard about his grandson. He was never around on the docks anymore.

And as much as she'd wished the sky would fall on Hutch Parsons, she didn't wish *this* on him. She remembered, back when they were still in the same grade, how every year the teachers would go around asking all the kids what they wanted to do when they left school. Cathy wanted to be an artist and Parsons wanted to captain his own boat. Always. Everyone else changed from year to year or didn't know or didn't care but the two of them knew for sure, always.

Maybe his family—and that geologist friend of his brother's—had been working on him, because when the career people came round last time to talk to the grade elevens and twelves, Parsons had said he might look at geology. But now what?

How would Cathy feel if she lost an arm? That started off as one of those clever questions where you don't expect an answer, but she suddenly pictured herself without her painting arm—no right hand and no chance of ever getting it back. She sat turned to stone, cold to her heart, frightened in a way she had never felt frightened before.

Cathy lay her right hand on her knee, studied it: the way the fingers all leaned towards each other ready to hold her brush; the way her wrist bent back a bit when she was gripping something, which put her hand in the perfect position to work on a picture; the way she could rest the side of her hand on the paper when she needed it to be extra steady. It was so amazing, how everything worked together. Until something went wrong. Her hands were shaking now.

Cathy tried to sketch the rocks in front of her, how they looked when the water frothed up between. Like her aunts back there with all their talk bubbling up in a rush. Rising and sinking. On and on. That spatter of laughter.

Her hands were still quivering—not so anyone would notice, nothing on that Richter scale—but it wasn't stopping. She stuffed everything back in her painting bag and scrambled to her feet. Walk. Take your mind off it.

She set off along the road and the ocean looked so big and empty: no skiffs, no kayaks. She liked to have people in her pictures. Parsons would miss the whole paddling season now and Jack Sheppard wouldn't have the heart to go without him and Jenny, and the other guys wouldn't go if they didn't. She'd seen Mr. Parsons taking tourists for trips round the harbour, but that was business not fun. There was no fun now in Mariners Cove.

Think good thoughts, girl, Cathy told herself. Her reading was as good as the rest of the class now. Not as fast as Rose Tucker, but then nobody was. But Sarah said Cathy was accurate, and that she now read as if she understood what she was reading. Sarah and Dad had both listened to her for hours. Even Mom didn't mind Cathy reading out loud now. Said she was proud of her.

But her writing hadn't changed for ages: same old spelling mistakes, missing apostrophes, that stupid silent *e*. She went back to her room and dug out her project book. This was where she had written notes about subjects she and Sarah discussed: Louis Riel, the Canadian Pacific Railway, the Northwest Passage, the cod moratorium in '92, and her very first notes about that picture of a Tunis market in Sarah's living room.

Sarah had wanted Cathy to make a list of everything she could remember about that picture. Jot notes in a different book from her journals. Sarah kept coming back to it every few weeks. Put your thoughts in order of importance. Put them in groups. Sentences. Now put the sentences in groups. Now write it all out so one group of sentences flows into the next. Now introduce it—something like *this is about a picture of Tunis*—and add a conclusion. *I'd like to paint in Tunis.* Now you have an essay. You said you couldn't write essays. Here's an essay. It's a bunch of thoughts about something, with a beginning, a middle, and an end. Like a painting. Cathy had said a painting didn't have an end and Sarah said a good essay should trigger the reader's thoughts, so it didn't really have an end either. But it had to be complete in itself. Like a painting. One day Cathy was going to win an argument with Sarah. It's not an argument, said Sarah. It's a discussion. Look it up.

Yes, Cathy's writing was definitely improving. And her arguing. Nothing was going to stop her getting to art school now. Nothing.

Home

✶

Hutch's mom had cooked dinner that first evening after he was discharged and the house smelled of turkey and birch junks instead of antiseptic and bathrooms. She gave Hutch first pick of the dark meat and there was salt beef and the last of their home-grown carrots and pease pudding and gallons of good gravy and real cranberry sauce—not those sick-looking rubber squares he'd been having for months.

They turned the lights down once everything was ready and the whole room glowed in deep stained-glass colours. The wood stove crackled and sputtered, sending shadows dancing up the walls. Home. Hutch never wanted to see cream and chrome again in his whole life.

He sat with a smile on his face and let the familiar voices flow round him: Brian and Lori rambling on about their wedding plans and Mom laughing about who was doing what in school. Dad talked about the trouble he'd had with the renovations for some summer visitor.

Gramps kept scraping his plate and asking for things and everyone picked at seconds and thirds and they wiped out two lemon meringue pies. Hutch sneaked food to the dog and Mom saw but let it pass.

Hutch tipped back on the hind legs of his chair so he didn't have to bend in the middle, but the chair overbalanced backwards. He grabbed the table edge to hold himself and everyone jumped and the dog yelped. Less weight at the front of the chair now: something else to be careful about.

The dog tried to sit on his feet but Hutch had taken off the prosthesis before the meal and pinned up his pant leg, so he was confused. He sniffed around the stump with his ears forward in his thinking position then settled back on his haunches, tongue lolling, ears flicking backwards and forwards, looking up at Hutch with his fluffy smile.

"Okay, Trooper?"

The dog always leaned on Hutch's leg or lay on his feet. He went round to Hutch's other side, trying to squeeze in between him and Gramps, whining because the chairs were too close. So they shuffled over to make room and the dog spent the meal leaning against Hutch's right leg, licking the back of his hand now and then. That heavy warmth was so familiar, so comforting, Hutch almost choked up.

+

Aunts and uncles and the younger cousins dropped by over the next few nights; the older cousins weren't home for Christmas yet. They brought in bursts of cold air and loud voices and the aunts brought homemade treats like shortbread and brownies and the kids brought CDs and the uncles brought the aunts and the cousins.

"How are you, my boy? Good to see you home." Uncle Em put an arm round his shoulders and gave him a squeeze, which wasn't his usual style.

His buddies had all finished grade twelve and left while he was in rehab: Jack and some of the guys had gone to St. John's, Andy to Camp Borden for basic training, some to Memorial, and Paul to Dalhousie in Halifax. They were coming back for Christmas except Paul and Bud. Others were gone to Alberta and didn't know when they'd be back.

The Saturday after the guys arrived, Hutch's mom and dad were at a party so the boys all came round and took over the basement. First they were all talking at once, telling him about their new lives, picking out the best bits, the fun things.

"...and you should have seen her face."

"...so he didn't try *that* again!"

Then Jack said, "Let's see it then—the famous leg."

Hutch pulled up his pant leg and showed them his fancy new leg and how he could dance around on it and they all said wow that's real cool and you'd never think. All evening they were laughing, and drinking the beer they'd brought in mother-proof bags, and watching the game.

And everything was just like always.

+

As the guys were leaving Hutch cracked another one-liner—he could never remember what, afterwards—and Andy gave him a punch in the shoulder. But he was just taking a step, good leg in the air, and the punch pushed him toward the peg leg side. His hip muscles weren't quick enough and there were no reflexes to tighten up his ankle muscles—no muscles to tighten—so Hutch couldn't correct the sideways sway, and started to fall. He put his good foot down but couldn't get it under his body in time. He caught at the door with his hand but it swung away from him. So down he went.

There was a huge crash then dead silence.

Then everyone was saying Jesus and holy shit and everything else and Brian rushed in and they all tried to pull him up, holding onto different pieces of him, and he just wanted to stay still until the pain died down.

They were all yanking him around so he roared, "Get off me!"

Another silence.

That vicious pain was round his hip and all down his leg and Hutch knew he wouldn't be able to put weight on it yet and he couldn't get either leg up under him and his back was in a knot and he didn't know what to do for a minute. Then he remembered his rehab lessons.

"Pull over that chair, will you?"

The guys leapt for the chair and Hutch managed to haul himself up and sprawl across it.

"Thought you were going to pull me up in quarters there," he said, with the best grin he could manage. "Felt like a side of moose."

And they all laughed more than the joke was worth.

Brian went out again and Jack said, "Shouldn't've had that last beer, buddy."

The others stood looking awkward and Hutch said he'd be fine in a minute and next time somebody else could do the floor show. He said he'd be seeing them, and after they said are you sure and will you be okay a few times, they piled out onto the porch. Jack stood for a minute looking back, with that blank face like he was remembering. "Talk to you tomorrow," he said in a flat voice. And then they were gone.

Hutch braced against the chair arms and lifted himself round a bit and tried to straighten out. He focused on the wall in front of him to take his mind off himself, but there's not much to see on a blank wall. It wasn't even painted: only a base coat to seal the Gyproc. Dad had been too busy finishing the living room extension to start on the room below, so Hutch and Brian and their buddies had taken it over, playing endless floor hockey with duct tape pucks. He could hear the thuds and grunts and loud breathing, the clack of sticks. Hours and hours. And Mom would bring snacks saying she'd rather they were here, playing hockey, than up to no good somewhere else.

Brian's face appeared in front of him.

"Done any damage?"

"Nope."

"Go to bed, b'y. I'll clear up." Brian found Hutch's cane upstairs, helped him up out of the chair, and stood by him until he could propel himself, somehow, across the room. "You're going to have to get used to that cane."

And with pain exploding everywhere, Hutch didn't have the breath to argue.

Rear-view Mirror

*

Mr. sheppard wanted portraits of Jenny and Eugene, and Cathy spent all summer painting them from photographs. It surprised her that Eugene's portrait was so much easier to paint, even though she didn't know him as well. Cathy captured the wide toothy smile so you could almost hear his big laugh. It was finished in no time. But Jenny.... Was it harder to paint beauty? Jenny's features were so regular and she had no lines on her face and the copper shine in her hair was difficult. The portrait looked wooden. It didn't help that Cathy had to keep wiping her eyes and got more paint on her own face than on Jenny's. She kept starting again and wasted a pile of paint before she was even half satisfied.

In the fall, Dad said Josh Parsons wanted a picture of his grandson, Hutch. Cathy had no photographs of him and the only good sketch she found was from grade four. Parsons had just jumped in a puddle, water spraying everywhere, him with his two feet off the ground and all folded up like he'd just pulled up his landing gear. Dad said she couldn't possibly paint that—not with the grandson having such fun on two legs.

He found one in his own collection, with Parsons standing in his Uncle Em's skiff, his uncle hanging over the engine and somebody else bent down at the other side. Off to do something with fish. Parsons was wearing those yellow coveralls with straps over the shoulders, the front sticking off, all stiff, and definitely rubber boots, although you couldn't see them. Sarah always freaked when she saw all the rubber stuff, said everything would fill up with water and sink so fast. And none of them wore safety gear.

Captain Parsons had been moved to Dan Parson's house after the stroke and when Cathy took over her small painting he was sitting in the window in a scuffed leather arm chair. His own chair, he said, from his old house. He could see the harbour from that window. Mr. Parsons had built out over the hill with another room under it. Dad had helped, said it was a real nice job. Josh Parsons had scoffed at first: what did they need all that for? Looked like a townie house with that basement. But now he liked the big window. No day bed in the kitchen for him. He loved his chair in that window.

Tears came when he saw the painting and Cathy hated to see him cry. He would never have cried before the stroke. Maybe the muscles round his feelings were paralysed too. She had brought extra-small muffins from her mother—easy to eat with one hand, Mom said. Cathy laid them on the table near his good hand and fled.

Gearing Down

*

Hutch was off his feet for a while after the fall. Then he tried to get out and about again. He walked over to White's Convenience, took his time and used the cane with an ice pick on the end, but he left it at the door. Mrs. White was stacking cans but she came round the counter with her arms out for a hug, her glasses smudged with something greasy.

"Great fingerprints for a crime scene," Hutch said, and she took them off and wiped them on her apron and smiled.

"None of your sauce." She called to her husband who was banging around in the storeroom, "Hutch is here."

Alvin White blew out his mustache and pumped Hutch's hand. "Wait now, I'll bring out that chair. Have it behind the door for when Old Mrs. Tucker gets one of her spells."

"No, no. Don't need…don't bother."

But the chair was placed with ceremony on their tiny bit of floor space, over the stew-coloured linoleum, worn and taped down for safety. Centre stage. Shit.

He didn't stay long.

Later, Hutch went with Brian to check his snares but the snow was deeper in the woods and he couldn't get through the thick brush, even with crutches. Still, he might manage where there was more of a trail.

And all through the season there were gatherings at the homes of neighbours and his parents' friends and relatives from both sides.

"You've lost weight. Have some of this chili."

"Will that tin leg rust in the fog?"

"Same young scallywag. Same grin. Haven't changed a bit."

It was all said with hugs and smiles and Hutch felt comforted—still himself in spite of everything.

When he squeezed past his uncle and said, "Excuse me," Uncle Cal said, "Why? What have you done?" And Hutch said, "Not telling," the way they'd been doing for years.

Then there was Phyllis Barnes. It was a surprise to see her at a Parsons event but it turned out she was dating Hutch's cousin Dave. Dave winked at Hutch so it was all good until Phyllis said, "That's going to cramp your style on a date," with a nod at his leg. She wasn't keeping her voice down either.

Hutch turned his back on her but he could hear her sniggering and Dave telling her to hush. To think he'd had his eye on Phyllis for ages before he took her out. They didn't go out for long either because her dad had put his foot down. Gave Hutch a tongue-lashing in the middle of Parsons Lane—had all the dogs barking and faces popping up at windows. Chewed him out for leading his daughter on. Ha! If he only knew. Phyllis did all the leading. Hutch had been part delighted, part shocked at how daring she was.

Now he blanked his face, pushing down a wave of anger and then a wave of worry that other girls might think the same way, and they flooded first one way then the other like water on a tray.

+

Over the Christmas break, Hutch saw his buddies in between family stuff, mostly in a group. But Jack came round alone on his last night, telling Hutch about this girl he'd dated a couple of times from St. George's Bay, sounding excited, telling Hutch how he'd be seeing her again on Thursday.

"What's she like?"

"Pretty. Nice smile. Short." He grinned. "Says I give her a crick in the neck."

Hutch swung down the steps to the basement three at a time on his good leg with the new handrails, Jack following behind him. They started a half-hearted game of foosball but Jack kept talking about his date so Hutch left off playing and just stood listening instead. Then he started to tell Jack about Phyllis Barnes, said in a sour voice at least Paul wouldn't have trouble finding someone new, with girls trailing after him all the time.

Jack stared at him, mouth open, looking mad—horrified and mad. "You really mean that don't you? You really fuckin' mean it." Jack stepped up so close that he started to blur and Hutch had to take a step back to keep him in focus. "Paul doesn't want someone new," Jack said. "He wants *Jenny*. They were together—"

"Hey, simmer down."

"He's not interested in chasing every girl, like you. He just wants Jenny. She told me she was going to apply for nursing school in Halifax so they could be together and...they had it all planned." Jack's face was turning red round his freckles. There was sweat on his forehead so when he pushed his hair back it stuck up at the front, like an orange rooster.

Hutch took a deep breath. "Dumb thing to say. Wasn't thinking."

He flicked a line of defencemen forward and back, forward and back, then gave it a vicious tweak so the players did a rattling somersault.

"Phyllis just made me think my injuries and stuff might turn girls off. Got me wondering, that's all."

"Oh, that's just Phyllis. Real bitch." Jack rubbed two hands through his hair and made it stick up even more. "She'll be putting down Dave the minute they're through. You watch."

They went on with their game in a twitchy, have-to-do-something sort of way.

"Paul's not like you, you know, starting up a conversation with a total stranger and best buddies in five minutes." Jack half smiled at him then was serious again. "Jenny could do it, though. It's like—she got things going and Paul joined in once things were warmed up. Anyway he's not into groups these days."

"How d'you know?"

"Called me. Month or so after the crash. Round Easter maybe."

"Never called me. Never came to visit either." But Hutch remembered Paul's face hanging over him, hazy. Maybe he had, once.

"And you never called him."

The buzzer went off on the dryer and his mom's feet clattered down the stairs. The dryer door clunked then clunked again. Hutch stopped even pretending to play.

"Paul tell you that?"

"Paul didn't call you because he didn't know what to say. Said 'hope you're feeling better' sounded frigging stupid."

"So what's he say to you?"

Jack had his back to Hutch now. "Talked about Jenny. Helped a bit. Me anyway. Both of us maybe." He was hunched over with his hands stuffed in his pockets, walking three paces one way, three paces back. "Can't talk to anyone home. I just stick to things that need doing: groceries and stuff. Mom...." He took a deep breath. "Mom's sick. We take turns looking after her. We try thinking up things to talk about but you got to be so careful. The littlest thing sets her off. Wears you out, thinking."

God. Mrs. Sheppard had been so full of life. Mom used to say she didn't know where she got her energy. Always dancing around, singing to herself.

"Dad keeps himself busy, off in the woods getting logs or cutting them up at the mill. Never had so many piles of two-by-fours. And nobody wants them." Jack shrugged and stood still for a moment then set off again. "I've tried to talk to the others but we never did talk much. It was always Eugene and Jenny...."

Hutch limped over to the nearest chair, lowered himself down with his arms, and eased out the leg.

"My brother, Pete, got Dad to let me go to trade school in St. John's," Jack said. "Said I needed something to work at and I could stay with them. He's just started out on his own, Sheppard's Electrical. His wife does the books. Says I can go in with him when I've finished but I think I'll go to Alberta."

The phone rang and his mother's voice answered, sounding surprised, and the dryer *thump, thump, thump*ed.

"You've lost a lot, Hutch. I know you have. But you haven't lost a *person*. You don't understand." Jack's voice was strained and he gave a swipe at his face with the back of his hand as he walked to the door.

"I've tried not to think about Eugene and Jenny on purpose," said Hutch. "Couldn't handle it on top of everything else." He spoke in a hurry, wanting Jack to understand before he left. "But you don't know how often things remind me of Eugene: guitar riffs or someone saying 'go on' in that way he had."

"Yeah. Catches you off guard, that stuff. Right in the middle of a conversation sometimes and you forget what you were saying." Jack zipped up his jacket, pulled up the hood. "Guess you would miss Eugene. You've just never said."

Jack was turning the handle of the door to the back porch. "Leaving early in the morning so...I'll see you at Easter." And as the door closed he said, "Talk to you before that though."

And he was gone.

New Look

*

"We're going into Gander to get your hair cut," Mom said just before Christmas.

"But it's a perfect morning for painting: eight degrees, dry, wind hasn't got going yet—"

"It's a perfect day for the drive into Gander. I've already made an appointment."

All the way in, Cathy slumped in the passenger seat and glared at the glove compartment. She didn't join in her mother's comments, didn't listen, so Mom talked to the phone-in guys instead: "Oh, for heaven's sake!" and "Well, I couldn't agree more."

There were three women working in the beauty parlour and the girl who washed hair was Jen Abbott. "You must be Cissy Abbott's great niece," Mom said to her, and launched into a load of questions about the Abbott family while Jen shampooed and rinsed and shampooed and rinsed, using enough shampoo to wash a Newfoundland dog. Yes, Jen had finished grade twelve last year and Cathy would have graduated this June past—maybe—if she hadn't had to repeat grade seven, so Jen was Cathy's age and already earning her own money.

Cathy stared at the ceiling all tipped back in a black plastic chair, her head dangling like at the dentist's, with a big lump sticking into her neck. She shuffled down a bit so the lump was in a better place. Aunt Maisie had always cut Cathy's hair. She cut a lot of the family's hair and everyone said she had a real talent, although they all ended up looking kind of the same. Except Cathy. You just went over to Aunt Maisie's with fresh-washed hair and bent forward over the wash basin so she could wet it again before she started cutting. Bending backwards must be a step up in the world.

Raylene was the main stylist so Cathy sat in Raylene's chair and saw herself in the mirror under a row of lights that took all the colour out of her face. How grouchy she looked. She sat up straighter and smiled a bit. Raylene studied Cathy's hair from all sides like she was checking out a painting, lifting up sections here and there, dribbling them through her fingers. Then she beamed at Cathy in the mirror.

"You have lovely, thick, heavy hair."

"Don't be talking," said Mom, coming over to stand behind Cathy. "Always hanging over her face. Dead straight. Won't take a curl no matter what you do. Curling irons, rollers, hairspray…soon as Cathy walks out the door it's all flat and in her eyes again."

"Yes," said Raylene. "This kind of hair likes to go its own way. It needs shaping more than curling." Raylene smiled at Mom. "We've just got some new magazines you might like. There's everything from wedding outfits to teen clothes." Mom had on her now-just-a-minute-young-lady face but Raylene kept going: "…and there's a pale-blue outfit in one of them that was just made for you." Mom's eyebrows went up and her thinking look slid in from the sides like there'd been a change in the wind. "Jen's Aunt Cissy told me all about your marvellous sewing and rug hooking—bet you could copy that outfit, easy as anything." Raylene called to Jen, who was sweeping up hair at the other end of the room. "Can you make Betty a cup of tea and make her comfortable? The magazines have got scattered around a bit." Next thing Jen was asking how much milk.

"Maybe we need something like this." Raylene thumbed through a stylebook and held it up. "It would suit your face, don't you think?" It looked a bit too…different for her mom to approve of, but by now she wasn't taking any notice. And Cathy actually enjoyed watching the cutting, seeing a shape come out of the mess like a sculpture. She'd never thought of hair as a medium before. And Raylene's makeup: that faint dab of colour bringing out the cheekbones—no, not a dab, a trace—and the pencil lines making her eyebrows thicker. You could do that kind of thing on portraits. Must look at her cousin Annie's fashion magazines.

Less than an hour later they were walking back to the truck, Cathy stroking her hair, feeling the smoothness, and her mom saying she wasn't sure about this.

"Let's wait and see what it looks like a week from now," she said.

And when the week was up Mom said it was still messy but not as bad as usual and maybe she'd make another appointment in February.

Bottom Gear

✦

Three in the morning and his thoughts were still doing laps. Hutch lay on his back watching moon shadows slide across the ceiling.

What he hadn't said to Jack, didn't think he ever could, was how bad he felt about Jenny. She'd been bossy and always so frigging sure she was right, but she was fun and she was the first to ask what was wrong if someone looked a bit down. She'd have made a great nurse. Only they hadn't got along those last few weeks because she said Hutch only ever thought about Hutch. And now he could never....

God. He lined up today's worries. Paul and Jack had been helping each other and Hutch had done nothing. Nothing. They didn't understand about his leg but he hadn't given much thought to them either. And Paul. How come Paul never told him about his and Jenny's plans? Because Hutch would have scoffed. Maybe he would have scoffed. Definitely. He was always shooting his mouth off about not getting tied down to one girl.

But Paul wasn't a crowd person. He never did like too many people, too much noise, too much of anything. And yes, one girl, the right girl.... Hutch sighed and his worries circled back round to himself again. He just couldn't help it.

✦

Before the crash, Hutch's worst punishment was being grounded and not allowed out in his boat. He'd never minded having to do chores in payment for pranks, but he hated being grounded. And right now his whole life felt grounded. Don't go there.

The lumps digging into his back were digging harder. He rolled out of bed and straightened the bottom sheet, hooking the corner back round the mattress where it had pulled off. He shook out the covers and punched his pillow a few times, tried to find a comfortable position on his side.

How long did it take? Gramps never got over Grandma Rose. Forty years and he still talked about her as if she sat across the table. And here Hutch was worried about what some girl might think that he hadn't even met yet.

Those scars *were* ugly, all the same. Well, the surgical ones weren't so bad—neat and tidy like pink zippers, with one in a crease so it hardly showed. It was the ragged tears from that piece of metal and from where the bones had poked through that he hated, lumpy and red.

At least his equipment was in working order. Dad had asked him about that his first week home. They'd been alone in the house, standing in the kitchen, Hutch cooking hot dogs for the two of them and the kitchen full of that boiled-wiener smell. Dad was back on, looking out the window, and afterwards Hutch realized there had been something about his stillness that had a feel of the woods just before the snow starts.

"Haven't lost your nature, have you?"

"No! God no."

And Dad said it wouldn't matter if he had, he was still a man and not to worry. But he had been worried, you could tell.

+

Just after the New Year Hutch wrote to Paul:

Hope a change of scene and being out of the province make things easier. Saw Jack at Christmas and he's hanging in there. Feels better being away. Found Christmas hard, like you would. I've filled out my application for MUN again and I might look at computer science but I don't know. The Marine Institute is out but I haven't given up on geology yet. I'll see how things go.

Let me know how you're doing when you have time.
Hutch

So there it was in black and white: he was not going to the Marine Institute. But he still might go out on the boats one day. And later that week Paul called, gave Hutch his Nova Scotia number, and told him about the house his folks had bought.

"Old and creaky and the plumbing clanks," he said, "but it's great." Paul had the top floor to himself and the apartments downstairs were rented to students. "There's one room on my floor that we didn't rent because it's so tiny. Can touch both walls at the same time. You could have it for next to nothing if you came to Halifax. Why don't you apply to Dal?"

+

Then he was back in school. Hutch had always enjoyed school because all his friends were there—now they weren't. Not that he didn't know this crowd—he knew the whole school—but he had no best buddies. He couldn't join in a lot of the talk because he hadn't been at this hockey practice or that volleyball game or the last hike with cadets. So he just listened. You need an audience as much as a performer, but it wasn't half the fun.

Endings

✦

Exams filled Cathy's head in those last months of grade twelve. And she worked—oh, how she worked—going over the set books with Sarah, going through old exam papers Mrs. Elliot gave her and having Sarah check them afterwards. They all said she was doing everything at grade twelve level now, just had to take her time. Don't worry about it. But when you can't write fast it makes timed tests some hard. Hated it when she didn't finish.

There was no time to paint although she would do a few quick sketches last thing at night to make her brain switch off. Mom kept chasing her out for a walk, said she was taking the polish off the floor with all that pacing. Then she graduated.

She, Cathy Russell, was a High School Graduate.

✦

It felt a bit like an end of everything when Sarah left, although Cathy was not as sad as she would have been before all the trouble. Sarah left before Cathy had heard back from either art school and Cathy's stomach was in a knot for weeks. Dad was back in Labrador, and she wasn't able to apply for a student loan until she had proof of acceptance. And she was trying to keep out of Mom's way because Mom was still upset about her going away. Upset wasn't the right word. Maybe there wasn't a right word. Mom was just worried about her and part of Cathy knew she just wanted the best for her but the other part wished she would leave her alone and let her get on with life.

"I was asking Nancy Stuckless up at the church about that bachelor of fine arts…" her mother would start. She was always asking somebody who knew somebody whose daughter/son/nephew had done a BFA and they all said you needed something else as well. "Useless degree, Donna Elliot said."

One daughter had done education afterwards and was a teacher now but she was teaching every subject on the curriculum except art. A son was trying to be a photographer on weekends but had to work in construction to pay the rent. The ones in town all had a "day job" in a restaurant or a store or something that didn't need a degree at all, and the ones round the bay moved back in with their parents because they couldn't afford anything else.

"I want to learn everything I can about painting, about art. That's all I want to do," Cathy kept saying. "I'll worry about a job when I'm finished."

But Mom was worrying already. Cathy heard her on the phone to Dad in Goose Bay as she came out of her room one night, stopped when she heard her own name—how Cathy wasn't cut out to be a teacher and she wouldn't take kindly to rude customers in restaurants and would spill soup on them on purpose and be fired on her first day, and she'd break dishes and march out in a huff and nobody would hire her anywhere.

Cathy didn't know what Dad said but there was a lot of "yes but—" at this end and "well, I know that," and then, "of course I'll support her. I'm her mother aren't I?" There was some listening and agreeing and, at the end, "I'm just saying."

+

But the Sarah thing was much worse and it all blew up out of nowhere.

Cathy had gone to Sarah's house with a painting—an end-of-grade-twelve-and-thank-you-for-everything gift. It was of Sarah in the garden in her old floppy gardening hat, on her knees with a trowel, Dog flat out in the background. Sarah had been so happy with it, rushing about showing it to anyone and everyone. And everything was perfect.

Then Sarah told her that she had been offered a one-year position at Memorial, and she and Dr. Brooks would be moving soon. Dr. Brooks had his pick of family practices in St. John's because so many doctors were retiring. And her job offer at the university was probably all due to Cathy and the case study and wasn't that wonderful?

"What case study?"

Oh, just how Cathy demonstrated this type of supplementary teaching—reading difficulties interfering with learning. They wanted someone with those interests. Academic paper...no names, of course. Absolutely no names.

So Cathy asked if she could read it. Read it through twice and said she didn't want other people reading that. Did Not. Yes, she could see how it made Cathy out to be smart *now.* But it said she couldn't use a dictionary at the start. Fourteen and couldn't even use a dictionary. It said she'd struggled with grade three readers, couldn't write a sentence. It showed she'd been Functionally Illiterate.

No, she knew Sarah never used those exact words but everybody would know she had been. Sure, everybody in Mariners Cove already knew she'd failed, that she'd been dumb back then. But they knew different now. What if someone at art school read Sarah's paper? And no, it didn't mention her name, but it said "small rural town" and that she planned to do a BFA. People would guess it was her.

Well, if Sarah thought someone wouldn't read it, she didn't know Newfoundland. Give it a few months and everyone would know. Everyone would be calling her Lighthouse and Crazy Cathy again. Cathy wanted to start off fresh, be just like everyone else. So Sarah could not send it to a publisher. She was very sorry, but *no.*

But it had already been sent.

+

It threw a shadow over everything: graduation, her chances of going to art school. It even hung over her when she was painting. If she started art school, especially at Grenfell, she'd be forever waiting for someone to say, "Oh, you're that girl who was functionally illiterate." Sarah had gone behind Cathy's back. Sarah said it was her work she was writing about, not Cathy specifically. But it *was* Cathy.

Cathy had tried to explain how she felt used, like she was a free sample or something, only she got in a muddle saying stuff. It wasn't fair. Said stupid things too, like that bit about the dandelion. It was because Sarah had talked about "her field" and Cathy said that made her feel like a dandelion, a dumb dandelion: a specimen in an experiment. She'd been pleased with that word, specimen—Sarah wasn't the only one with good words—but then she'd been so sidetracked thinking about the word that she forgot what she was saying. And Sarah said Cathy wasn't listening and Cathy said Sarah wasn't either and they both spoke at the same time then neither of them.

+

Cathy avoided Sarah after that but a letter came from her a few days later. Guess Sarah was avoiding Cathy too. She didn't tell her mother. Cathy always picked up the mail when Dad was gone. She almost tore it up, would have done a few days before, but she was more sad than angry by then. Just wished it hadn't happened.

Dear Cathy,

I'm so sorry you were upset...I wouldn't want to upset you for the world. And I really don't think anyone will recognize you from that article, although I know you disagree.

I was trying to explain what worked for you so it might help other people wondering about the same thing. It's only lately teachers (and people like me who just want to help) are discovering reading and writing problems early enough to do something about them. The earlier people with reading difficulties start, the easier it is to catch up.

Cathy could picture her saying that, her voice all tight, leaning on the counter with her fingers turning white from the pressure. And Cathy—standing with her arms folded, glaring at her feet—squeezing everything in so she wouldn't fly apart.

And to prove things were working, I had to show some of the changes you've made—and you've gone ahead in leaps and bounds, Cathy. You've made such amazing changes.

Well, fine. But Sarah wasn't the one stuck out there wearing the Dummy label.

Small journal...few readers.
Teachers mostly.
Extremely unlikely.
Sorry. So sorry.

Sarah was only sorry Cathy was upset, not sorry she'd sent that paper. She had to have known how Cathy would feel, and she'd sent it anyway. Didn't tell her until after she'd sent it because she knew. Told her just before she left so she didn't have to see Cathy much. Sarah just wanted a job. Didn't care about Cathy.

Cathy took Sarah's letter up to the lighthouse. When she hung round the house Mom kept asking what was wrong. Cathy looked down at the water hurling itself at the cliffs below, backing off and trying again. Not for the first time, she tried to picture herself jumping and couldn't. She tried to remember that desperate feeling of not knowing which way to turn. But it was like trying to remember being freezing cold when you were warm as toast in bed. You could try to think *shiver* and *pain* and *numb* but you couldn't feel it. And now she couldn't imagine ever wanting to stop living.

Sarah didn't save her. If Cathy had really wanted to jump that day she'd have done it straight away, wouldn't have hung around thinking about it. She'd have changed her mind about jumping if she'd thought about it—might have hit that beige-looking shelf that ran all round the cliffs just under the water. Looked like it was undulating—Sarah's word—the way a snail's rubber foot did, because of the way the waves moved. Not for the first time, Cathy felt dizzy and stepped back.

She stood in the spot where she'd first seen Sarah. She could still see her, collar turned up and wool hat pulled right down with that hair puffing out round the edges. Sarah had looked all worried—not about academic papers, about Cathy. And Cathy had asked her to help and she had.

Getting Through

*

February, on the anniversary, they held a memorial service at St. David's. Hutch would rather have remembered Eugene and Jenny alone with Jack, outdoors, but maybe everyone remembering together was good—made you tougher because you had to act strong to get through it.

He was up there with the choir because everyone had been nagging at him to sing the solo. He'd never been in the choir although the teacher had been after him for years. So here he was in full view while the minister talked about all those things Hutch tried not to think about. The back of his throat ached and his tonsils felt like they were being squeezed up into his nose.

He thought about meeting the crowd at The Café yesterday—how everyone had been cracking jokes, laughing. Hutch had sipped his hot chocolate and got foam on his top lip, leaned over to Cathy Tizzard and said, "Want to share my drink?" He gave her a kiss so she got foam on her lip too, kind of sideways, and the girls giggled and the guys said woo hoo and he felt like one of the crowd again, just for a moment.

Half the coast had come to the service, and the townies, except Paul, and the hockey crowd, including Gus Sheppard, who had flown all the way from New York.

It was so slow getting out. People shuffled down the aisles then log-jammed, nobody moving, digging for things to say when everything had already been said. Hutch felt better at the tea the women had put on across the way—just another bystander wrapped round a plate and a Coke. He gripped Jack's arm as he passed and they nodded to each other without speaking. What else could you do?

Hutch really missed the gigs at Jack's. He used to go up there after supper sometimes. The guys all sang but it was Eugene who kept them together with his accompaniments. He'd be crouched over the guitar on that kitchen chair in the corner, foot on an old Sears catalogue, freckly hands sliding up and down the strings. He'd be listening and tightening knobs, ear almost touching the sound box. He could make that thing dance. Hutch wondered what had happened to it. He didn't think anyone would touch it now. Same with the old Silverado, up on blocks behind the mill.

Pete had left his old guitar behind when he went off to St. John's so they all had a go on that one. Sometimes they'd played at weddings out around, Eugene with his own guitar and one of the brothers on the other one. Usually there would be a DJ and they just played when he took his break but now and then they played for a whole wedding. Parents and grandparents were always requesting old stuff like "Wild Rover" and "Old Time Rock and Roll" and "He'll Have to Go" But they usually managed to play "Wonderwall" for the younger crowd, and maybe a couple of Green Day's hits like "When I Come Around."

Jenny had a fantastic soprano so people kept requesting "I'll Always Love You," which went on and on. You could get tired of that song. Jack never sang at the weddings. They called him Jack the Vac because his voice wandered around at the bottom like a vacuum cleaner—which didn't stop him singing back home when he was in the mood. Proper thing. Never in the mood now.

+

So. There was school and there was family and there was the computer, and more and more Hutch turned to his computer. Even with that he had to mess with chairs to find something that didn't kill his back and he changed positions a lot. But by the time school ended he was almost enthusiastic about computer science. He had provisional acceptance at both Memorial and Dalhousie.

Hutch had been hoping to try his kayak when the ice was gone, maybe just on Uncle Em's pond the first time, but the position that made his leg hurt worse than anything was sitting with his legs straight out in front. Well, he couldn't even do that yet, things were still too stiff and tight, and the closest he could get set off that awful nerve pain.

He worked at stretching things, especially that exercise where he was in a kayak-sitting position only lying on his back with his feet up the wall—the effort he put into his schoolwork was nothing compared to this—but the pain shot everywhere. And not just while he was exercising, but for hours afterwards. He knew they would tell him to stop, that he was making things worse. But he had to. Had to.

And for all his efforts nothing changed much—or at least not enough. So Hutch sat his final exams and thought he'd done okay, even with English, and watched the kayak season coming, and knew he couldn't do it.

Part Two

"Tomorrow's illiterate will not be the man who can't read; he will be the man who has not learned how to learn."

—ALVIN TOFFLER'S *FUTURE SHOCK*, 1970

Fresh Start

*

The day her father left for Labrador, late in May, it came as a shock that Cathy herself might be gone when he came home in October. So she wouldn't see him until Christmas—more than six months, more than ever before. Cathy didn't know how to say all that. Words still didn't come when she wanted them. But her father just looked at her and smiled.

"It's only a few weeks longer. You'll be too busy to notice." He hugged her tight. "You know what you want. You've always known what you want. You'll be fine."

Another big hug and he was gone.

Then in July, after Sarah had left, NSCAD said yes. Cathy couldn't keep still, wanted to write and accept straight away, but Mom said no, wait, wait, went down to the mailbox every day, looking for something from Grenfell. Cathy made herself wait four days, but when there was nothing in Friday's mail she sent her acceptance to NSCAD and the application for a student loan and started checking out accommodations in Halifax.

"But Mom, it's a bird in hand, like you always say."

Her mother freaked. Went off to Aunt Dot's and Cathy had to get her own supper two nights in a row. When Dad called from Goose Bay there was a silence on the other end for a bit, then: "Well, we'll just have to manage, won't we?"

On Tuesday, Grenfell said yes and Cathy had to write and tell them she wouldn't be coming.

Mom had a Mood round her all summer. She was less free with the hugs and just pulled muffins out of the freezer when someone was coming instead of baking them fresh. She sighed more. Now and then Cathy would put an arm round her and Mom would pat Cathy on the hand and say don't mind her, she was just sad when people went away—and the farther they went the less likely they'd be to come back. Cathy said that she was only going to learn about portraits and then she'd be home. Promise. And Mom would pat her hand again with a wobbly little smile and look at the floor. If only Mom could send emails whenever she felt lonely. All those tricks she'd learned, to manage without reading and writing...but they wouldn't work long distance.

"I'll phone, Mom. You know I'll be home. I wouldn't want to live anywhere but here."

Mom was different shades of sad all summer, which made Cathy feel guilty. So she swung from making a big effort to talk and listen and be there with her mom, to taking off with her painting bag and staying away until suppertime, then back again. Sarah was out of her life and Dad was in Labrador and school was over and Cathy no longer had to keep working non-stop. All of a sudden, life was a big empty space.

She loved not having to think up things to write in her journal anymore and dumped the latest one in the box under her bed with the rest. She missed using Sarah's computer but she'd written out all those QWERTY letters and she looked them over now and then, practicing on a paper keyboard so she wouldn't forget.

Cathy did try to always have a book on the go, and even went into Gander to the library whenever someone was driving that way, had a session on a computer there when there was time. She did phone Sarah to tell her about going to Halifax, but it was during working hours so she left a message. And Sarah phoned back and left a message saying how wonderful. Cathy counted the days to going away.

The only thing that gave Mom a boost that whole summer was planning Cathy's wardrobe. There were the usual arguments—"Mom, I'll never wear that. But, but, but"—and one day they drove into St. John's and stayed overnight with Aunt Dot's daughter and managed to agree on new pants, a few everyday tops, boots and sneakers, and a winter jacket.

Compromise: verb: *to meet half way.*

Cathy saw a beautiful sweater in shades of green with such elegant trim but they didn't buy it because the price would turn your hair white, Mom said. She said the same about the price of art supplies and they bought the minimum of the basics on the list from NSCAD and Cathy began to realize how much this all might cost and that the more she practiced, the more supplies she would use.

In that last week Mom seemed to pull herself together, said how proud she was that two art schools wanted Cathy. Cathy overheard her making a big fuss about it to the aunts and telling Aunt Gert, "Cathy was born to be an artist and I don't want to hear another word about it."

At first, Mom was just going to drive Cathy to the bus in Gander. Then she was going to drive her to Corner Brook. Finally she and Aunt Dot would take her all the way to the ferry at Port aux Basques. Having Dot there made everything easier. She told funny stories about when her daughter, Marianne, first moved away: how the oven in one apartment was on a slant so everything flowed sideways and came out burned on the thin side and soggy on the thick; how, on her first trip to a laundromat, there was a guy in shorts and bare feet in February because everything he owned was in the washing machine. Every time Mom started to sound sad, Dot came up with another story.

They stopped for a big lunch in Corner Brook at this cafeteria-type place with turkey and all the fixings and Mom and Aunt Dot told Cathy to enjoy it because it would be the last one she'd get for ages. They made such a racket about it that the women behind the counter were all wishing Cathy well and said to come in for a feed on her way home at Christmas and people at other tables were clapping and cheering for her and Cathy's eyes filled up. Didn't cry when she said goodbye to the aunts and cousins but had tears in her eyes for a bunch of strangers.

She felt all stirred up for a while after that but on the highway to Port aux Basques they pulled off the road to watch a herd of caribou and Cathy went all-out sketching them until Mom said it was getting late. Cathy had never seen caribou this close. They stayed up in the hills usually. They were so lovely, small and fragile-looking compared to moose, and with such delicate colouring. It was like comparing Jenny Sheppard or Sarah Brooks to herself. And caribou were always in a group. Moose were lumbering loners with big feet. Thinking about that took her all the way to the ferry terminal.

Mom wanted to go on-board with Cathy but Dot said no, let's say the goodbyes here.

"Phone me when you arrive," Mom kept saying. "I'll be waiting."

So Cathy left them standing by the truck, shoulder to shoulder, and she walked alone, loaded to the ears with bags, up the ramp of the huge Nova Scotia ferry. It was so much bigger than ferries serving the islands around home. She waved from the door and Aunt Dot had her arm round Mom now and Cathy blew strings of kisses then turned and went inside.

+

It was awkward squeezing along corridors and up and down steep skinny stairwells with both hands full and a lumpy big backpack with bundles hanging off it—Cathy even had her ticket in her teeth for a while. It was ages before she found a seat with room for everything. The throbbing from the engine came up through and gave her a headache. The oily smell and used-up air and that slow twisting and untwisting made her queasy, but it was too hard moving her stuff to go out on deck. Boats were only good in pictures. She kept counting her belongings, checking and re-checking.

She ate the sandwiches Mom had packed, drank her water, felt a little better. She slept on and off in the seat, waking with each change in the motion or when someone walked past with a swish of clothes or a stir of air, or when her head fell forwards and yanked on her neck. For once she had no urge to draw.

She felt lightheaded when she was waiting for the Maritime Bus to Halifax, felt she couldn't get enough oxygen, like she was in a bottle. Everything looked faded and smudged. Every colour was a bit grey as if some dirt had been mixed in, every sound muffled and off-key. She had been too excited to sleep the last week and now she was too exhausted to see straight. Halifax was a blur of streets and traffic and noise and fumes and Cathy ached all over by the time she reached her room. Her fingers and the fronts of her elbows felt stretched. It was a strain on her painting hand—her heart beat louder for a moment. Her shoulders burned and her neck had a rubbed patch where she'd hung her art bag with her valuables.

"Guard it with your life," Mom had said.

+

The student loan was not as big as they'd hoped, hardly enough to cover the basics, but Dad said they'd be all right for now so long as Cathy was careful. Maybe she could look for a student job in Halifax.

She had spent her last weeks in Newfoundland looking up accommodations and finally took a single room at the top of a house on Vernon Street. Cathy wasn't up to sharing her space with strangers, even though it would have cost a bit less. And for once her mother agreed. She estimated she could walk to the college on Duke Street in twenty minutes in good weather, and it was still cheaper than many other options.

You could tell it was a rental place from way down the road: all those neat lawns, then this yard with its mess of dandelions, weeds, buttercups, and those tangled threads that spread over everything like a hairnet and have tiny blue flowers on them in the summer. Near the sidewalk, litter was trapped in fat trenches—ruts from winter tires, by the look of the deep clear patterns they'd left. There were raised shapes like the potato prints she'd made in grade one. If only her camera weren't so far down in her bag....

Inside, the walls were the colour of cream gone sour—that thick beige skin. The floor was covered in bumpy, cracked linoleum in overlapping geometric shapes, browns with a ginger line here and there. Worse than drab. Ugly. No pictures, no plants, no rugs, and a sign in her room about no thumbtacks on walls.

The bed was a futon in a dead-looking gold with flecks of brown, the brown of the ruts outside. The two yellowish blankets on the shelf had been dead even longer. She had brought her light blue sheets from home and the colours glared at each other—or would've glared if they'd had the energy. But there was a tree outside her window—not a tree like home but green and growing—and she was here and it was all good.

The house was full of students. She was to share a bathroom with a girl in the other single room, but Cathy never saw her, although the others said she came by every week to pick up her mail. She was living with her boyfriend and this place was a cover-up to please the parents. Expensive cover-up, but nice not having to share.

Mom sounded shocked when Cathy told her about it on that first phone call.

"Cathy! What kind of people are living in that house? Is there a good lock on your door?"

Aunt Dot would have to calm her down. And Cathy would have to be more careful what she told her mother in future.

+

There were three girls and a guy in the apartment below: two sisters and two cousins. That first Friday the one called Heather invited her in. She introduced Cathy to a couch-load of people and they squeezed together to make room but Cathy chose an upright chair back against the wall, behind the circle of chatter. She hated being in the middle. At first they turned in their seats to talk to her.

"Did you really grow up in a lighthouse?"

"Yes."

"Wasn't that lonely?"

"No." Silence. "Well, *I* never thought it was."

After a bit they stopped turning round so she watched and listened at the start. There were postures and expressions that caught her eye, but the talk was just sea-moan.

Cathy was the first to leave and Heather's eyebrows floated up. "Already?"

Cathy said how she'd enjoyed herself and everyone was so nice and thank you but she just wasn't very good at parties. She went to her room and sketched everything she could remember and was still drawing when the front door banged for the last time. She strained to remember details but they'd melted away as she walked up the stairs. Only the simple things stayed with her: the way that twitchy guy's face was all grooves and spiky lines and how the girl in pink was like Mom's cat—stacked circles, purring—and how that Jeff guy suited his name with his light brown baby-fine hair that flopped over his eyes like the tops of a double ff.

+

Those first few days she listened so hard in class she went home with a headache. Then came her very first drawing class.

October 20 2000

Foundation Drawing. The Prof took newsprint and screwed it up in a tall shape and messed with it until it would stand on the table without tipping. She walked all round checking from every angel then we sat at the table and drew it. We looked at all the sketches after. How ~~difrent~~ different they were. There was a great discussion about ways to show shadow—stippeling, crosshatching, squiggels. The whole ~~seshen~~ session went by in a flash.

She only wrote special stuff in her journal these days and this was special. The part about painting was even more special and took even longer.

And now its Studio Practice and this is my first real Painting Class....

She had been waiting for this all her life. She was so full of light and air she could float away or burst. The room was bigger than she had pictured—big sinks, cans full of brushes on counters, cupboards full of supplies, washed-out paint splodges all over, and a smell like wood and pressboard being wet and dried and wet again over and over—kind of musty but not a bad musty. Rain flooded the windows and she couldn't see out so it was a separate world. Her world.

They painted a jug of flowers with acrylics on boards three feet by two. Eight pictures stood on easels and at the end everyone crowded round to critique each one. Critique was not the same as criticize.

Criticize: verb: *to indicate faults in a disapproving way.*

Critique: verb: *to make a detailed analysis and assessment.*

Sarah said always say the good stuff first and be gentle with anything bad. Only say part of the bad stuff if there was a lot.

The first three paintings were like photos. One looked exactly like the real flowers; one was a bit heavy looking; the third had lots of detail in one part but nothing much in the rest. The prof asked other people first and when Cathy was asked for her comments she just repeated what another girl had said—she had nothing to add.

The next one was that full-of-himself guy who tipped his head back and looked down his nose. He'd painted geometric shapes, which didn't seem right because the flowers were softer than that, and there was a funny face in the shadow on the jug, which Cathy had noticed but not painted because it didn't match her flowers. The prof asked Cathy first. She said she liked the funny face. She said it wasn't how she saw the flowers but everyone saw things differently so that was fine and she liked what he'd done with the colours. She was proud of herself for being diplomatic but he glared like she'd said it was garbage. She wondered about that afterwards, whether she'd used the wrong words. She decided no, but critiquing was harder than you'd think.

Cathy's was next. She had painted the flowers like butterflies. They were fabric; silk maybe. One was like a flame lying on the table and had curly bits—tendrils, like smoke—so that's how she painted it. She made the stalks more bendy and the jug more open so everything was looser. The first person said wow. Nobody else said a word. The silence went on too long so she sneaked a look round and full-of-himself looked mad and the others just looked…she didn't know—maybe how she used to look with a set of English questions in front of her, not knowing where to start. The girl who said wow said she didn't want to go after Cathy because hers was so great. Cathy knew it was the best thing she'd ever done because she was feeling the best she'd ever felt.

But Ive had more ~~practise~~ practice because all I ever do is paint. Those guys have a life.

+

The girl in class who liked Cathy's painting came up to her that same day and asked all kinds of questions. Her name was Jessica and she was from Halifax. She was real nice and invited Cathy to sit at her table at lunch. Two other girls joined them. They were doing different classes but all of them wanted to do a bachelor of fine arts. Cathy didn't say much, just answered when they asked her anything.

She sat with them a few more times, until a few days later when the three of them were walking down the hall. They didn't know Cathy was just inside the bathroom and one of the girls said to Jessica: "She's like a big black cloud and she hardly talks and I can't understand half of what she says when she does talk."

Cathy wasn't going to be anybody's big black cloud. No way. So she made sandwiches for lunch after that and ate them down by the water, or inside the ferry terminal. It was cheaper anyway.

On the second Thursday of classes, that guy Jeff from her building caught up with her as she was walking to school. Not too many people could do that, but his stride was even longer than hers. He worked in a restaurant downtown, Thursdays and Saturdays, "at least until classwork gets heavy." They started walking down together every Thursday.

He was nice too. There was that lazy word again: nice. Well, he was friendly and he was kind. Not great looking but not bad either, and he was only a bit shorter than Cathy. He just yakked about his classes at Dalhousie and his girlfriend and his family back home in New Brunswick and he was funny sometimes and Cathy didn't feel she had to answer with something smart.

He asked her about art school, said he'd never met an artist, and next thing she was telling him all about her wanting to paint forever and he didn't seem a bit bored.

+

There were a lot of artsy hairstyles around campus: streaks in wild colours and whole heads in blue or green. Orange and yellow streaks would have been fun, but Cathy couldn't afford them. At least her hair had a shape these days, thanks to Raylene, but as it grew longer the front bits got in the paint or the spaghetti sauce, or the wind blew it in her mouth. She took a section of hair from each side of her face, tied them together with an elastic at the back, and practiced doing it in front of her mirror. At first it pulled her skin tight and made her eyes water, but after a bit she learned how to make it stay together in a looser way, prettier.

She bumped into Jeff in the hall and he said, "Nice hair."

Cathy looked at the floor and grunted. Muttered thank you so low that maybe he didn't hear, so she said it again a bit louder, but that was overdoing it so she said about her hair being like her Russell grandmother's, although she'd never seen her grandmother, but people back home said it was and....

She stopped in the middle of this puddle of words and lifted one foot up and put it down on dry land, then the other foot. Then realized she'd moved away from Jeff, which looked unfriendly, so she moved back. They headed for the door and Jeff did that two-handed struggle thing with the locks.

That uppity guy had complimented Jessica yesterday in art class. She had been wearing a scarf tied in a cute way and huge earrings and bangles. He'd looked her up and down with a sleazy grin and said,"Hmm, nice." Cathy would have scowled or turned her back but Jessica smiled showing all her teeth—the way Jenny Sheppard used to—and said, "Oh, thank you, Fraser." And she just stood there, not at all uncomfortable, and she looked good.

Jeff had the door open now and when they were out in the sunlight he looked at Cathy's hair again and said it was pretty. So she straightened, stuck up her chin, and smiled a bit.

"Thanks."

First Year

*

When Hutch arrived Paul was out on the sidewalk. "New jacket?"

"North Face," Hutch said with a nod. He had on his new fleece, a checked lumberjack shirt with a white tee, his best jeans, and his favourite trucker hat.

"Nice."

"Mom bought it in St. John's end of the winter last year. She hid it until she was sure I was going away, said no way I was going to wear my red-and-black plaid in Halifax." He grinned as he remembered her face. She'd probably have burned that plaid if he'd tried bringing it. "Got me a Columbia winter one too." He stopped then. Didn't mention how they'd had to cut off his Ski-Doo jacket in the ambulance.

Paul took the biggest bag and Hutch slung on the bulging backpack and picked up his laptop. The first flight of stairs had a handrail but the next flight didn't. It was tight and steep with a narrow tread and his backpack kept pulling him backwards. Hutch had to lean ahead and slide up the wall, good foot up first each step, and he had to slam his phony foot right to the back to make sure he didn't overbalance.

"Sorry," said Paul. "Old house. We had to buy small furniture so we could get it up the stairs; you should have seen the trouble they had with the fridge."

"No sweat. Just being careful." Might have to use the cane on this.

"I ordered pizza. Should be here any minute."

They went into Paul's area first: a high-ceilinged room with two trestle tables, bar stools, and a sink, an easel, a three-way mirror, and paint stuff stacked everywhere. "My studio," Paul called it. A big old fridge, which he'd bought for a song, rattled and chugged by the door—too big for his apartment.

There was a great view of roofs and the sunset through Paul's wide vinyl windows like the ones Hutch's dad had put in at home. The rest of the room was tall walls and cracked plaster and a dingy stucco ceiling stained with damp marks.

"The folks had a new roof put on but we haven't got to the ceilings yet, and the old windows were about to shake themselves out into the street, so they had to go."

There was a door in the corner into an apartment full of Paul's stuff and they ate the pizza at a little table in the kitchen with cold beer to celebrate Hutch's arrival. Paul said Hutch's room was only big enough for a rabbit—hutch-sized—and pointed out where he could store his overflow in the studio and said please use the fridge.

Hutch was just glad to unload his bags, make up the bed, and fall into it, saying he'd leave the evaluations until morning.

+

School was the easy part, once Hutch was used to Dal's layout and the distances he had to walk between classes. He enjoyed the classes, got on with the other students. He sat on the end of a row where he could to give himself stretch room, stood up now and then when he was at the back. One prof asked him about that after class and when Hutch explained he just nodded and said carry on.

A guy who looked like he worked out a lot came up to Hutch in the cafeteria one afternoon. Sean.

"You sound like a Newfoundlander," he said. "Where're you from?"

Sean was from St. John's but it turned out his brother had known Eugene. They got talking and went for a beer after class that day. This was Sean's second year, so he knew the ropes. He was friendly, greeted everywhere he went, stopping to chat to each person. Lots of backslapping and tall tales, but he listened to people too, remembered what they'd told him last time so they could carry on where they'd left off. There was another round of Q and A when he introduced Hutch. It took a long time to reach the bar.

Sean ran his hands through his hair all the time when he was thinking, just like Jack, but instead of looking like a ginger birch broom, Sean's hair always looked Hollywood. "Designer casual" Mom would call it. He was a good-looking guy and girls' eyes followed him even more than Paul, but he wasn't into fashion. He recycled the same five T-shirts through the whole school year and the holes in his jeans grew big enough to need safety pins.

Sailors became Hutch's favourite bar in Halifax. First because they didn't check his ID, but later, when he'd seen inside a few more bars, for a whole slew of reasons: mostly because there were always people in there whatever the hour, and he liked being in the middle of things; the noise level was just right; it was dark enough to be interesting and scruffy enough to feel friendly, but the glasses all shone. And the beer was cold and foamy and good.

Sean was having a party that Saturday and invited Hutch to bring Paul along too. A girl in Hutch's math class said there was always a party at Sean's.

+

A few weeks into the semester Hutch sat next to the window on the bus in his usual morning stupor. A big woman with a puffy brown jacket squeezed in next to him. She overflowed onto him from shoulder to knee. He pulled over as much as he could but she just spread out more. She radiated warmth like a hot water bottle. The bus was swinging and bouncing and someone almost fell in the aisle. Never been this bad before.

"Driver had a fight with his woman and he's still mad," the guy in front said.

"Too much coffee," said the guy's neighbour with the big mole on his cheek.

"...shouldn't be allowed."

"...should have his license taken away."

The comments came from all around. Hutch smiled slightly. It took a shared gripe to make people talk to each other at this hour of the morning.

Then the woman next to him said, "There's going to be an accident."

Pain shot down both legs so sharply Hutch gasped. He could hear metal screeching, Jenny screaming. There was glass bursting and he put his hands up to cover his face. But when he opened his eyes there was no glass, just the guy with the mole and the hot-water-bottle woman digging around in a bag on her knee.

"Excuse me. Getting off next stop."

Hutch could hardly get the words out. What his eyes saw didn't match what he could hear. His stomach roiled and he could taste acid at the back of his throat. He wasn't sure he could walk.

The hot-water-bottle woman swung one leg out into the aisle and hauled herself up by the back of the seat in front. She was saying something but Hutch couldn't hear because of the noise in his head. Her canvas bag had a picture of Fidel Castro on the side and she was only holding one handle so it tipped and things started spilling into the aisle: a newspaper and some pink knitting with the needles stuck through a ball of wool. He heard Eugene yelling, "Oh my god," and there was a tight band round Hutch's ribs so he couldn't take a breath and he tried to say thanks but didn't know if any sound came out.

He staggered down the aisle and thought maybe he'd stood on her knitting and there was a tug, but he felt strangled so he didn't look down—just had to get off that bus. And later he thought maybe he'd seen something pink by his foot as he stumbled down the steps. He staggered across the sidewalk, bumping into something or somebody he didn't see, and he wondered after if that bus had flown off through the lights trailing pink knitting. He grabbed the top of a low railing and held on like it was the only thing stopping him from hurtling into space. Everything was spinning with a rushing noise and a gurgling, then gradually it shrank back to a kind of sobbing gasping stillness.

Someone asked if he was all right and he managed to say he'd be okay in a minute thank you. His voice sounded strange and his head pounded and he could feel his foot twisted around and the exact position of every inch of both legs. He could even feel that slice of metal stuck in his side, making him double over. Hutch just stood there holding on for grim death. Good expression, that. He wanted to lie down and die. He wanted to go home.

He stayed leaning on the railing for ages until he felt more like himself and the leg pain had shrunk almost to a normal bad day, although his stump was real sore. But when he set off back to the apartment the pain round his hip got worse and worse. The cane would have been handy but it was under his bed. He'd shove it in the bottom of his bag from now on. He was surprised he still had his backpack. It took a long time to walk home.

Hutch kept hearing Jenny and Eugene. Ages later—felt more like days later—he crawled up the stairs, took a handful of painkillers, and fell on his bed fully dressed, yanked off the leg and let it drop on the floor, let everything go. But the tears he'd been holding back had solidified into a lump in his head.

He awoke to knocking on his door. Paul. It was almost dark.

"What happened?"

"Oh, bit of trouble on the bus. Long story."

But Paul looked like he was putting two and two together.

Change of Style

✦

"Have you seen *Miss Congeniality*?"

"No."

"I'm going tonight…if you want to come."

"Okay."

"This isn't a date or anything." Jeff stared straight ahead as he walked along. "I have a girlfriend back in Shediac. Corinne. I've mentioned her before." Yes he had, every Thursday. "It's just nice to have company."

"Yes."

So they saw the movie and chatted about it on the bus home and about how they loved Sandra Bullock as the lead. They walked the ten minutes from the bus to their house, being extra careful on the black ice, and when they parted in the hallway Jeff caught Cathy by the shoulders and gave her a quick kiss.

"Just for being sweet."

As a first kiss it didn't rate, wasn't even on the scale: it was so quick it was more of a bang on the lips. He had a little bristly bit that he'd missed shaving, and their lips were freezing cold instead of burning with passion. As she brushed her teeth Cathy pictured Paul kissing Jenny. He'd have been shy at first but he was so in love he would have forgotten about that once he got started. She had toothpaste foam dripping down her front before she pulled herself out of that little dream.

Still, a kiss was a kiss. Don't knock it.

+

All the Fine Arts crowd was going to the Christmas dance. Some were going in couples but there were enough singles that Cathy thought she'd go too.

What to wear? She looked at every item in her size in the thrift store. The racks were packed tight so she had to pull things out to look and some items were left spread out on top, hiding stuff underneath. Cathy walked up Sleeveless Tops and down Short-Sleeved Blouses and tried to picture herself wearing them until her eyeballs hurt.

She walked round the block to clear her head and went back to Women's Long-Sleeved Blouses and picked one in a dark fuchsia with a wide neck, and another in gold. She tried them both. The gold one was loose and the other fit perfectly but showed up her shape and she'd never worn anything like that, so she left it outside the fitting room and took the looser one to the checkout.

There were three people in front of her in line: one woman bought half the store and one had six wine glasses, which were being wrapped separately with enough paper to keep Cathy supplied for a month. The last girl was counting up a handful of small change and digging around in her pockets. Cathy shifted from foot to foot.

You're Junoesque, Cathy. And models are all tall, Sarah had said. *Think of the clothes you could wear. All those things that make me look like a dust bunny.*

Mom had spent years trying to get Cathy into pretty clothes, but pretty didn't suit Cathy. There was just too much of her. Black and baggy was comfortable and easy and she didn't have to think about choosing stuff every morning. Hair, she could manage, but the less she had to think about the rest of her, the better.

The girl with the coins was dribbling them into the cashier's hand. Cathy pulled herself up to her full height and marched back to the fitting room and hung up the gold top. All of a sudden the checkout was empty so there was no chance to dither. Next thing she was walking home with the fitted fuchsia shirt under her arm. And when she tried it on again in front of the bathroom mirror it looked—sexy.

Well, she couldn't hide being six feet tall and when she slouched she just looked like six feet folded at the top. Sarah's words. The rest of her was built to match and she couldn't hide that either. Cathy was practicing *tall* more often these days, although she still forgot when she sat down. But she was not used to showing her shape. Flowing and loose was good. An extra layer to hide the paint marks was good. But Cathy Russell was no chicken. If Hutch Parsons could parade around with a fake leg and still act like he owned the place, then Cathy could show off her figure.

Some artificial flowers caught her eye at the dollar store. *Anemones* it said on the label—made of fabric in deep colours the same tones as her shirt, one maybe exactly the same, with bendable green stalks. There was some ribbon in the same purple. She spent nine dollars, which was almost as much as the top. But she loved the necklace it made and there was one flower left to stick in her hair and her neck no longer looked so very bare.

Cathy went to the dance in her best pants that only had one paint splash, which she'd hidden with some black marker. There was a lot more paint on her sneakers but she didn't have markers that colour and who looked at feet, anyway?

She tall-walked up to Jessica's group. Some of the guys were looking as if they liked her outfit, looking surprised, looking like they thought—sexy. Well, good. She sat down with them. *Don't slouch.* She liked the feel of hair on the back of her neck. Kept that part warm. All this bare skin was drafty. And the anemone necklace was a bit scratchy but three girls said they liked it so it was worth the discomfort.

One guy called Luke asked Cathy to dance and she almost said no. But how difficult could it be? She didn't step on anyone and didn't look any sillier than anyone else. Dancing was like art. If you stood on one leg with both arms in the air and yodelled nobody would take any notice if you did it with—whatever that word was of Sarah's. Something with fruit in it.

Aplomb: noun: *calm self-confidence.*

Cathy had to stop thinking about Sarah.

She kept looking out for Paul but he wasn't there. She'd only seen him a few times since the start of school, in a hallway or in the cafeteria. He'd stopped the first time and said he was glad to see her at NSCAD, asked how she was doing. But that was it. Just a smile and a hello ever since.

And after an hour or so Jeff turned up. He had said he might drop in after work. She wasn't too sure she wanted him there because Luke was kind of nice, but at least it was company for the walk home. So Jeff talked about hockey and she listened, and she talked about art and he listened and they drank a few beers—well, she drank one and he drank three or four, and they tried a few dances.

In the hallway back at the house Jeff kissed her for longer than last time and pulled her a lot closer. He breathed nachos and beer and peppermint in her face, mumbling about her being sweet, until Cathy pulled away with a thanks and a goodnight, and ran up the stairs in a way that said Enough.

She hung up her shirt on the outside of the closet door where she could see it and lay in bed reliving her first dance with a little smile. She bounced out and hung her necklace over the shirt on the hanger and fell asleep with the light on, looking at it.

+

Cathy wasn't going to send anything to Sarah for Christmas but Sarah sent her a book about colours—a kind of encyclopaedia. A *thoughtful* gift, Sarah would have called it. So Cathy made a big card for her and painted a bit of Halifax Harbour on it. She wrote a careful thank-you letter like one she'd seen in a magazine at a checkout when she'd been stuck in a line for ages. *Thank you so much for the beautiful* (bad eggs are useless to ill folk ul) *book. I shall always treasure it.*

Cathy.

The ferry home to Port aux Basques was easier this time because she knew the ropes, had less luggage, and was better at packing anyway. She was glad she wasn't trying to fly to St. John's like Paul because they were having so much snow—flight cancellations and blocked roads and people stranded. Western Newfoundland was having a far easier winter for once. In fact, snow on the Avalon Peninsula would become Mom's main topic of conversation on the phone for the whole winter semester: how a hundred or so stranded motorists spent two nights in a church hall because the Trans-Canada was blocked; how there was a blizzard every four or five days, everything closed; how snowbanks in St. John's were over ten feet high and had to be trucked down to the harbour and dumped; how they had to close one highway when the thaw set in because the snowbanks were unstable and could collapse onto the road and bury traffic.

But now, on Cathy's first night home, Mom baked a delicious ham with roast potatoes—pies for dessert of course—and everything was perfect. Cathy was excited. She had brought three of her smallest pictures and explained what they were about, explained the techniques, and Mom was beaming and Dad patting her on the shoulder and they both looked proud. So then she started talking about art school and how wonderful it was.

"There's art everywhere and so much space to spread out in and it all gives you ideas and then you want to go and try things and there aren't enough hours in the day to do everything."

"Well, you have room to paint here too, Cathy." Mom sounded offended somehow. "And you always did spend all day at your art."

"I know. I don't mean..." She couldn't think how to say what she did mean. "It's just that everyone is interested in the same things as me, and thinking the same way maybe, and there are people to talk to about things I've never been able to talk about before."

"Yes." Mom was twiddling her rings and nobody spoke for a while. "Yes, I suppose."

Dad crossed his legs the other way and Mom picked up her knitting and made a big show of counting the stitches.

"So what else do you do besides painting?" she said eventually.

So Cathy started telling them about the sculptures they were making in Modelled Forms and how Dad would like one of the guy's models of a blue jay and a chickadee, and that led to Dad talking about some of the wildlife he'd photographed in Labrador, and the evening turned comfortable again. But at some point Cathy must have mentioned Jeff. She wasn't sure what she said because she was thinking about art, not him, but her mother pounced.

"Who's Jeff? What's his last name? Where's he from?"

"He has a girlfriend, Mom. Don't get excited. He's just a guy who lives in the house."

But her Mom was off at a gallop and there was no stopping her.

+

The whole clan was having a party for Great Grandmother Dora Hill's ninetieth birthday and they had rented the community centre because there would be over sixty family members before you counted neighbours and friends. Cathy had thought she'd wear her new shirt, be an Artist in the Making. She was even looking forward to it.

Late in the afternoon she helped her mom take over cold plates and pies and put up tables and arrange chairs and hang up streamers. Cathy blew up balloons until her ears hurt. Of course some of her aunts were there and her mom couldn't resist mentioning Jeff. Aunt Joanie stopped what she was doing and gave Cathy a hug as if she'd just announced her engagement—"Oh my, how nice!"

Then her cousin Annie heard.

"What's this? Tell me all about him."

Cathy said Mom had it all wrong and he was just a guy in her building, told Annie about the girlfriend.

"Do you like him?"

"Yes, but…."

When the aunts were distracted, Annie asked if Jeff had kissed her and Cathy was so surprised there was a pause before she said no and Annie made a crowing noise and said, "Girlfriend in wherever…what a load!"

So in half an hour they practically had her married off.

After that Cathy didn't want to go to the party at all but even Dad was going. At first she decided she'd go in her usual black stuff and slouch and ignore everybody. Then she decided she'd go in her new shirt, walk tall, and tell the lot of them to take a hike. All her clothes lay piled on her bed while she thumped around in her housecoat, scowling.

When Mom called out that they were ready to go and hurry up, her mood had swung toward tough-it-out. So a few minutes later Cathy marched out in her artsy outfit and both her parents just stood and stared. First they looked a bit shocked then Dad had the tiniest smile, which got bigger at the hall when the commotion started. Twice Mom opened her mouth to say something and maybe it was the look on Cathy's face that made her stop, because she never said a word.

So Cathy wore her new shirt and anemone necklace and the cousins all exclaimed and said how great she looked and Aunt Gert said she didn't approve of showing off your shape like that. Aunt Dot said, "Oh Gert, leave her alone, she looks gorgeous," but on the quiet, later, she said to Cathy, "I know you're not used to buying your own clothes but next time maybe get a size larger?"

Cathy took no notice of Aunt Gert but she always listened to Aunt Dot, so the next day at home she studied herself in the mirror and Critiqued. The shirt was not too tight; it just fit well. Nothing was stretched or buckled or pulled taut. It fit perfectly. And she was not going to hide inside sacks and tents anymore.

But at the party, when the fuss about the shirt died down, the cousins weren't at all interested in what she did at art school and bit by bit the conversation went back to the usual he said/she said stuff and they closed up into their gossipy little circles without her, just like always.

Moving Right Along

After the bus incident at the end of October, Hutch couldn't wear his leg for three weeks because of the rubbed skin and the pain: back pain, stump pain, phantom-limb pain, remembered pain, nerve pain… whatever. He didn't know what he'd done to make the stump so red and sore—maybe twisted the socket out of kilter getting off the bus then walking home. And he always had the phantom stuff when the stump hurt. He would have stayed home except he didn't want to be alone with those voices. So he filled his days, squeezed out the spaces, stayed in the lab working until they locked the doors. Twice he crashed at Sean's place after one of his parties.

People looked shocked when they saw his pinned-up pant leg, but most were just shocked on his behalf; said they had no idea because he managed so well. Then they were back to normal.

Hutch walked to school, taking forty minutes now—he could really cover ground with the crutches. He listened to the weather forecast first thing in the morning, and only started trying the bus again when the sidewalks were wet or icy. He always watched how it was being driven as it approached, sat on an outside seat, stuffed in his headphones, and turned up the music.

Sean's parties were different. Most people just looked surprised at first then carried on. Some even made a conversation opener:

"Can I borrow one of those? It's been a rough week."

"Can you tap buddy on the shoulder with that, please? The one with his back to us in grey?"

And Hutch would oblige and buddy in grey would ask what kind of ammunition the crutch took or if it had a retractable sword.

Paul took him to his aunt's for a Sunday lunch in November. The roast was so tender you could cut it with a fork, there were little puffy Yorkshire puddings full of great gravy, more vegetables than he'd ever seen at one meal (not that he was big on vegetables), and wine so fantastic he decided maybe he wasn't just a beer man after all. The Mercedes that took Hutch and Paul home probably ran on red wine too, the way it purred. Hutch could handle a bit of pampering now and then.

He counted down the days until he'd be home for Christmas.

+

Hutch was back in his peg leg later that month but he carried the fold-up cane in the bottom of his backpack. He was only reminded of the crash with something specific, like metal scraping on metal, or hearing the Beatles—not just "Love Me Do," but any Beatles—although that didn't happen much these days. He learned to put it out of his head by concentrating on something else: going over a complicated math formula or listing all the countries in Africa and their capitals. He'd been shamed into learning those after a bad trivia night at Sailors.

So Hutch was ready for a bit of fun by the time the Christmas parties rolled round. He met this girl, Samantha, at an art party of Paul's and then she turned up at another party of Sean's and was coming onto him all night. She said if Hutch took her home she had nachos and dip. And he thought, *why not*? Some guy was leaving and gave them a ride. It was all so easy.

It never crossed his mind that she didn't know about his leg.

And it started off so well: they were laughing at a horror movie that was so bad it was funny, sprawled on this saggy green couch with a two-tone squeak. Hutch would rock from side to side to make it squeak and then try to think up lines of songs with those notes in them. Things were going fine until she asked what that lumpy thing was she could feel through his shirt and did he wear a holster? She was giggling then, but after Hutch said it was a scar from the accident it was as if she'd pressed Pause. Everything stopped. And when she pressed Play again she was looking—polite, and her voice went all phoney-polite-interested….

"Oh. Were you in an accident? How awful."

"Yes. I was in a bus crash a couple of years ago. You might have heard about it on the news. Two of my buddies were killed." He tried to keep his voice casual but it came out louder than he meant, and stiff.

"Oh, god." She frowned slightly and said maybe she did remember it and she sounded more normal for a minute. "Didn't they die when the back of the bus went through the ice on a pond?"

And the way she said it in that casual, it-might-rain-today way made Hutch's stomach clench. Jesus. They *died.* They both started to sit up and her foot hit his peg leg and she stared at him with her mouth open, frozen. That only lasted a second too then she was back to her social-worker look.

"Yep," Hutch said. "That's my fake leg." He took in a breath then decided he wasn't saying anything else. He saw Phyllis Barnes's face with that big sneer all over it. *Told you.*

Samantha said she'd make some coffee but Hutch said not to bother and started hunting for his jacket and stuff and all the while she was saying don't leave and how much fun he was and how she had enjoyed the party and they were planning a party here soon and he must come….

She was probably still at the social chit-chat as he was walking up the road. It was a long way home.

+

Christmas was all family and food and catching up. Hutch's relatives were full of questions and enthusiasm: Did he have photos to show them? Had he met any Newfoundlanders in Halifax? How was Paul? But there was a divide now in the conversation between his buddies who had been away and those who had stayed around, and neither side seemed all that interested in what the other had to say.

So Hutch stuck to family and his closest buddies. He caught sight of Cathy Russell on the ferry on the way back, but she stayed downstairs and he was out on deck as much as the cold would let him. He was out to the bus stop and into the last seat on the first bus before she even came off the ferry.

When he got back to Halifax, the winter semester flowed along without any complications: every new class interesting, every new girl fun, but he kept things casual—just a few dates and then move on.

By the end of the school year, Hutch had decided to try for a summer job in Halifax and dropped his resumé all over the city. He just had two responses, both student-only jobs. He saw the interviewer noticing his leg. Hutch wasn't sure if the plastic showed when he sat down or if it was the way he sat, but she gave him a sympathetic look—maybe it worked in his favour. He wanted to say he didn't need the pity thank you, but if it got him the job.... They offered him four weeks of data-entry work in the Media Arts Department at NSCAD, starting the week after exams finished. Not a manly job, but it would pay the rent.

The girl who did his orientation was a real eye-catcher. Her hair was a mass of red, orange, and purple streaks. Petra.

"Love your hair. Need sunglasses."

She had heavy mascara and a thick line at the edge of her eyelids. He thought they must get tired holding everything up. Her earrings were painted corks from wine bottles. She ought to have looked weird, but instead she looked—inviting. Of course the low neckline helped. There was another cork bouncing around just above that fantastic cleavage.

Petra told him she worked part-time to put herself through art school. She wanted to specialize in film. She asked him how he got his limp. Hutch had not realized he had a limp. He must be getting sloppy. So he slowed down and concentrated more on equal step lengths, equal time on each foot.

Petra asked him about his limp again when she saw him a few days later with his cane, so finally he told her about the crash. Then she wanted to know about his injuries. When he mentioned surgeries, she wanted to see the scars. So after his second Friday, he went back to her apartment and showed her. And, oh boy, Phyllis Barnes had nothing on Petra.

He took Petra out three more times before he left for home, even tried to look her up in September but she was gone. Part of him laughed, knowing she only went out with him because he was a freak, but it helped to balance the scales.

Change of Place

✶

The house on Vernon Street had been sold. The new owners were planning renovations over the summer then moving in themselves. In Cathy's first week home that summer, Sarah called.

"Your mother told May Parsons you would need a new place to live next semester—"

Frig. You couldn't sneeze in Mariners Cove without somebody at the other end of town passing you a tissue.

"—so I mentioned it to Lena Wilson—you know, Paul's mother—and she said you could have a basement apartment in that building they bought a couple of years ago if you wanted. But of course you don't have to take it. I only asked her because I know what it's like looking for a place to live when you're far away."

Paul's building.

Paul.

Sarah mentioned alternatives in some high-rise with a load of student apartments, but only if Cathy was willing to share.

"You have plenty of time to think about it; you don't have to decide right away."

Paul.

Cathy said yes immediately. Yes, yes, yes. Thought about it all summer.

Dad wasn't happy about the higher rent but said he supposed they'd manage. Mom was pleased about the move because it was more connected to home. She was more upbeat about everything this summer. Cathy made a point of asking her about cooking for one because she'd be able to cook a bit in this new place. She'd lived on sandwiches all last year. What recipes did Mom know for one person with a hot plate? Mom kept recipes in her head so Cathy had to stand over her and measure stuff as it went in the bowl.

"Yes, but how much is 'not too much?'" she had to ask. "How big is 'just a tad?'"

+

The new apartment was dark because the windows were up near the ceiling and wore layers of sheer curtains to hide the feet on the sidewalk. Cathy stood sizing up the picture she could make: it would be the same shape as the window frame, railings across, sidewalk shining in the rain, greys with blurred colours in the puddles and so many feet, each with a different story. She would need a good lamp.

She turned and paced through the rest of the apartment. The walls were cream again but not sour this time; when she checked them against Sarah's colour encyclopaedia, the best match was Antique White. The floating floor tiles were a mix of browns on cream but looked fresh and clean, and there were touches of Fog Green around the windows and doors. It was soft on the eyes and the name made her smile.

The apartment had two rooms with no door between—and one room was full of bed—but there was more space overall than her last place. There was a tiny ensuite bathroom—how elegant was that—a camp-sized fridge, a stovetop with two rings, a miniature microwave, and a cupboard with a mix of saucepans with dented lids and a buckled-looking frying pan. There was way more storage space here, which meant more floor space for her easel if she kept things tidy. A big step up.

And at the top of the building was a studio filled with light, shining over the city, full of Paul. He invited Cathy up for a look on her first evening. He said she could paint up there sometimes—they'd do up a schedule later. And just as she was about to leave, the door opened and in walked Parsons. Parsons! Her voice rose to a squawk.

"What are *you* doing here?"

"And a happy Thursday to you too."

Paul had picked up an envelope and was passing it to him. "The tickets," Paul said.

"Letter from St. Paul to the Philistines," said Parsons, waving the envelope at her with that stupid grin.

"What?"

"Forget it." The grin disappeared and he shut the door a bit hard as he left.

Second Year

*

"You really gotta share your studio with that lump of misery?"

Hutch was sitting at Paul's kitchen table, swirling his coffee round and round, seeing how far up the sides of the mug he could force it without it sloshing over the top.

"I'll try and schedule her for when I'm out. But she's not that bad."

"Yes she is. Not an ounce of fun in that girl. Ruined a real good snowstorm one time—"

Coffee flooded over Hutch's thumb and Paul rolled his eyes. Hutch licked his hand clean with a lot of *mmm*ing and lip smacking.

"Had this big storm early in the season back in grade ten, or nine maybe," he said. "You'll be cursing the snow in May when it won't clear off, but it's perfect in October on a school day. Everything closed. Temperature around freezing so the snow's all sticky—great for holding a shape.

"I take off before Dad grabs me and line up a couple of dozen snowballs at Roberts Corner. Perfect spot for an ambush. And I lie in wait. And wait and wait. Hoping for a bunch of girls. I could take on three or four with my stack of ammo. They'd swarm me in the end but that's the best bit." He leered at Paul. "And who comes along but Cathy Russell. Well, I wasn't wasting good snowballs on her. Only she turns up the shortcut and there's a tree on the corner just loaded down with snow, at least a foot deep on a branch over the track. She doesn't have her hood up. If I aim at that big pile just at the right moment...."

Hutch was aiming at an imaginary target across the room. "And I got her. Right on the head and down her neck. Beautiful. Couldn't have done it better."

He paused in his story and reached for the radio fast to turn off Britney Spears singing "Baby One More Time," but Paul got there first.

"So what happened?"

"Nothing. She just kept right on walking." Hutch shrugged. "Didn't even look round to see who'd done it. Didn't even knock the snow off herself. No fun at all." He shook his head in disgust. "There I was with the sun coming out and my snowballs all melting and nobody around for a game."

And here she was in Paul's building like a black hole. Paul's parents and Sarah Brooks had cooked it up between them, even to her having studio time, which was a bummer. At least he could forget about her when she was in the basement. Hutch could hardly remember the guy who had that apartment last year, probably only saw him twice.

+

Hutch was well into the semester and swinging along nicely. It had been two months since those planes had crashed into the Twin Towers in New York and it was still the main topic of conversation, but everyday things were squeezing back in and classes were no longer disrupted. The anthrax scare in October brought terrorism even closer somehow, because postal workers were dying from handling contaminated packages and his Aunt Liz ran the post office back home. Not that terrorists would have ever heard of Mariners Cove, or Newfoundland for that matter.

He was surprised how much he enjoyed his classes, even calculus, but his English course was still a pain. It was just the grammar, a bunch of stupid rules, but it was like walking—when he was in a hurry he limped.

It was great seeing familiar faces again, to be back at Sean's parties. And he was going out for the third time with this girl from PEI, taking it slow and casual. Ever since Samantha Hutch had been cautious. Maybe he'd been a bit pushy on dates when he was younger. He didn't rush anything these days and the less he pushed the more they pulled—must be some law of physics.

His back was much better after the summer. They'd said it would improve with time but he hadn't really believed them. But things felt more solid, like he could rely more on everything working. Didn't hurt as much—not all the time, anyway—and usually he could work out what had stirred things up. Then he could decide whether it was worth doing whatever again and paying for it, or not—like running for the bus that time or helping Sean move all those crates of bottles.

Paul had said some girl needed computer help, something about her having trouble with photographs. Hutch was all smiles. When he heard who it was, the smile fell off his face altogether.

"She'll drive me crazy, Paul. Not doing it."

So Hutch was not in the best of moods when he knocked on Cathy Russell's door. But she said all the usual come-ins and thank-yous and looked straight at him instead of somewhere past his left ear. Acted normal. Her apartment was bigger than his own, but you could hear cars gearing up from the corner and smell exhaust fumes. At least his room wasn't level with the traffic.

Her only table turned out to be one of those wobbly things you let down from the wall with a pull-out leg.

"Can't trust these one-legged things," he said and looked at her sideways but she didn't crack a smile.

He went all the way upstairs for his cane and by the time he came back down his leg was bugging him. Paul owed him. Hutch adjusted the length of the cane and rammed it under the edge of the table to stabilize it.

"Neat," said Cathy.

He found an outlet nearby, hauled up the one chair, and opened up his laptop.

"So what do you want to know?"

"What Paul bribed you with to come and help." Cathy was bringing over a fold-up metal chair from the bedroom.

Hutch snorted a laugh and said, "Three six-packs." Then he straightened his face and said, "No, no, I don't mean that. Just teasing."

"You weren't teasing when you said it was too much bother to be polite to the lighthouse."

"What?" He caught himself gaping and closed his mouth. "What are you talking about?"

"One summer. By the ramp. Jack Sheppard was trying to hush you up but you didn't feel like keeping your voice down." Cathy shrugged. "Maybe you thought I was too dumb to know what you meant because you said, 'Nobody remembered to switch on the light in that one.'"

"I never." His Mac was flashing at him but Hutch was staring at Cathy.

"Maybe you don't remember, but I do. Every word."

He looked down at his laptop. Felt like walking right out and almost turned it off, but a little memory was dancing around just out of sight. Jack. *Hear you in Bonavista.*

"Well, if I did, that was a mean thing to say and I'm sorry." He drummed his fingers on the table, wanting to get started. "Sort of thing kids that age say, I guess. Stupid." Stop making excuses, Parsons. "Sorry." He started connecting to a photography site. "But I called you Lighthouse since about grade two because there were two Cathys in our class. I called Cathy Tizzard Tizzy. *She* didn't mind. Told me she liked it."

"She would. Thinks the sun shines out of you."

And what was he supposed to say to that? "Called you Lighthouse for *fun.* And you never told me not to." He glared at her. "Don't know much about fun, do you?"

"Being called dumb is not fun."

"Well, if you think I'm going to crawl on my belly for some stupid kid's comment I made back—god knows—back when I was a stupid kid, you can think again." He powered down his computer, yanked out the plug, started winding up the wire.

"Sorry." She hunched up her shoulders, grabbed her elbows, and squeezed herself in. Lord, she'd do herself an injury. "I'm sorry I said that. After you apologized."

Hutch laid his laptop on the chair, lifted out the cane, and started to put it back to its normal length.

"Can we start again?" she said. "Please?"

He stood with the cane halfway fixed and there was a watchful little silence. He almost said no effing way but she looked like she meant it—those big eyes looking all sorrowful.

There they stood, staring at each other like a couple of idiots, and it was one of those moments where you sometimes act stupid because you're annoyed. But he could hear his folks: "Be nice to Cathy. She doesn't know how to be with people." He tightened up the cane and whacked it back under the table with so much force that the whole thing shuddered. He sat back down.

Cathy looked embarrassed and pleased and angry all at once. How did she do that? She was the least comfortable-in-her-skin person he'd ever met. Polar opposite of Sean. He wondered what Sean would make of her. Of course she wouldn't get near him for all the girls orbiting. He could imagine Sean wondering, *who is that black bear in the corner*? Hutch almost smiled, but grabbed it just in time.

"So what do you want to know?"

It took nearly an hour but in the end nobody had thrown anything. He risked giving her his phone number and said to call if she had problems.

+

Faraday's was a little bistro on the student beat which prided itself on good cheap food. It had wrought-iron tables and chairs and it must've taken algebra to work out the maximum number of seats that would fit in that minimum irregular space. Earlier in the fall they'd had chairs out on the sidewalk too and in their tiny backyard. It was Hutch's favourite place to eat.

On Mondays they had a special: soup and a big bun with as much coffee as you could drink. The soup was usually beef-vegetable or split pea—something homemade and filling—followed by a bologna sandwich back in his room. The Monday special almost felt like home.

He wasn't up to socializing on Mondays after a heavy weekend so he would have liked someone easygoing to sit with, but a lot of the guys had class, including Paul, and Sean never went anywhere without a girl. Hutch didn't have the energy to tidy himself up for a girl. So he went on his own. All the tables were for two and the place was always packed, so two Mondays in a row he ended up opposite someone he would rather not have ended up opposite.

The first was a girl who kept trying to flirt with him. She seemed to think he must be out for a pickup if he was on his own. He was too tired to fake interest, even if she looked like that fantastic girl on the Coke commercial, or Jennifer Love Hewitt, or...well, maybe then. She was probably a nice enough girl and afterwards he felt a bit mean for cutting her off, but he just wanted to enjoy his meal and linger over coffee. He nearly scalded himself drinking the second cup too fast.

The next week he hid behind the latest *Sports Illustrated*, his Christmas gift from Brian and Lori. But there was an article on sports injuries and the guy sitting opposite him just *had* to be doing kinesiology and just *had* to explain every juicy detail about the inside of a knee joint. The beef in Hutch's soup started to look human and there were some bits floating around that he couldn't identify so he almost didn't scrape the last bit of glaze off the dish like he usually did.

That Saturday he poked his head into Paul's studio and Cathy Russell was there. She was painting a glass with an off-centre light. Hutch remembered Paul doing the same piece last year. He walked over to take a look, ignoring her glare.

"That's really good," he said, surprised, "The way you've caught the light." Paul's hadn't had such a shine.

"Thanks."

She sounded like she wanted him to get lost, and kept right on painting. Just what he needed at Faraday's. One word every half hour would be perfect. He thought of mentioning it. Nah. Cathy Russell? Nah.

"Paul around?"

"No."

"Know where he is?"

"Out."

"Well, I guessed that much." Hutch was heading for the door. "Know where?"

"Not really. Gone for a run."

"Tell him I dropped by. Please?"

She said okay, but she probably wouldn't bother—or she'd be too busy painting to remember. Then again she might because it was Paul. She could be like a scarecrow at Faraday's, frightening everyone away.

+

Hutch had managed one quiet Monday on his own at Faraday's, but had to skip the next two for a project deadline. Then it was Christmas. So it was January of his second year before he was ready for the Monday-night routine again.

He strolled into the studio on the first Saturday morning back at school to find Paul was out for a run again. Crazy idiot on all this ice. Cathy had breakfast spread out—she was painting it, not eating it—and was staring at a jar of marmalade.

"Nice shadows," he said, just for something to say.

Cathy kept staring at the marmalade.

"All that black shows up the shapes."

She looked irritated so Hutch kept prodding, trying to get a rise out of her. "Round jar's nice. That one of your mother's?"

"Yes."

Was that her teeth grinding? He felt a laugh building but froze it, tried to look innocent. "But couldn't you find a better plate?"

"No."

"Just sayin'. There's a chip in it. Did you see that?"

"Of course I saw it." She stopped painting and glared at him. "Artists *see* things."

"Always knew you were crazy." That got her. Ready to choke him. "Joke," Hutch said. "Just a joke." He sat down, lifted his leg out a little. "Looking at things right is science, not art," he said in his best lecturer voice. He'd had this conversation more than once with Paul and some of Paul's artsy friends. "In science you measure everything. Over and over the same way. Accurate. An artist paints his own view of stuff. Interesting maybe, but not accurate."

"He or she," Cathy said, turning away and looking at the floor, not at her artistic breakfast. "And it's *more* accurate. Shows more than just boring measurements." Cathy frowned at him. "And shadows aren't just black stuff. They can be all different shades."

She stopped and her eyebrows went up a notch and she stared past him, said maybe that was why ghosts were called shades sometimes. "They'd have to be different from each other because of the people they'd been." Her voice had grown softer, dreamy almost. "Shadows have the tiniest bit of purple in them sometimes or blue or green. A pale one might have a flick of yellow."

"That's when you take it to a doctor."

"What?"

"Come on, Cathy, you're supposed to be the one with the imagination! When a shadow gets pale you take it to the doctor."

She just looked at him like he had two heads but her lips squeezed together a bit and maybe curled up a fraction at the corners. Two degrees max and he wouldn't bet on it. But her lips still looked good even pressed together. What a waste of great lips, hanging them on Cathy Russell.

He started designing graphics in his head with lips running around on high heels then added some guy lips in sneakers chasing them, then realized he'd seen something like that on a commercial.

"That's not for you to eat," Cathy roared suddenly. "That's for my picture."

"Oh. Sorry." Hutch was finishing up the toast. And on the spur of the moment he said, "Want to come for soup and coffee at Faraday's next week? Make up for the toast."

Cathy's mouth fell open but no sound came out. Before she could say no Hutch explained about the Monday special and said he couldn't stand these chatty people sitting opposite him but the food was too good to miss.

"So I'd come to fill a chair." Her face was blank, voice flat.

"Well…er…kind of." Not to be rude or anything, but better not give her ideas. Holy shit, no. Not that she looked like she had any—more likely to thump him.

"As long as I'm just filling a chair, I'll come."

Still the blank face. Hutch hated it when people did that.

Change of Outlook

✶

Cathy had been floating on dreams of breathing the same air as Paul Wilson that whole summer before she moved into his building. Now it was ruined by that piece of pollution up there. She paced her apartment the first night, swinging from anger at Parsons to anger at herself for letting him upset her. Sarah would say it was just another problem to tackle but Cathy wasn't going to think about Sarah either.

She would forget the dumb jokes that Parsons creep played on people. He couldn't help his sick sense of humour. And he may not have done everything—just because he never missed a chance to throw snowballs in someone's face doesn't mean it was him dumped that load down her neck at Roberts Corner. And it could have been Jed Batton who spray-painted her pictures up at the lighthouse. Probably. Batton's jokes were meaner.

But she would never trust Hutch Parsons and never let him near her sketchbook.

✶

Cathy only began to notice a world bigger than her own after Nine Eleven. She followed the news every chance she had—not just to help vocabulary and listening, but for the first time to actually find out what was happening. She started asking why—and found the reasons were different depending on who was doing the answering.

She began to realize how little she knew and, also for the first time, she felt the need to learn more about world things, people things. She wished she could talk to Sarah, ask her what to listen to, what to read, what she thought about it all. Sarah knew so much about what went on outside. This was something for Cathy's Projects Book. A guy in her class loaned her a copy of *The Economist*; it took her a month to get through it. Cathy listened to talk shows and conversations going on around her and thought about the human race and she even said something now and then when kids were chatting in her classes, in corridors, the cafeteria—just like everybody else.

She thought several times of phoning Sarah but never quite got as far as pressing *Talk.* And Mom was too full of all the planes that had been grounded in Gander after Nine Eleven to think about anything beyond. But even that was something different. Usually there was a pattern to those phone calls:

"What did you cook for supper tonight?"

"Just let me tell you what happened at the bake sale...."

"You'll never guess what Gert said this time."

Cathy's part in these conversations were scattered yeses and nos to keep things flowing. Now and then there'd be something new—"Missy brought home a stray tomcat last week. Scary-lookin' thing with a squashed face and half its tail missing"—and Cathy wanted to ask if Mom had offered it a bowl of milk and a muffin on one of the good plates, but she couldn't get a word in. By the next call the stray had disappeared.

Dad had asked Cathy to phone home every week and Cathy wanted to, but she tried to call when she was in the right mood and sometimes days would go by when she wasn't. And even though she knew it was stupid, she always felt guilty because she wasn't home for her mother to talk to every day.

+

Saturday morning was one of the times Paul said Cathy could use the studio, so she went up at six o'clock that first weekend. She began working on views from windows upstairs and down, as well as doing projects for school. By Christmas she had ten sidewalk-feet pictures and called the series *To and Fro*. She showed them—only five because of limited space—in a little display given by her class. Her apartment was getting crowded so Paul let her store some pictures up in his studio.

Classes were all about technique, technique, technique. Cathy practiced everything so much she was over her budget for art supplies in no time, which she told her mother late in October in her phone call home.

"Mom, don't buy me anything fancy for Christmas, please. Just need money for art stuff."

Mom sighed.

+

Parsons came by the studio on two of her Saturdays looking for Paul but Cathy didn't say a word. He tried cracking his dumb jokes but she kept her face straight. Needn't try his tricks on her. In January, when he asked her to Faraday's for the cheap night, she almost dropped her paintbrush. Of course he just wanted someone to fill a chair. It was like Jeff with his girlfriend-in-Shediac. Jeff just wanted company. Parsons was using her more like batik—she'd be the wax on the canvas so the paint wouldn't stick.

At first she was going to say no and leave him to the bistro customers. But even though he was no friend of Cathy's he *was* a bit of home. She was sick of mainland voices and words she didn't know and people not understanding her accent even after all the work she'd done. She missed all the different ocean noises and being able to watch the weather change and it was somehow comforting to know he would miss them too. Cities didn't smell right. Stale. Her room didn't smell right. She missed Mom making her a cup of tea at night, even missed her chatter. Mom made you feel comfortable. Dad must miss that when he's in a tent in the wilderness.

Not that that had anything to do with Parsons. But he always understood what Cathy meant, spoke like home, dressed like home—those green/grey tees and sweats, a baseball cap glued to his head—although he was wearing townie jackets now, like Paul, and less ball cap. He even had a face like home. She hadn't realized, until she left, that there were faces you could pick out as being from Newfoundland and his was one: rocky and square with peat-pool eyes.

Anyway, she would go to Faraday's with Parsons. She was getting tired of beans on toast. And Parsons might notice her sitting opposite, ignoring him, more than the long-distance ignoring she was doing right now.

Faraday's

✶

Most Mondays Hutch met Cathy at the bistro. If they happened to meet on the way they walked together in silence after the usual "Hi, how's it going?" They stood in line then poured themselves into chairs you could never pull out far enough because of the seats at other tables. Lack of shuffle room sometimes bothered Hutch but these chair backs were vertical and rock solid and suited him perfectly.

Cathy didn't seem to expect anything of him, or notice that he was scruffy and yawned a lot, so Hutch could sit and daydream about the weekend just gone. The girl from PEI had found somebody else but the girl who sat behind him in his math class was even nicer.

A scattered time Hutch felt like talking on a Monday night but he always had to start the conversation.

"Soup's like Mom's," he said one day. "Brian and I made pea soup a few times. Never turned out like hers."

"You cooked your own?" Cathy sounded shocked.

"Mom said just because she was the only woman in the house didn't mean she was going to do all the cooking and cleaning. Said she was a mom and a teacher first. Drudge wasn't on the list."

At first Cathy was all stiff and called him Parsons like she was mad at him, but after a bit she eased up, called him Hutch. It was relaxing—more than he'd expected—and he could just sit back and soak in the smell of coffee, voices, the clatter of spoons. There was just enough drag-and-clang noise of iron chairs to keep him awake. "Convivial," Cathy called it: cheerful, sociable. That was from the dictionary in that bag of hers, that Santa's sack in geometric shapes of red, purple, and green. Her mom had made it. She used to carry a sketch pad in it too back home—probably kept that paper company in business—but she never had it at Faraday's. In fact he hadn't seen it in Halifax at all.

One Monday he came out of a snooze and Cathy was chatting to a guy at the next table with the biggest mop of hair Hutch had ever seen. The only bits of face not covered were his eyeballs and nose. When he left, Hutch asked her why she'd told that guy he had a hair suit. She said she didn't; said he was h-i-r-s-u-t-e. Hirsute.

"What the frig does that mean?"

"Hairy."

"So why not say hairy?"

"Just learned that word."

"People'd know what you meant if you said hairy."

"Use it or lose it."

"Jesus, Cathy, it's a chat not dictionary practice."

And Cathy went on and on about how unusual words were more interesting, like messing with colours. So many shades in the dictionary going to waste. Then she started in on him.

"No need to get mad," she said.

"I'm not mad. Yet."

"You're blowing down your nose."

And Hutch said something about her jumping around, off topic, and that arguing with her was like trying to spar with a punching bag on wheels.

"I'm not your punching bag."

"I didn't say you were," Hutch said, exasperated.

"Yes you did."

"Now *you're* getting mad."

"No I'm not."

Her head was coming forward more and more, so Hutch stuck his own head forward and they were almost nose-to-nose and her eyes had tiny gold flecks in them. He used his soothing voice just to annoy her.

"You're turning a conversation into an argument."

She sat back, chin up. "It's a discussion. An argument's a heated exchange of conflicting views."

"That's my point."

"*You* might be arguing," said Cathy. "*I'm* discussing."

"You have flecks in your eyes, like gold dust."

Not sure why he said that. It just popped out. She'd been all ready for the next round but she stopped, looking taken aback. He watched expressions flash across her face: shock, embarrassment, suspicion, then blank—drapes closed.

"I have boring brown eyes like most of Mariners Cove," she said. "But thanks."

"Nothing boring about you, Cathy." And that was true; she was too full of surprises.

Cathy gathered her stuff and stood. Meeting adjourned and drapes still closed. She didn't say another word all the way back to their building.

+

Hutch asked Cathy about Paul's art once. How was his style different from hers? Chalk and cheese, she said.

"But you should ask him. He's real good at analyzing and critiquing."

"Aren't you good at that too?"

"No. I just like doing it. He likes thinking about it."

And to every other question the answer was the same: ask Paul. She did say once that he knew a lot about artists, and was always reading biographies. She said that was something she wanted to do when she ran out of projects, but she never ran out. She was always behind with art history, although using a desktop with spell-check at the college made the writing a bit easier. He'd forgotten Cathy had trouble with reading. There must be a lot of that in art history.

"How did you ever survive in school?"

The moment the words were out he wished them back in. Cathy glared at him, eyes like lasers. He held up his hands, saying, "Okay, okay. Just thought it must have been a real pain having reading troubles. No offence."

Cathy switched off the lasers but kept looking him in the eye. "It was."

"Library sessions must have been torture."

"They were."

"I saw a drawing you were doing in there once. It was real good. You were drawing books instead of reading them." He smiled at her. "Sitting on the floor in the corner, ducked down so Miss Tucker couldn't see. You almost made it to the bell before she caught you, too. I've gotta hand it to you."

"Yes, I remember," Cathy said. "Still have that sketch. Didn't keep many from those days but I liked that one."

She was looking past him, seeing it all again....

+

She'd been feeling so down that day. It was true: library times were the worst. Grade seven—the first grade seven—and kids all at the tables leaning down on their elbows over books, some of the guys sniggering over one, and Cathy Tizzard so deep in hers she didn't notice Parsons hiding her bag on a trolley full of books. And Tizzy could read so fast. You could see her eyes zooming across the lines, moving up to the top of the next page, and she kept smiling to herself. Smiling at something in a book.

Cathy had sat cross-legged in a corner, hidden, staring at the nearest shelf. The books were all closed up with their backs to her. You could see by the tops of the pages that some of them had never been opened, the pages fit together so tightly. Others had pages that had been read a lot—not creased exactly, just less ironed-looking so they weren't as snug.

She could see a corner of a page tucked down. Miss Tucker would have a fit. People had meant to come back to that corner or they wouldn't have bothered to fold it, so they must have liked the story. One book had corners folded in a few places and there was a gap between the back cover and the stitching. It had been read a lot. Cathy remembered thinking how like Parsons that was: jacket half hanging off like he didn't care about wind chill and stuff. Showing off. But maybe he really didn't care.

She sneaked a look at him now across the table but he was sipping his coffee, staring around.

The books had all been different heights and widths and colours. Cathy remembered rearranging some into a pile between standing books and leaning one at an angle and putting that dark red one next to the rusty one.

She sketched them all in pencil but crayoned in the dark red one with the jacket hanging off and the green one with the gold tree on the spine and a thin new-looking one, the colour of her bedroom curtains. She'd just finished when the teacher caught her.

+

Hutch had learned not to ask Paul about art. It made him blue. He had thought it was only missing Jenny that made Paul blue and had tried the art topic to cheer him up, but talking about art, his own art, brought him down even more. He seemed disappointed with it. Everyone said Cathy was so talented but you never heard any comments about Paul. Paul had a stack of Cathy's pictures in his place that he had to pass by every day and one day there was a sheet spread over them. Paul said it was to protect them.

But there was more than painting in the curriculum. Maybe he was good at something different. But whenever Hutch asked about his classes at the college, Paul would say something about them being easier or harder. You never heard Cathy use those words—she'd say more interesting or less interesting. She still loved painting more than other art forms—especially "people pictures," as she called them—even though a lot of students turned up their noses at portraits these days. Cathy didn't care, said they were *her thing.*

Ask her anything with the word art in it, and she was good to go for an hour. She'd be leaning forwards, eyes as big as they could stretch: "They say you can't...but I wonder if...I'm dying to try...." Everything was so exciting to Cathy. Just let me at it. And she always had questions—questions you couldn't answer, like how do you paint silence. Or air.

"There's more to being at university than just doing the syllabus," Hutch said to her one time. "Why don't you go to some of the after-school things or the socials?"

Cathy said she didn't have time. There was too much art stuff to do, to practice. She learned by doing and there was just so much to do. Hutch only ever saw Cathy out being social once, at some off-campus party with Paul's art crowd, early in the semester. Hutch was there because there was nothing going on at Sean's. She was wearing a sexy wine-coloured shirt with weird-looking flowers round her neck. Forget the flowers. What a shape. And then he remembered her standing in the shallows back home in a clinging wet tee, lifting her hair back with both hands. He'd been too mad at her to enjoy the view at the time.

He'd been about to go over for a chat but a girl he'd met a couple of times pulled him into her group saying she wanted him to meet this bunch of people, and by the time they'd scattered again, Cathy was gone. He'd walked all through the rooms to check, but she was definitely gone.

+

There came a day when Cathy asked him why he was called Hutch. That wasn't how he was christened, was it? So he spent a long time making a good story out of the first part so that maybe she'd forget about the second.

"Oh, I had colic as a baby, according to my mother, and screamed from when I was six weeks old until I was four and a half months. To the day." Hutch pointed a thumb at his chest. "Family says that's why I've got great lungs." They'd tell him to Hush, and Oh, Hush, and Hush Down, and probably much worse things they never told him about.

"So my first word, after I pulled myself up on my feet in the crib and dribbled all down my front, was 'Hu-ch.' Mom said I couldn't manage the *sh* sound. Said that was typical too because I never did hush."

"So Hutch stuck," Cathy said. She looked at him for a moment then said, "So what's your real name?"

Hutch sighed and put on his blankest face. "Arthur. Arthur George, after Mom's oldest brother. Died at sea before I was born."

A slow smile spread across Cathy's face and her mouth opened wider than he'd ever seen it. He could see a couple of fillings in back molars on the top.

"Your name is Art."

She started to laugh—out loud, which she didn't do very often. He'd never heard this laugh before. It came from her boots, and rang round the room like the whole brass section of a frigging big band. Half the room was looking now, grinning and wondering, and all Hutch could do was shrug and shake his head and wait for the fuss to die down.

He was probably looking a bit pissed off by the time she stopped because she wobbled out a sorry. And now and then on the way home she went off into a fit of stupid giggles and she'd probably keep the whole frigging building awake all night.

+

It was March when Cathy came straight from some one-off class with all her books and art supplies. She couldn't find her wallet when it came time to pay, and started rummaging around in her backpack in a panic, laying things on the table: dictionary, notebook, plastic box with pencils, and a cloth bag with tubes of paint, pastels, and paintbrushes inside. Holy shit, what a pile. And a sketchbook. He reached over to lift the sketchbook but she grabbed it right out of his hand. Almost made him jump.

"Just going to have a look. My hands are clean."

"You're not having a look." And the way she said it would take paint off walls.

"Suit yourself."

It was because of those pictures of Paul, years ago. How was he to know the book was full of Paul sketches? He'd just expected boats and gulls and maybe a few Mariners Cove faces. And anyway Jenny had nearly taken his head off at the time.

"Still mad at me for taking your book that day? It was just a bit of fun." He wasn't going to apologize. "Anyway, you had your revenge: you put a scrape in *Dolph*'s side where she hit the dock. Still shows. Pisses me off every time I see it. So you're even. More than even."

But what did a stupid scrape on his boat matter now? He scowled into his coffee and left it half drunk and got to his feet. Cathy could keep her frigging book.

+

No way was he going to Faraday's again with Cathy Russell. What a crabby female. Always scowling and carrying on. You'd think he was a criminal the way she went on. Maybe he'd try the bistro by himself again, straight from his class at five. Not sure if he would even bother to tell her, although he wouldn't mind leaving a message on her voicemail: "I won't be at Faraday's." Let her wonder if he meant this week or ever.

Then Paul invited him to the studio that Sunday to meet his cousin Amy and her friend before they went back to Montreal. The cousin was a female version of Paul, tall and athletic, the same Scandinavian good looks—elegant.

"I've been hearing about you for years so I bullied Paul into inviting you over for a coffee," she said with a smile. And Paul said something about it taking a lot of bullying.

"Pleased…"

"…my friend, Laura."

"Bridesmaids at a family wedding."

"Awkward time…"

"…more important things on their minds than student schedules."

"…heading into exams too?"

"Studying soon as we're on the plane."

"…crying babies like the flight up."

"English majors. Both of us."

There was a knock on the door and it was Cathy, all in her painty black clothes, a yellow streak down one cheek. Hutch looked at the floor.

"Ah," said Paul. "Glad you could come at such short notice, Cathy. Let me introduce you."

Then Laura said how she had really wanted to meet the person who painted those lovely pictures and was saying, "Tell me about this one…."

And Laura led Cathy over to the stack leaning against the wall, her back to Hutch, blocking his view. Laura had a fantastic voice, low-pitched and clear as ice water. Bet she could sing. She sounded all enthusiastic and bubbly, kind of like Jenny. Hutch took a quick look at Paul but he was pouring coffee, being the perfect host. Hutch hadn't really noticed Laura until she spoke—she was mousy-looking compared to Paul's cousin, pretty enough but ordinary.

She turned back to Hutch. "Everyone who's any good at math seems to end up in computer science or engineering," she said. "My brother's working with fibre optics. What are you interested in?" She was looking at him like she really wanted to know, wasn't just being polite.

It was nice chatting with a girl who could ask sensible questions. Then Paul called a taxi for them, so Hutch and Cathy left the studio. Hutch was still thinking of Laura.

"Nice girl," he said.

"Which one?"

"Well, both, but mostly Laura."

"Thought you'd go for the gorgeous Amy."

"I'd go for either of them but Laura's real easy to talk to."

There was a little space.

"She's like Jenny."

They had both spoken at once and they stopped there at the top of the stairs with their eyebrows up.

"Didn't think you'd—" said Cathy at the exact same moment as Hutch said, "Thought you'd just see—"

Cathy's eyebrows crunched together for a second then she said, "Hope Paul's noticed too." And they nodded at each other. Cathy smiled a bit and nodded again. She started down the stairs saying, "See you Monday then."

Hutch walked a few steps towards his room without answering then said, "Good enough."

Change of Heart

*

Back on those first Mondays at Faraday's neither of them said a word. Parsons looked so half asleep Cathy thought he might fall in his soup. Then one time, when they were finished eating, he straightened up.

"Well, if you're going to make all this racket, I'm going home." There was no grin until he looked at her sideways then just a little one and she couldn't help grinning back.

In February Parsons asked her about her basement window paintings. He'd seen some up in the studio, mentioned how the feet and ankles looked so real. She told him about the anatomy class they'd had at the hospital with real bodies. Cadavers. And one girl had passed out right next to the table where a body was lying and another had rushed out and thrown up. But Cathy had seen plenty of skinned rabbits and quarters of moose so she could focus on learning about the muscles and bones that gave a person their shape. Faces and hands were covered up because the prof said that was what upset people the most.

Then she noticed Parsons's expression and it was not an I've-been-hunting-too look, it was an awful I've-seen-people-die look.

"Oh god, Hutch, I'm sorry. You must have seen them. I didn't think."

"No. No, it was pitch-black."

But he still looked kind of sick, and Cathy didn't know what to say so she reached over and put her hand over his on the table.

"I hear their voices sometimes," he said. "Just before...at the end. Eugene and Jenny." Then he seemed to recover, wake up again. "Don't ever say that to Paul."

"No. Oh, no."

And they both took their hands off the table at the same moment and Cathy rushed into telling him about her latest class project and gabbled about how the others complained over all the homework he gave them and Hutch said yes, he had a prof like that too.

She noticed him squirming around in his chair sometimes, looking uncomfortable, and the way he limped when he was tired, or maybe something was hurting. And, once, this woman had a look on her face when he wasn't wearing his leg—like he was doing something disgusting in public.

Cathy began to enjoy Mondays at Faraday's as a change in routine, and sometimes she and Hutch would see someone from one of their classes and they would introduce each other as "a friend from home" and all chat together for a few minutes. It gave Cathy a wonderful feeling of being part of the crowd—a student among students, a Cove person among Cove people. Everything here felt foreign and even Paul spoke like a townie. Hutch was a Cove person to his toenails.

Then he said she had gold dust in her eyes, said it with that little smile. First her heart sped up and her stomach went into a knot and she wanted him to say more, wanted to look in his eyes while he said it again. Then she remembered the grin and how he played all the girls like salmon on a line. Couldn't trust Hutch Parsons. She was not going to be tricked into anything more than filling a chair at Faraday's.

But maybe he wasn't an enemy anymore.

+

One day Hutch asked why Cathy never talked about Sarah these days. He said some of the guys used to call her Sarah-Said back in grade nine. He was looking at her, straight-faced but with a tease in his voice. Did they talk on the phone? Did they email? Cathy poked at a couple of scraps of carrot she'd missed on the side of her bowl and wondered what to say, and how much.

After a bit Hutch said, "Did you guys have a fight or something?"

"Yes." Her voice came out a bit snappy.

"Since you've been in Halifax?"

"No. Back when I graduated."

"Jesus, that's nearly two years ago. Her fault, was it?"

"Yes. It was."

"Two years is a frigging long time to hold a grudge, with all Sarah Brooks has done for you. What happened?"

And Cathy was so mad that Hutch should say she was holding a grudge when it was Sarah who had been so awful, that the words just blew out of her before she could stop them. "She wrote a paper saying how I was illiterate back in grade seven. Couldn't read a dictionary. Trouble with grade three readers. Sent it off to be published without even telling me. Never got my permission or *nothing.* Waited 'til they were leaving before she even said."

Someone at the next table had turned round and was staring. God, she was almost shouting. Cathy lowered her voice. "She used me. To put on her CV. To help get a job. Never told me because she knew I wouldn't let her." Her hand was shaking. "I trusted her."

Cathy was out of breath. She felt the lump in her throat she always got when she thought about this too much. Her coffee had slopped over and she dabbed at the puddle with her napkin. It soaked through and she reached over for Hutch's. Hutch wasn't saying a word. She never meant to tell him this. Never.

"I can see how you'd be upset," he said gently.

Hutch finished his coffee. Cathy left the rest of hers. They headed back to their building in silence.

When they were nearly there Hutch said, "I was thinking. 'Bout what you said." He gave her a quick look then kept his eyes on the ground as they walked. "If you did all this up on a spreadsheet: the publication thing on one side, and what Sarah has done for you over five years plus you not speaking to her for two years on the other side, I'd say you're about even now." He had one foot on the step and his key out, looking at her sideways. "Waddya think?"

And his voice was so warm and...and understanding, that she choked up completely.

And the worst of it was, part of her agreed with him. It really was almost two years and in all that time nobody had ever mentioned the study. Maybe Sarah was right and nobody had read it, or connected Cathy with it.

Hutch had accused her of holding a grudge and she didn't want to be mean like that. Maybe she should try and let this go. Jenny Sheppard wouldn't have held a grudge. No, and Sarah wouldn't either. But Cathy couldn't speak. She just shook her head and didn't look at Hutch. And after a bit he opened the door and she turned down to her room without a word.

Food for Thought

*

Sarah Brooks called in late March, inviting Hutch to dinner that Friday. Dr. Brooks was coming for a conference. Hutch couldn't really spare the time this close to exams but—free food.

Paul and Cathy were invited too and he wondered if Cathy would do her black cloud imitation all night. But when he arrived at the hotel she and Sarah were so deep in conversation they didn't even notice him walk in. It was the necklace Cathy was wearing; apparently Cathy had made it and they were discussing colours and bead sizes and length so she could make a similar one for Sarah. Well, that was unexpected.

Cathy looked good in a cream and black top, and the way Sarah was saying how glad she was that it fit so well, it must have been a gift from her. And it did fit well. Whatever was wrong with her motor, Cathy Russell had a great chassis. She was wearing regular shoes too instead of her usual winter tires. In fact she looked almost elegant. Hutch was glad he'd shaved and tidied himself up and worn his good shirt.

They had a round table with Tim sitting between the ladies, and Paul and him opposite, so Hutch took the seat next to Cathy and wiggled his eyebrows at her. There was the usual shuffling at the start.

"This my glass or yours?"

"Sorry. That your toe?"

Sarah delivered a pile of messages from all their mothers and there were questions for a while about the state of things in St. John's and Mariners Cove. Hutch asked after Dog.

"Took him a while to get used to a townie leash," said Sarah. "Pulled such a face when we first put it on. You'd have laughed. But he's getting old now and stiff. Doesn't mind short walks in a straight line from hydrant to hydrant. Doesn't even bark at cats."

Then the waitress arrived with the menus and the list of specials, which she recited in a top-speed monotone. The French didn't sound very French. The next little while was spent chuckling over the specials and choosing and some of them were still undecided when the waitress came back with the wine. Only Tim and Paul were ready to order. But the waitress went round with the bottle anyway, and Cathy started drinking her wine ages before the food came, saying she was thirsty. Her voice started to rise but a group was just arriving and settling in, so mostly it went unnoticed.

Sarah indicated the water, said she herself was afraid to take even a mouthful of wine on an empty stomach. Cathy kept right on sipping. And Hutch watched her, sitting back with one arm dangling over the back of his chair, and he saw Sarah looking at him but didn't even try to hide his grin.

Sarah said, "Have some of this bread, Cathy. It's warm, and delicious with the butter all melting."

"No, thank you," Cathy didn't want to spoil her appetite. Hutch flicked a quick look at Sarah, who was looking concerned, and back to Cathy. His grin kept right on growing. Paul's eyes made a quick circuit round everyone's face and went back to his napkin.

"It'll soak up the wine so you won't get lightheaded." Sarah's last try.

"Great wine," said Cathy, draining her glass and looking around for the bottle. "Very nice." The tip of her nose had turned a bit pink.

"We saw *A Beautiful Mind* the other night," said Tim. "Anyone else seen it?" Nobody had, but Paul said he and Hutch had gone to see *Black Hawk Down* after Christmas. Then there were those blockbuster movies everyone was talking about and Hutch sat forwards again and stopped looking at Cathy and enthused about the technology in *The Lord of the Rings*. Cathy was reading the trilogy and had started the second book. She was indignant at the way Tolkien treated the character of Sam Gamgee.

"Just because he didn't have the same schooling as Frodo and the other rich hobbits he's made Sam act stupid, childish—clapping his hands when he's excited and jumping up and down and stuff. It's derogatory."

She looked at Hutch. "Disrespectful."

"I know what derogatory means. Like you when you talk about guys who work with computers."

"It's computers I'm derogging, not guys who work with them."

"Oh? *Guys who spend all day following orders from a machine*, you said. *Turn into brainless robots,* you said."

Paul was smirking and looking down at his napkin again.

"So did you go see the movie, Cathy?" said Sarah. No, she was going to wait and watch them all on the VCR at home because it was cheaper.

"They're on DVDs these days, Cathy," said Hutch, straight-faced. "Digital video discs."

It was lucky that the waitress appeared with plates just then—no, scallops here please, leek and potato soup over there—and the talk turned to admiring the contents and appearance of each person's plate and the cutting and chewing and savouring. Hutch was starving, so he focused on his food and forgot about conversation.

When they were well into their main course and his stomach was feeling less neglected, Hutch asked why Cathy had pulled her plate away and turned it 180 degrees.

"My asparagus clashes with your broccoli. It's spoiling my appetite."

"I'll eat yours too if you like," said Hutch. "My stomach's colour-blind. And the greenery in that vase thing is broccoli-coloured. Should I ask the waitress to take it away?"

"Eat your dinner, Arthur," Cathy said.

Shit.

Paul spluttered round his wine, grabbed his napkin, and apologized, all at once, and Hutch turned in his chair to look at him—anything to take the focus off himself. He hoped to god Cathy wouldn't do this again. Hutch offered to pat Paul on the back and Paul said in a scratchy voice, between coughs, "Not one of your pats, thank you. Haven't recovered from that Tigers game."

"You're following college sports?" Tim said. And the conversation turned to one sport after another ending with the FIFA World Cup in

South Korea, which would start at the end of May. By then they were choosing dessert and Cathy's nose had lost most of its glow.

Tim paid for a taxi to take them home because the weather had turned sour again: *snow and blowing snow*, and Hutch said, "So that dinner will keep us alive over the weekend."

Plans

✶

Cathy felt better about Sarah. It would never be the same but maybe that was all right. She was grown up now. And she would enjoy making Sarah that necklace when she went home.

She meant to tell Hutch all that but he was back to being half asleep at Faraday's on the Monday after the dinner. Hardly said a word, so she didn't either. She tried not to feel disappointed. His social life must have picked up. Cathy started listening for extra feet coming back with him, girls's feet, but she didn't hear him at all. Maybe he was crashing somewhere, or at some girl's place.

Hutch had watched her a lot at Sarah's dinner, smiled a lot, teased her in front of people. That's how she'd seen him behave with girls he was chasing, like Jane Butt and Phyllis Barnes. So what was he up to on weekends? Cathy reminded herself that he was not to be trusted. He was not cute. But every time she went in and out she looked for him. She listened for his uneven thump on the stairs, watched for his feet outside her window. She'd catch herself doing it and tell herself to get real. She would turn her chair away from the street and turn up the radio—only to find herself straining to hear over the music. After that one Monday, end-of-semester deadlines put a hold on Faraday's altogether, so she didn't have a chance to see if he seemed interested. And it was back to beans on toast.

She'd be doing a third-year course with Michelle Papineau in September—Madame Papineau, the reason Cathy had applied to NSCAD in the first place. Cathy felt awkward calling her Michelle but the visual arts professors liked to keep it casual. And Cathy already knew exactly what portrait she wanted to paint for the final project. All the paintings she'd done of Paul were small, in watercolours. Hutch's portrait would be larger than life, in oils.

+

The end-of-year dance was coming up but Cathy hesitated. She went looking for a dress. If she found something she liked she'd ask him, if not she wouldn't—let Fate decide.

At least she didn't have to worry about shoes. Seeing Michelle around campus had made her notice shoes; Michelle wore very high heels—cute little bows on the front of one pair, pearly things on another—little tiny shoes that clipped along the corridor and sounded so dainty.

Cathy's sneakers were enormous and fat and scruffy. They squeaked. She started keeping her eyes open for regular shoes but they were hard to find in her size. And she was wearing out her sneakers tramping around looking. She couldn't believe the prices. Then she saw a sign, *All Merchandise Must Go*, and the only sizes left were teeny like Madame's, or giant like Cathy's. And lined up at the back of the seventy-five-per-cent off table there was a pair of plain black shoes that fit her, with a small enough heel that she wouldn't wobble. Only twenty-four dollars. A week before, she would have said no way was she paying twenty-four dollars plus tax, but she was wiser now.

So she trailed around large stores and small, much-loved and just-arrived, looking for a dress. She was heading home empty-handed when a colour caught her eye in the window of a tiny store, hardly big enough to have a window. A warm bronze that would bring out the gold dust in her eyes. She tried it on and was surprised—the silky texture, the way it hung. Cathy had never looked this good. She watched herself in the mirror turning, lifting her arms, pretend-dancing, and couldn't believe it was her. When Cathy checked the price she found out the difference between a store and a boutique. Her Visa would curl up and die. Dad....

She bought it anyway.

Heads or Tails

*

Hutch shouldn't have come to Faraday's tonight—he still had one more exam—but he was starving and had no groceries. He'd really been cracking the books because he wanted a good co-op placement for the summer semester. He'd had to work half the night after that dinner with Sarah and Tim Brooks and every night since. Still, he was here now. Hutch sagged back in his chair and looked round, saw he'd finished his soup without tasting it.

"Will you come with me to the end-of-year art dance?"

There was a beat before the question registered.

"I don't dance."

"Does that mean you won't come, or you'll come but you won't dance?"

If he'd known this was coming he would have thought up a watertight excuse. "Can't you ask Paul?" Shouldn't have said that.

"Three girls have asked him already and he said no, of course. Thrice. Said he might drop in for half an hour."

"Thrice." Hutch gave a half laugh, half snort. "What were you reading that had a thrice in it?"

"Do I have to ask you thrice?"

"No. No. And no."

"Does that mean you definitely won't come or are you just saying no I don't have to ask three times?"

"Shit, Cathy. This is like multiple choice."

"A simple yes or no. Will you come to the art dance with me or not?"

Hutch had been tossing a mental coin and it had come down on the edge. It wobbled around and finally fell on its face.

"No. Sorry. Used to like dancing but I can't stand dancing going on all round me when I can't join in."

"Okay." Cathy finished drinking her coffee and started gathering up her stuff. She didn't look mad or upset or anything, just looked like he'd said no to a second cup of coffee. Shit. He stood up, clanging his chair into the one behind.

"Oh, all right, I'll go."

She looked at him with no expression on her face at all. Just pointed her eyes at him and looked.

"You don't have to if you don't want to."

"Said I'll go. So I'll go." He wound his way over to the cashier and started digging out coins and Cathy came over with a handful and they counted it all out.

He stumped out of the door and up the street calling back to her, "Have to go to the ATM."

He phoned the Wednesday before the dance.

"How dressed up is this thing on Saturday?"

"No blue jeans."

"Dress pants and a good shirt then. What time?"

+

It was the kind of rain that bounced, that night, and Cathy had on rain gear when he knocked on her door. Part of her hair was up on the top of her head, the rest hanging down, and she was wearing big loopy earrings. Didn't see her in jewellery much, or hair up, or makeup. Made her eyes look huge. Luscious lips. Holy shit. He remembered how Paul had pulled a knowing face at him when he'd heard about the dance, almost a smirk.

"You two seem to be hitting it off."

"God, no—nothing like that." She was much more interesting than he'd ever thought she could be, but she was still just Cathy Russell.

Cathy had the tickets and swished in ahead of him up the steps. He was more used to her scuffing than swishing. And she was wearing a dress. With legs. Everyone was shaking umbrellas and stamping feet and exclaiming about the rain and Hutch heard his name. He turned to see a friend of Paul's behind them, calling to him over a group of people chattering in Japanese, and they stood shooting the breeze. By the time Hutch turned around again Cathy was standing by the coat check with an older couple, faculty maybe, being introduced to the woman, shaking hands.

He reached the coat check and handed in his jacket and the big black umbrella he had bought in a thrift store; it had two bent spokes that gave it a sort of list to one side, which was why he'd bought it. He'd only used it once. He was pulling down his shirtsleeves when he saw Cathy next. She was standing away from the crowd, looking around.

Hutch just stood still and stared.

This was a different girl. This was someone you would notice in a room full of people, someone you would want to meet. When did this happen? She was looking at him now, motionless amongst the bustle. His feet felt glued to the ground and he had to peel them off and force himself forwards, one robot step after another. He wanted to say how wonderful she looked, how amazing it was, how stupid he was for not seeing all this before.

"Hi, Lighthouse. Looking good."

+

Cathy went over to a group of people and one of the girls, Jessica, leaped to her feet and gave her a hug saying she looked fabulous and there was the usual manoeuvring and scraping to expand the circle by two more chairs. Paul joined them for a bit and even he looked twice at Cathy. And one guy said he recognized Hutch from Cathy's sketches, which pulled him up short.

"What sketches?"

"Well, you know you won't escape her pencil," said buddy with the shaved head and the eyebrow ring, Tristan. "She has everybody committed to paper five minutes after she's met them."

And they talked about her as if her art was fantastic and seemed surprised that Hutch was surprised. Well, he thought her art was fantastic too but what did he know?

So when he had a chance Hutch said, "You've done sketches of me?" His eyes flicked over to Tristan and back to Cathy. "I'd like to see them. Please."

"Just preliminary sketches. I want to do a painting of you, a portrait."

This was a Very Bad Idea. This was much too up close and personal, although Cathy maybe didn't see it that way. It was probably just another project to her, like a bowl of fruit.

"Would I have three eyes all looking different directions? If you did one, that is."

"Looking at three different girls? Maybe." She was smiling, looking as if she just might do that. But she didn't mention the portrait again all night.

Hutch had said he didn't dance so it was ages before he could legitimately say he needed to move around a bit and how about it. "Just be careful not to push me backwards or to the left."

He and Cathy danced every slow dance after that. And something changed out there under the strobe lights, with his arm round her and her hand curled up in his. This was a girl to hang onto, somebody special. He pulled her a bit closer and she turned to look at him. Her eyes were warm, the expression in them was warm. Beautiful eyes. Usually she looked ready for a fight but tonight, for the first time ever, she looked as if she might like him more than just a bit.

But as they left the dance, his feelings buried themselves again. The rain had stopped and they'd be back too soon in a cab so he suggested walking, even though his stump was starting to grumble. He needed time to think. This was too far too fast. He had no clue what to do.

Any other girl…

…but this was Cathy. Cathy Russell.

Holy….

He didn't want to be tangled up with someone who…what? He felt like an animal that senses a danger it can't see or hear or smell, just absolutely knows it's there. Cathy was—not a predator—more like a trap.

It was awkward living in the same building. It would be so much easier to part here and go in opposite directions, give himself some space. It would have been easier if Paul had stayed around and they'd all gone back together. He realized Cathy was talking.

"Sorry. Miles away."

"I was asking if the dancing bothered your leg."

"Oh, no. We weren't jumping around or anything."

He went back to thinking yes-no-yes-no right up to reaching her door. He had a feeling she'd said more but didn't ask. He stood looking at her, outside her door, still not knowing what to do, seeing those big eyes on him. Part of him wanted to hold her so close they would sink into each other and the other part wanted to run.

She moved forwards and gave him a little sisterly kiss and started to step back saying thank you, and his arms went around her of their own accord and he kissed her in a not-brotherly way from plain instinct. Then put his arms down in plain fright. Cathy smiled and turned to unlock the door, went inside, and shut it quietly behind her.

And Hutch stood watching the dust motes floating in a beam of light, roused from their dormant state and hovering, waiting to land.

Heads or Hearts

✶

The effect her dress had on Hutch was everything Cathy had hoped for and more. He stood absolutely still with his mouth open, blocked all the people behind him who were trying to squeeze round and didn't even notice. Cathy could feel his eyes on her all evening.

He even danced with her, which she hadn't expected, and he held her close but in a casual way. She was surprised how broad he was, how deep chested. Then halfway through he pulled her closer and she was aware of every inch of herself. And him. She wanted the music to play forever—"My Everything" and "Crazy" and all kinds of songs she hadn't thought she liked. Their faces were level when she was wearing the heels, so now and then their eyes met and he was smiling—not that saucy smile, just good-humoured. And in the last dance he leaned his cheek on her hair and she thought that if nothing else happened, at least she had that.

He was not smiling on the way home, at least she didn't think he was, and he was not listening. And when he was outside her door he looked serious and just stood there without moving and there was a silence she could touch, and it made her nervous so she gave him a little kiss to say it's okay, you don't have to do anything. But instead he wrapped himself around her and kissed her and kissed her and she couldn't breathe, couldn't think, couldn't hear anything but the booming of her heart, fabric squeaking, and the scraping of his chin. She felt the silkiness of his hair and how the curls wound round her fingers but were so soft, not as wiry as she'd thought they'd be. She smelled shampoo and aftershave and skin, tasted the inside of a mouth not her own and the sound his tongue made roared around like waves in a cave. And when he let go suddenly she had to take a quick step to catch herself.

He looked—like he thought he'd just made a mistake. Cathy turned away so she couldn't see that look, would rather remember the part that came before. She opened the door and just glanced once as she closed it and smiled at him. He never moved. Only his eyes turned to watch her.

She leaned against the inside of her door in darkness, trying to fix it all in her memory to look at again and again. She went over each sensation, like studying a poem for an exam. And after a while through the door she heard his feet moving away.

The next day she caught the ferry home for the summer.

+

Cathy was still feeling dreamy when she reached Mariners Cove. She walked all her favourite trails, sat in the sun by the back door and listened to her favourite bit of ocean, ate everything her mom laid before her with enthusiasm, and listened to her mom's chatter with a smile on her face. In a fit of nostalgia she pulled out her box of journals from under her bed just to see how bad her writing had been and how far she had come. But it brought back more than a feeling of pride. It brought the memory of desperation and need, of her determination to learn. She could see it in how hard she had pressed on the pencil, in how her writing started to wander after one or two lines but kept right on going. She could almost feel herself gritting her teeth.

She remembered some of the events, too. Recalled her mother tripping on the lamp's cord and breaking the shade and of herself thinking how much easier it would be to draw the scene for Sarah, rather than write about it:

...lamp on the ground and Mom with her hands in the air in that stupid way, like someone was pointing a gun at her, and the cat taking off in a straight furry line like a flying eyebrow.

Except every other word was mangled and misspelled and she'd written *flying Ibrow*, which made her giggle.

+

Sarah called, in Cathy's first week back home. She'd been checking out galleries in St. John's and there were a few that took work from unknown artists if the owner and manager liked them. Would Cathy like to come for a visit and bring in two or three of her best pictures, all framed and ready for display, and they could make an appointment for a showing?

It was kind of Sarah to take the trouble but Cathy had mixed feelings about spending hours and hours alone in Sarah's company. She'd love to have a real good talk with her about the state of the world, because it was Sarah who had first talked to her about outside things. She wouldn't mind Cathy asking dumb questions or making a load of false starts before she managed to voice an opinion. Dad wouldn't either, but he was off in Labrador and Mom was more into local stuff. But there were a lot of thoughts Cathy didn't want to share with Sarah. Still, she was glad the gap between them had closed a bit. She'd already started the necklace, spreading it all out on the kitchen table to show her mom the design. Maybe she could finish it in time.

"D'you think I could crash with Dot's daughter for a night?" Cathy asked her mother. "One night with Sarah, one with Marianne?"

Mom arranged everything with Dot, gave Cathy bus money without even a sigh, arranged a lift to Gander.

Cathy brought three of her best pictures on the bus, and loved every minute of her trip round the St. John's galleries with Sarah, spent the whole day with her. After her appointment, the manager agreed to show one piece at a time over the next few months, but told her to please not be disappointed if they took longer than expected to sell. Cathy promised she wouldn't. He said about sometimes having to wait a long time before the right customer walked in, the customer who saw things the same way as the artist. The shop took an awful big percentage if one was sold, but how else was Cathy going to get her name out there?

She had dinner with Sarah and Tim that night, and over coffee Sarah said, "I can see changes in your painting since you started at NSCAD—more professional. Of course. But you've kept your own style. Don't lose that."

Cathy wasn't sure what her style was, although Sarah wasn't the first person to say that. Then in her positive, Sarah way, she nodded and said, "You've fulfilled all my expectations and more."

And Cathy felt a rush of affection she hadn't felt since the trouble started and tried to put it into her thank you.

Distance

✶

It was Hutch's first ever flight. He'd given himself plenty of time but every stage took longer than expected and his leg set off the alarms so by the time he was through all the gobbledygook they'd started boarding and his stomach was in a knot. He felt like a rookie, wondering which row the numbers above the seats belonged to, almost sitting in the wrong place, fumbling with his seat belt, reading all the safety instructions in the pocket in front. He only began to enjoy himself when the engines came to life and the plane started to move.

He was in an aisle seat and the old guy by the window was reading the *Globe and Mail* and kept turning the pages. Every time he turned one he spread the whole thing out in front of himself and the window and half of Hutch, like he was going to hang it on a frigging clothesline. Then he'd fold and shake, fold and shake, until it was all squared off to the right size. Two minutes later he'd do it all again. Half the time Hutch had to make do with looking out the windows on the other side of the aisle.

The plane coasted across a lot of tarmac then made a slow turn until it was pointing down a runway. It paused, then the engines roared up and the plane shot off as fast as it could go, like a pole vaulter heading for the bar, pushing Hutch back into his seat with the force of it, the power. The horizon tilted and now they were in the air and the wheel sounds stopped. There was a rumbling thump that scared him for a moment but it was just the undercarriage being hauled up. And Hutch realized he was smiling—a stupid big grin on his face like a little kid. Excitement. Adventure. Like taking off in his kayak.

And here he was in Kanata, Ottawa's tech haven. Big names he'd been hearing about forever: Corel, IBM, Adobe, and that huge fancy Buckingham Palace of a campus, Nortel's Carling Campus. He'd applied for his summer work term to a start-up company, on the go for four years, and early next morning he was walking in their front door clean-shaven, wearing his interview shirt, hair brushed until his scalp hurt, and a spring in his step.

He worked his ass off those first three weeks. They were using a scripting language designed for web development that he didn't know, and every night he had to go back to his room and dig in, working until all hours so he could catch up. It was like one of those long hikes with cadets—every time you got to the top of a hill there was another one up ahead. He'd seen a big bull moose one time, all knobby knees and headgear, bouncing along in that casual way—making it look so easy. There were a lot of fit moose around Kanata.

When Hutch was well into his second month, Mike, his mentor, hooked him up with three other guys for a group project. Life was easier after that. It was still a long day and he was on the go every minute, but things wound down after supper and he was able to look around the city a bit.

He went for a hot dog sometimes with the guys but they just talked computers, spent their leisure time playing computer games. Hutch wanted to forget about technology when he wasn't working. What he really wanted was something physical, to get behind a puck or a ball with his two feet on the ground, to reach and drive and pull and strain, feel the wind chill from his own speed. He even missed the stairs in Paul's place, which he'd cursed daily for two years, so he started walking up two flights and taking the elevator the rest of the way.

They were okay guys, the others. They were all from Ontario, although Sanjay was born in Mumbai and Hutch sometimes had to ask him to repeat things. The other guys teased him about that, saying Hutch's accent was way thicker than Sanjay's and they were the ones that needed a translator. Hutch liked the fact that every region back home had its own flavour: Bonavista Bay, St. John's, the Southern Shore, Burin, the Northern Peninsula—not just the accent but words and expressions. Here everybody was the boring same, except for the second-language guys. No personality at all.

He started to notice a girl's voice through the wall of his room sometimes, singing. It wasn't loud but it had such a clear ring to it that it carried. It was Jenny's kind of pitch, a soprano, but cleaner somehow, more exact. Sometimes she sang the same phrase over and over, with tiny changes, then went through the whole piece again. He enjoyed the concert as he was getting ready for bed. Then on Sunday morning she started to sing "Farewell to Nova Scotia," so he joined in.

Twenty minutes later there was a knock on the door and a girl was standing there: curly dark hair, nice figure, pretty smile.

"You can sing," she said. "I didn't know nerds could sing."

"Hey, I'm not a nerd."

"Anyone who works over there is a nerd." She waved her hand vaguely in the direction of Nortel.

So they stood in the doorway talking about singing and she was going to her gig and would he like to come?

+

That was how he met Fiona and a bunch of guys who really knew their music, and how he had the bars of his musical cage permanently bent out of shape.

New*found*land, says the guy, Jay, on the keyboard; New-found-land says Hutch. Like *un-der-stand*. And Jay grinned like he'd known all the time, then turned the "Ode to Newfoundland" into jazz and blues on his keyboard. And a saxophone joined in and drums, and suddenly there were snatches of styles Hutch vaguely recognized but couldn't put a name to and Fiona threw in a bit of rap and it was all so expert-sounding you'd have thought they'd rehearsed for hours, not improvised everything just then. Eugene would've loved it.

Turned out they were all music students at the University of Ottawa. Fiona drove Hutch downtown for the gig and afterwards took him on a walking tour along the Ottawa River and past the National Art Gallery;

it looked huge and impressive and Cathy would get lost in there and forget to come out. They drove along Sussex Drive and past Parliament Hill, which was crawling with tourists, and over a bridge to the Museum of History and Civilization and circled around a bunch more places until he'd lost all sense of direction. Fiona said that, being an outdoors sort of guy, he'd have liked Gatineau Park but the traffic up there was shocking on Sundays.

On the way back Hutch said, "So why are you staying way over in Kanata?"

"Oh, it's actually my brother's room. I'm just staying there for two weeks while he's in New York. This is his car I'm driving too."

Fiona had said she needed to "get away" for a bit, never did explain from what. But Hutch thought it might have something to do with the big dark-haired guy who played trumpet and trombone. Hamish. It was the way Hamish looked at Hutch like a bear standing over its catch—just try it. Very big guy. Don't mind me, b'y—ten days and I'm outta here. Fiona didn't seem to notice those looks when she waved to Hutch from the stage now and then, winked at him, and linked her arm through his as they walked out.

Hutch went out for coffee with Fiona most nights over the next week. A couple of times, a guy hailed him from another table. His accent again—it was hard to be anonymous here. This guy was from St. John's, doing a work term up the road. His mother grew up in Gander and as soon as Hutch said Mariners Cove, the guy mentioned the Sheppard family. He'd seen Gus play the night of the crash and did Hutch know anybody on that bus? Hutch said he knew everybody on that bus. It was a small place. He made sure his leg was out of sight and let the other guy leave first.

He went to Fiona's gig the next Sunday too. It felt good just to listen, the way he felt good after a hockey game. Something inside had a workout.

This was the day her brother was coming back so, before she drove to the airport, Hutch took Fiona for supper at a little place she knew. It was a lot like Faraday's only the chairs were uncomfortable and the talk was all music: he should join a choir, take up an instrument.... Yes. One day. She dropped him off in the parking lot and they exchanged a little goodbye kiss, ignoring the idiot who took the devil's own time parking opposite with his lights up on high beam. The little kiss turned into a big one but it was still an everyday kiss. Fiona wasn't Cathy.

Cathy would have been home all this time. How often had he thought *must tell Cathy*—some Newfoundland-related thing or some funny incident. He loved the way she tilted her head when she was listening. He wanted to make her smile—he loved her smile—and she didn't smile easily; you had to earn it.

She'd probably think he was up to something if she heard about Fiona but he was a free man, and anyway she would never know. But that guy from the coffee shop turned up at the airport, booked on Hutch's flight, and he was there again when Hutch's leg set off metal detectors and asked him about it. Once they landed, he kept up a monologue for thirty minutes at the luggage carousel in St. John's. He was smirking all over his face when he said, "Pretty girl you were with Sunday, in the parking lot. Fiona. Meet her up there, did you?"

+

Hutch had to hang around St. John's for orthotics appointments for seven whole days while they made changes to his leg, staying at Uncle Em's sister's in Mount Pearl. That gave him less than three weeks in Mariners Cove and he made it into the last week before he came face to face with Cathy.

There was no—whatever that was on the dance floor—in her face. She looked troubled and her eyes felt like searchlights scouring the back corners of his head.

"What's wrong, Hutch?"

He wanted to say he thought kissing her that time was like a promise he didn't mean to make, but he couldn't.

"You met a girl in Ottawa."

Holy shit. It was a statement, not a question.

"Not really. Just had coffee with this girl a couple of times. Didn't mean anything. I'll never see her again."

"Didn't mean anything." She said each word slowly. "You never mean anything, do you Hutch?" She shrugged and turned away.

+

Back in Halifax Hutch didn't see a hair of Cathy. Didn't want to. Jesus. He could hear the frigging chains clanking. *You never mean anything.*

Paul had been in Montreal with his cousins all summer: jazz festivals and art shows, practicing French, cottage by the lake. But making decisions too.

"Applying to do a master's in art history in Montreal next year. At Concordia." They were on their second beer at Sailors when Paul asked about Cathy.

"What do you mean, *me and Cathy*?"

"Well, b'y, you looked pretty taken with her at that dance."

"Yeah, well…that was then. This is now."

Change of Direction

✦

Once school started Hutch could feel the pressure ratcheted up from second year. All the profs started the laying on of homework and questions about student goals for the semester and he was so buried in projects by the end of the first week that he could put Cathy right out of his mind.

He thought of her the next Monday but he wasn't sticking his neck out so he invited some girl from Sean's to Faraday's instead, and was bored. She kept up this chatter about nothing the whole time. He had liked that at Sean's with a few drinks in—now it was annoying. Why couldn't she just talk when she had something to say? He noticed she was wearing blue, like most of the girls in there.

"Lot of blue around tonight."

"Yes. This season's hot colour. Gotta be up with the fashion."

And hadn't there been a lot of blue around at home last visit? Well, he liked blue but what a bunch of sheep. Cathy didn't follow the flock. In anything.

Hutch avoided the studio until Paul happened to say Cathy only used it for half a day on Mondays now. So then he took to working in there on Saturdays when Paul was gone because there was more light and air and he could stroll around while he was thinking.

He was there late in October when Cathy brought up a pile of pictures. He was taking a break, standing by the window flicking through an old copy of *Popular Mechanics*. She paused when she saw him, nodded, and leaned her pictures against the wall in groups. She left and returned with another pile, without either of them saying a word. The second time she left she didn't come back.

Just as he'd managed to focus on his screen again, she walked in and stood in front of him until he looked up—which was not immediately because he was buggered if he was going to keep being interrupted by her flapping in and out. She looked all stiff with the drapes closed and was grabbing at her elbows.

"Would you sit for that portrait I mentioned last semester?"

Hutch waited for more detail but that was it. And as usual, half of him said *go* and half said *stop*.

"What would I have to do?"

"Just sit here for however long you can manage at a time...maybe five or six hours altogether."

She was looking at him now with her eyes up on high beam, a CAT scan, a CAThy Scan. He kept staring at her, daring her to read his mind, wishing he could kiss her enough to make her eyeballs spin. So why didn't he? Because she'd slap him upside of the head and say don't try your tricks on me. But that never stopped him before, just added a bit of spice. Any other girl.

"Can I be on my laptop while you paint?"

Cathy hesitated. "Some of the time maybe, but some of the time I'd need you just sitting looking straight ahead—a bit sideways to me."

It was a foot in the door. Did he want a foot in the door? It would give him time to make up his mind....

Which was how he ended up sitting for his portrait in Paul's studio, wearing the fisherman-knit sweater his Aunt Liz had made him, every grizzled Saturday morning from October into December.

Hutch brought down his CD player that first session and put on *Navy Blues*. Sloan was a Nova Scotia band but he'd had this back in Mariners Cove. He didn't want to be sitting in silence, listening to the paint drying. Cathy didn't comment. In fact she was so engrossed in positioning her easel and himself and all that painting junk on the table that she probably didn't even notice, which was fine by him.

+

Cathy's Santa bag was often hanging on a hook on the back of the door with a sketch pad sticking out of it. He didn't risk asking at first but shit, she was the one with something to lose. So the next time he said, "You haven't shown me the sketches you drew of me before. The ones Tristan mentioned."

She looked straight at him for ages, studying him, and he didn't move a muscle. He just stared right back. Then she said okay, next time she'd bring them up with her. He wondered if she'd accidentally forget but she didn't. She passed one of those sketch pads to him with two hands, flat, like something on a tray that might spill. And he took hold of it just as carefully.

He went through it page by page, taking his time, asking questions now and then. And after a bit he forgot about being on probation and became absorbed in the sketches: street scenes, the waterfront, faces, groups. There were pages full of the tree just down from their building in different light and different seasons, leaves turned inside out in a gale or weighed down in the rain.

"Fantastic," he murmured.

There was one sketch of Paul and five or six of Hutch, and he didn't say a word about those. He looked okay. His face had more angles than photos of him, harsher maybe, especially one that was all straight lines, but it was certainly him.

"Lots of talent," he said when he reached the last page. "As far as I can see, anyway. And you know I have no clue about art." He passed it back. "Thanks for letting me look."

She just nodded, no expression on her face. And whatever she'd felt after he'd taken that other book, maybe this made her feel better.

+

Cathy said the portrait was almost finished, but she never let him look. Well, he'd seen it once because he'd refused to sit again until she showed him. He'd liked it. It was waist up with a background of rocks and ocean, him just sitting there like a regular guy. He liked the way some of the colours in the rocks were in his sweater, some of the shades in his face were in the rocks. Simple. Once he knew he wasn't going to be embarrassed, he hadn't pushed it again.

He'd felt like an idiot at first, sitting there, didn't know where to put his eyes. But Cathy had that intent look she always had when she was drawing, or looking at something with her Art Eye, seeing the fisherman she wanted to paint and forgetting all about Hutch Parsons. So he could relax and study her and after a few sessions he tried out a joke or two and she smiled in a half-listening sort of way. So one morning, just for something to talk about, he started telling her what all the gang was up to these days.

"…and Jack sounds serious about this girl from Burin. Had to go all the way to Alberta to meet a girl from Newfoundland."

"All the way to Burin to meet someone you hadn't been out with first."

"Bullshit. I didn't go out with that many girls. You can count them on one hand—three fingers."

"But you *chased* every girl on the east coast. Except me of course." She paused. "Well, you never really saw me…."

She didn't see him coming. She jumped when he started to take the brush out of her hand.

"I see you now," he said.

He had an arm round her but she wouldn't let go of the brush and they both reached back, fumbling for a surface to put it on. Then they were wrapped up together, all arms and mouths.

Feet in the corridor, a cellphone ringing outside the door, Paul saying hello, the door handle rattling. Hutch took his arms away and stepped back, breathless, and Cathy staggered a little so he put his hand out to steady her and that was how they were when Paul came in sideways with about five bags of groceries in one hand and his phone in the other, which gave them a bit of time. But Paul was taking everything in and there was this little grin on his face when he looked at Hutch.

"Hope I'm not interrupting."

Cathy was putting caps on her paint tubes and clearing up with her head down, blushing, and Hutch said no, no, they were just finishing, in his best casual voice.

And that was it for the rest of the day.

All week Hutch kept trying to get back to Cathy, but he went with Paul to his aunt's on Sunday, denying everything when Paul started to tease. There was an extra lab and some tutorials and once he saw Cathy leaving the building just as he was heading her way. Every time he thought *now*, something happened. He could have gone late at night but that was a bit.... At least he knew what he wanted. He wanted Cathy Russell. A future with Cathy Russell. Starting now.

Friday, Paul was off somewhere for the weekend and Hutch told everyone who might come looking for him that he'd be gone too. He spent ages getting ready. He was so careful shaving he cut himself. The deodorant fell out of its case and rolled all over the floor gathering a month's worth of moss, then he had trouble cleaning it off and got the waterproofing all over his fingers.

He tried to prepare himself for anything; instinct said she felt the same way as him but caution said she didn't trust him—and anyway, you just never knew with Cathy. Just before eight he knocked on her door. And when he saw her smile—those beautiful eyes and those fantastic sulky-sultry lips smiling at him—he knew it would be all right.

And it was.

+

They had one week to themselves in a dazzle, making meals together, squeezing round each other as they cleared away. I'll wash, you dry. Kissing over the dishpan. Laughing when they messed up each other's breakfast—Cathy leaving the dial on the toaster up on Burn and Hutch leaving it down on Hardly Warm because he was always too hungry to wait. Cathy's easel was moved closer to the window and Hutch's laptop stayed on the fold-out table, cane wedged in place. Nights were full of whispered confidences and fumbling, awkward—and, on one occasion, fantastic—sex. But even the fumbling was great.

Paul saw him coming up the basement stairs on that Wednesday morning and laughed his head off, called him a dark horse. He said he'd knocked at Hutch's room a few times and wondered where he was. Paul went out through the front door mimicking Hutch.

"Just 'someone from home,' he says. 'Nothing like *that*,' he says. 'It's only Cathy Russell.'"

"Keep it under your hat, b'y. Please? Don't want Mariners Cove to know. Not just yet."

It was lucky Paul was a guy Hutch could trust to keep quiet. Now and then Hutch wondered why he didn't want people back home to know. He'd never cared before. Was he afraid it would spoil something? Was it because this was too important? Or was he embarrassed because it was Cathy? Was it because of his leg—that every Jed Batton and Phyllis Barnes in the world would say he couldn't do any better, now he was a cripple? No way. He wouldn't let guys like that influence him. But all those thoughts had gone through his head, so he had thought them. He made himself look them in the face but he still didn't know why.

+

Then it was Christmas, with so many family events there was no opportunity to be together anyway. They'd discussed it and agreed they didn't want the gossip so they let things slide for the holidays. Then in January, Hutch went back to Ottawa for his third-year work term.

They emailed, short and basic: work and weather. But always there was a line at the end about missing each other.

Hutch went for a scattered hot dog with the other work term guys—one in particular from St. John's. The two of them tossed about ideas for work after graduation. Both wanted this same placement again for the last work term, in September. They planned to keep in touch.

He checked out a couple of choirs—he'd meant what he said about that—but they had their auditions in September. All he could find was an advertisement for voice lessons tacked onto a notice board in a grocery store. So he ended up heading downtown on the bus every Saturday, singing scales and learning breath control on the third floor of a skinny brick house in Little Italy, squeezed in between two pasta places—a free supply of garlic and coffee fumes with spices he didn't recognize. He was always starving when he left. The teacher was a tiny woman with a soft speaking voice but when she let rip with a line of song to demonstrate a crescendo, Hutch couldn't believe the huge sound that came out of her little rib cage, without any effort that he could see. Her voice would have been handy on a trawler in a storm. She had him sing a simple folk song each class and started teaching him sight-reading.

It wasn't as good as a real gig but it was something.

Staying Around

✢

Cathy had finished her third year—two semesters to Hutch's three—and was working a few shifts a week so they could be together. She would paint in her spare time. Hutch had finished his work term and was back in Halifax for the summer semester. So he moved in.

Cathy had worried about how to break the news to Mom and Dad about not coming home until August. Cathy had mentioned taking Hutch to the art dance last year, which was a mistake because Mom asked about him every single phone call after that, even when he was in Ottawa.

"No idea, Mom. He's in Ontario."

And when he was back Cathy was vague: "Oh, he's around. Yes, I saw him the other day. Yes, I bump into him now and then." No way was she telling them he'd moved in. Then her mother asked what day she was coming home.

"Got a job in a hamburger place for a few months, Mom. Kind of like McDonald's. Paul says I can use his studio until it's rented so I'll be staying here a bit longer." Cathy listened patiently while her mom rambled through a ton of reasons why she should come home earlier.

"I'm going to paint things to take into that gallery in St. John's, Mom. Make some more money, maybe." She'd made five hundred dollars on one painting the gallery had sold last year and three hundred and fifty dollars on the other, even after the gallery guys had taken their cut. Cathy still felt a flood of pride about that although the money hadn't gone very far.

Her mom's voice got a bit croaky and there were more and more little breaks between words. "But Cathy, you could come home and paint here. Dad's gone to Labrador already. Dot says I should stay with her, but her daughter's coming for a month. In July. With her husband and children." She was almost whispering now. "I'd be in the way if I stayed. So I'll be home. By myself."

"I'm sorry, Mom. I'll be back in August. It's only a bit longer." Cathy was hunching up now, feeling guilty about Mom, guilty about Hutch. "Sorry."

And it didn't take long for Mom to put it all together. "Is this anything to do with Hutch Parsons?" Her voice had picked up again, sharper, full of Mother's Instinct. "I know he's up there until August because May Parsons was telling me. Are you seeing Hutch?"

"Well, now and then."

"Cathy." Shock. Horror. "Cathy. Don't get caught up with him. He's a nice boy and he's had a rough time, but he's a scamp."

"He's just a friend, Mom. Don't get excited."

There were a few ums and y'knows and then Mom said he was known for being a scamp around girls. "Don't let him try any of his tricks."

"I know, Mom. Don't worry," was all Cathy could think of to say.

+

Hutch used a cellphone and made a point of never answering a call on the apartment's landline because it was always Cathy's mom or Sarah. Cathy hadn't told Sarah about Hutch either because she didn't want Sarah to know if Mom didn't. Anyway, keeping it secret added a bit of—something.

Mom stayed with Dot until her daughter arrived in July and for the first few days back in her own house she seemed more content, said she thought the world of Dot but she was awful messy and she wasn't a very good cook, and Mom couldn't take over the cooking the way she wanted to because it was Dot's house after all. And she'd missed the cat. Dot didn't want it at her place—allergies—so Mom had to keep popping over to check on her. So even though Cathy felt awkward on the phone these days with Hutch creeping around pretending he wasn't there, that call was easier than some.

Once Hutch stuck his face up close while she was on the phone with her mother and crossed his eyes and did that stupid trick where he closed one eye and pretended to take out the other eyeball, rolling it up in his head so just the white showed, then pretending to put the eyeball in his mouth and swill it around and put it back in the socket again. And all the time Mom was yakking in Cathy's ear and Cathy was going purple trying not to laugh and finally let out a cough-snort-choke noise and turned it into a fit of coughing.

"Sorry. Crumb gone the wrong way. Call you back."

And when she hung up she pounced on Hutch, which was what he was waiting for, and it turned into a scrambling, love-you-love-you scurry out of their clothes, out of enough clothes, and into a wonderful, *the* most wonderful, she-didn't-want-it-to-stop-ever wonderful....

+

They still went to Faraday's on Mondays and Cathy wondered if anyone noticed the difference now they were together.

Together: adverb: *with each other, in a close relationship.*

There was a light shining inside her now, for sure. Maybe she glowed like Mary Pratt's fruit. There was no room for all this happiness and some of it must have to stay outside, like haze round the moon. Did it show to other people?

She'd never bothered about how other people saw her—or even *if* they saw her—but now she did. Now she was aware of everyone in the room, of her clothes touching, of the heavy stick-to-your-ribs smell of pea soup being carried to a table behind. The raspy "thank you" and the waitress saying, "careful—it's hot" in a flat voice that told you she'd said it fifty times already. She was aware of a big tall guy squeezing between tables, ducking to avoid dangling lights, neck looped over to talk to someone like those flamingos in *Alice in Wonderland.* She was aware of a low-pitched argument across the way:

"That's not what I said."

"But it's what you meant." Both voices with sharp edges. Cutting.

Strange, how the only mean comment that had really bothered Cathy years ago was from Hutch. *They forgot to switch on the light with that one.*

That had hurt. That had been etched into her brain: first the needle, scoring the words, then the acid, pressed in with each remembering, making the wound deeper. Maybe it wasn't her brain—maybe it was her heart, even then. Hutch.

+

They went home together, shared a taxi from Gander, played it down when people raised their eyebrows.

"We're studying in the same city," Hutch said. "Staying in the same building even. Makes sense to share a drive home. You don't have to be married to share a frigging taxi."

Some nerve he had.

They met at The Café a few times and in White's Convenience, strolled along Main Road together once. Cathy took a small painting of Hutch to give to his grandfather and the three of them sat together for an hour or so. But twice they met on the quiet, up the track to the lighthouse. They pushed their way into the woods for an hour by themselves. Cathy so needed that. And Hutch's last work term was in the fall semester this time so they wouldn't be together until January. How was she going to manage?

Art First

*

Cathy poured all her time and effort into art after Hutch went to Ottawa that September. She had not realized you could miss someone so much. They phoned at weekends and emailed often, but that was just an hour or two out of a whole long week. Paul was gone and a couple was renting the top floor including what used to be the studio. So she rearranged her apartment to make the most of the space, taped down all the extension cords. When Hutch returned she would rent locked storage space down the hall for her pictures. In the meantime she had to step around the piles leaning against the wall.

She'd been thinking of improvements she could make to Hutch's portrait and that he might be a good subject for her entry in the fourth-year art competition. It would need to be bigger—maybe oils on Masonite this time—and different light, different shadows.

*

And suddenly it was the winter semester, a study term for both of them. Hutch was sitting there in cargo shorts with the leg off, like every Saturday morning around the apartment, even though it was snowing itself into a frenzy out there. "Freedom," he said, and she was only painting him waist up, after all.

She stood, thinking, and Hutch relaxed back into his chair, snoozing still, with that little smile. She wanted to snuggle into him. He looked so perfect there, broad shouldered and muscular, strong in a way that didn't need a hairy chest to prove it. Didn't need a scruffy chin, although he had one today. Didn't even need two legs. Which made her wonder. She did a pile of sketches and wondered....

+

The start of May and Cathy sat in front of the finished portrait and dreamed. She would get a top grade for this, she was sure of it. And she had a good chance of it being the one chosen to go in the national competition. Just think. If she won it—a two-week internship with that painter whose name she could never pronounce but whose work she drooled over. It could happen. She hadn't let herself think about it before but it could happen.

When Hutch came home she led him, smiling, round to the painter's side and flicked off the cover with a magician's flourish.

"Ta daa!"

Silence.

"Jesus. You've painted...you've...Jesus, you've put my leg in it."

Cathy's heart started booming in her head. Her beautiful picture.

"I can't believe it."

She unfroze enough to notice him rub his face with both hands. She'd never seen him do that. Then he pounded a fist into his other palm, started walking up and down, *ker-plonk, ker-plonk*, hand on the wall at the turn-arounds, speeding up, the plonks getting heavier and his body tipping sideways more with each one.

"Did it never cross your mind to ask me? To find out if it was okay?"

No, she'd just been thinking about the best way to paint him.

"You had to know I'd hate it."

He pulled up facing her, head down like a bull charging, eyebrows clenched down over his nose. She'd never seen his mouth so tight and his voice came out with a hiss.

"I'd never have let you do that if I'd seen it. But you wouldn't let me see it, would you? Would you? You knew I—"

"No. No, I didn't think—"

"—no. You never fucking think. That's the trouble with you. It's art, art, art. No room for anything else!" He was shouting now, spit flying. "I thought maybe—but I was wrong. You'll never change. Same frigging lighthouse with the light switched off when it comes to people."

"Stop." Cathy put her hands over her ears, squeezed her eyes tight shut. "Stop."

Hutch stood still, shook his head. "Sorry. Didn't mean that. It's just...." He looked bewildered, hurt. "Why?"

Reasons skidded round her head, tripping each other, but when she didn't answer straight away he started looking mad again and Cathy said she was just trying to think of how to say it. So he waited, standing there looking ready to blow if she didn't say something soon while she tried to line up the thoughts she'd been putting together as she painted him.

"When you sat there for the first sketches I thought...it struck me... how strong you looked, how strong you *are.* And that leg is part of you and kind of makes you look even stronger—like dressing a big tough hockey player in pink frills or something. The contrast...and you sat there all comfortable like it was just—I don't know, like it was just another part of you. Which it is. But you looked like—take it or leave it. And I tried to paint you like that."

"Sure you don't want a pink bow on it?" That was in his normal voice and the weight on Cathy's heart lifted a little. "But you'd need the hockey player's permission for that wouldn't you? Wouldn't you?"

He turned away awkwardly and wobbled and let out a whole string of curses at his legs and not being able to do stuff and something about that guy in the supermarket with burn scars all over his face and the fried arm and how she'd probably paint him just as he stood and never care if it wasn't what he wanted to see hanging on his wall and....

"Yes!" Cathy shouted over him. "Yes I would. You won't really look at yourself, will you? *See* yourself. You just think you're a useless cripple. Still. After all this time."

"I do not. You don't know how hard I work to look as normal as I can, to *be* as normal as I can with this frigging—this *thing.* And I don't think I'm useless. I just can't do things I love—get out on the water. Can't even...be with you the way I want to and, and, god...."

His voice cracked and he rubbed his face with both hands again.

"Hutch, I love you and I don't care about your stupid stump. I was thinking how—how whole you are, even with a piece missing, and all you can think of is how to hide it. You're still trying to be what you were before and you don't see that you're *better* than what you were."

"Better!" he scoffed. "What a load. Get real."

But the fire had gone out of him and Cathy wanted to hug him for comfort but was afraid he'd push her off and she couldn't bear that. She turned away, sighing.

"I'm just trying to level the playing field," Hutch said after a minute. "You don't know how many times I've felt less than the other guy because of this damn leg." He began walking up and down again but in an absent-minded way. "I'm doing okay at school, got good work terms. But I feel like I have to prove I can be as good as them, better maybe, all the time. Never used to care about marks but I do now.

"Even found myself working at being funny at parties. Can you believe it?" He looked sideways at Cathy. "And girls." He stopped in front of her for a moment, touched her arm for a second. Then the anger was back in his voice and he said, "But you should know better than anybody. It's how you felt when Sarah published that paper." And his voice rose a bit further. "Jesus, you've done exactly the same to me."

God. Maybe she had. No. But she couldn't let herself worry about that now, couldn't weaken now. Hutch swung away again, paced a bit more, speeding up again.

Finally he said he was getting lightheaded. He was starving because he'd worked through lunch and he had to get a sandwich or die. Cathy said how about that spaghetti she'd made, and they ate in silence but when they were clearing away the dishes he said could she cut the bottom off the picture? It would only be a couple of inches, ten per cent max. The rest of it seemed okay, although he'd really only looked at the leg.

Cathy tried to pin herself to her books but kept thinking what on earth she would do if Hutch insisted on having the bottom cut off.

My god, he wanted to amputate her art.

✦

Wednesday after school Hutch looked crumpled and exhausted but after supper he said okay let's have a look at the rest of it. They walked round to the front of the portrait with Hutch's arm laid across her shoulders and he studied the picture for ages in silence. But after a bit his arm slid down. The smile melted and his face flattened.

"What's wrong?"

"Nothing. It's great. Fantastic, even. But..." Hutch was frowning at it, head dropping forward.

"But?"

"I don't like the thought of you showing this to anyone."

"What?"

"I don't want just any old person seeing this. I'm not talking about the stump, or not just the stump—I mean the rest of it too. It's...I don't want people gawping at it."

"Why?"

Cathy's heart jumped around in a panic and Hutch stood and stood and finally said he didn't know.

"But this is my project for the semester," she said. "I get marked on this for my final exams. I've got nothing else." Her shoulders hunched up and she was pressing her hands together, squeezing them so they sounded all wet-rubbery. "It's the very best thing I've ever done." That came out in a whisper.

"I know, Cathy. Well, I don't know but I can see it's really great. But...I just don't want people looking at me. Like this."

"But what bits don't you like?"

Hutch was gnawing his lip and said it was that look on his face. She tried to see what he meant but she couldn't. He turned to her with something like pain in his face and said couldn't she use something else—that first portrait of him, or Devils Cove in the fog, or that tree? And she said they were ordinary and this was her best work ever.

"I know you want to show it, and maybe you'd win prizes and stuff, but you *can't.* Jesus, Cathy, can't you see?"

"How can you do this to me at the last minute?"

And he got that stubborn jut to his jaw, that exasperating, stubborn.... The silence was radioactive and neither of them had any warning, any protection. Everything screamed *danger* and Cathy's feelings careened around in red spirals looking for a way out. And Hutch looked worried and sad but so frigging stubborn. It felt like she was dangling from a ledge and no way Hutch was going to throw her a rope until she let go of the picture. And she couldn't. She couldn't.

For two days she chewed at the problem, weighed and measured, looked from close up and far away. She woke Thursday night and Hutch was out looking at the picture with a flashlight, leaning on a crutch. Cathy pretended sleep.

She'd worked towards this moment all her life. She had to be true to herself. She had the right to use her very own work. But Hutch had the right to not want his face, his amputated leg, out in public. Well, he should have thought of that before he agreed to sit. He was giving permission to show the painting when he agreed to sit. But that was bending the truth, being—what was that word. Anyway it was taking advantage. And it wasn't the same as Sarah because Sarah knew Cathy would be upset, hid the case study from her on purpose. Cathy hadn't really thought about how Hutch would feel, just about the best way to paint him.

She didn't understand why he felt so uncomfortable with the picture—the stump maybe, but not the rest. He looked fantastic. It showed him at his best. She understood that people hated her portraits when they were too truthful—unflattering as they saw it. She'd learned a bit about how much she could get away with from people at home and from Sarah and from art classes. But he said no, it wasn't that he looked awful but he didn't want people seeing that look on his face. Said it was private. For her. And yes he did have that little smile for her but other people saw it too, so what was the difference? It was something nobody but him would think about.

Because she *was* going to take it into school. And it would be hung up in the gallery with the others. And she hoped it would be chosen to enter the national contest.

+

On the Friday her final project was due, Hutch was gone all day and Cathy began gathering cardboard and bubble wrap and tape to protect the portrait when she took it into school. Had to search everywhere for scissors and found them in the kitchen. Hutch had been cutting into the plastic casing round some batteries—breaking them out, he said, and what did people think the poor batteries would do if they got loose?

But she was sacrificing Hutch. He was going to be so upset, mad. He would think she'd let him down, or didn't care. She might lose him. And what was one picture compared to being loved by Hutch? What use was a picture of him if he was gone? It was all about her again, not about Hutch's feelings at all.

She would not take it. She would not put art before Hutch.

Cathy stood with the scissors in her hand and stared at a can of beans on the counter, *through* the can. Her eyes saw it but the message froze on one foot, not registering in her brain. But after a while Cathy noticed the counter digging into her hip and she moved and rubbed her hip and saw a can of beans on the counter and decided she was hungry and hadn't eaten breakfast. So she put down the scissors and had beans on toast and coffee.

But she might never get another opportunity to enter a competition like this. She'd been fifteen years working on her art and she had been with Hutch for less than one. Art deserved to be put first. If she didn't put the picture in for judging she would regret it for the rest of her life. If she lost Hutch she would regret it for the rest of her life.

She washed the dishes. She turned on the radio to give her brain a break and some chicky with a long-lashes-cute-blonde voice said it was three hours to the weekend.

Deadline.

Panic.

+

Cathy spent almost an hour protecting and wrapping the picture and stringing it up so she could carry it then another age getting it up to the main floor. She could have used Hutch's help with this. She had to lean against the outside door to stop it slamming in the wind and manoeuvre her package through and the taxi wasn't there. So she stood, back to the wind, one side of the portrait against the wall and the end on top of her sneakers, until the taxi arrived. It was heavy on her toes after a while.

She had thirty-five minutes to spare by the time she delivered her precious package. The prof ticked her off the list.

"And the title?"

Cathy had thought about that for weeks, all kinds of fancy names. But the one that seemed right was quite simple: *A Man*.

She walked home with her stomach churning and chest tight, tried to rehearse what to say to Hutch. He would see the picture was gone from the easel and she wanted to be there to explain—she walked quickly. But what would she say? Maybe it would be better if he arrived first. She slowed down almost to a stop and someone *tutt*ed as they swung round her. Her thoughts leapfrogged over each other. She still hadn't decided what to say when she reached her building and opened the door.

And Hutch was walking up the corridor, wearing a backpack.

"I'll get the rest of my stuff tomorrow," he said in his polite-stranger voice, face blank, cold. The pressure in the hallway was going to squash her flat—purple and black clouds with sizzle lines.

"Where are you going?" Her voice wobbled and shredded as she forced it out.

"Sean's."

"When will you be back?" Stupid question. Dumb, dumb question.

"I won't."

All at Sea

✦

Three days went by after Hutch left and, oh, how slowly the time passed. Cathy liked old-fashioned clocks with second hands rather than guessing when digital numbers would jump to the next minute. Now. No, *now*. The minute was always too long.

She started getting up at three or four in the morning, turning on the big soft-white light over her easel. She would pull on her old black sweatshirt and set up a piece of Masonite. It was not a project, just laying acrylics on a board. It was not the picture that mattered this time but the escaping. And that worried her—she wanted to be going *to*, not running *from*.

People used to ask if it was lonely living in a lighthouse. She'd always said no. But you didn't understand lonely until you'd been the opposite. If you grew up with no sunshine, drab was normal.

Lonely: adjective: *sad from being alone or without friends.*

Well, Cathy had never felt like that. Art had always been enough. She hadn't needed a person. Before.

She spread the paint without really seeing it, thoughts floating in a no man's land between waking and dreaming. Her hands just did what they always did. Finally, when she saw what she'd painted, it was like nothing she'd ever done in her life. The colours were strange: pale grey-blue, grey-white, and pearl, like a bathroom mirror when the steam starts to turn into water and the glass is a big blur with the light all wrapped up in the steam so you can't tell where it's coming from.

Cathy slept in, didn't wake until her mother phoned and she must have sounded logy, sad maybe, because Mom said Cathy wouldn't feel down anymore when she was home and started listing the reasons.

"...and take a break from packing up and paint something, only paint something you *want* to do, Cathy, not something you *have* to do. You'll feel better." Mom surprised her sometimes.

So Cathy told her about the weird picture and her mom got all interested, probably because Cathy said it was like a dream—Mom and Aunt Dot were big into interpreting dreams.

"Sounds like one of those shiny days in the north," said Mom. "Can't tell what's water and what's sky. Mel says pilots hate that kind of day in the Arctic. No sun, no horizon, no edges—hard to know where you are. Dangerous."

Fancy being in a place where you couldn't trust your eyes.

For class, Cathy always had to be careful with the *way* she painted. Technique. But she was so used to that now, it was almost automatic. It was like sports—if a hockey player had to think about what his feet were doing, he'd trip over them. Maybe that's what art school did; got you to the point where you didn't have to think about your feet.

Anyway, she hadn't thought about technique last night, although she'd changed from a knife to a brush part way through, for some reason. Never before had she painted something without Seeing it first.

Analysis: noun: *a detailed examination of the features or structure of something.*

That was Cathy's whole notion of painting, even if you changed those features, distorted them, changed them into something else altogether. But this painting wasn't seen. It was felt.

Maybe that was what she'd done with Hutch's portrait. The seeing and the technique were there for sure but there were feelings from deep inside too. All mixed together. Maybe that's why it was her best picture ever. She'd always been the observer, an outsider recording what she saw and analyzing from a distance. With Hutch's picture she was involved, part of, together with. Her emotions were in that picture as well as Hutch's.

She was afraid then. Afraid she'd never paint as well again.

+

Cathy looked at last night's picture with new eyes. She could add a touch of ice and cloud, turn it into a seascape, but this was a self-portrait—her mood in paint. So she started a second one, calling them both *All at Sea*. But that sounded muddled, like she wasn't going anywhere. It was not how she wanted to be. So when she had finished the seascape she leaned the two paintings against the wall next to each other and studied them. *It plays tricks with your eyes, with those silvery colours all running into each other and the light bouncing back.* Mom had said that. So Cathy changed the name to *Catching the Light*.

She phoned home to tell her mother and Mom said how she was dying to see the pictures and they'd need a shoehorn to load everything into the truck, and in three days and six hours they'd be in Halifax. And for the first time Cathy started to feel a bit excited about the graduation ceremony and going home.

She began emptying drawers, sorting and throwing: old term papers, a torn T-shirt she'd planned on mending and hadn't, odd socks. She started packing. How much junk she'd collected in four years! There was a shirt of Hutch's at the back of the closet. She stood with it pressed to her face and such a wave of regret rolled over her that the tears came and this time she let them flow. She wore the shirt to bed that night and cried all over again, then scolded herself: *pull yourself together, girl. Get up at a sensible time and have a sensible breakfast and do things. Make plans.*

There was an exhibition to think about at that gallery in St. John's where she'd sold two more paintings last fall, making four altogether. Four paintings before she'd even graduated. She had the dates and the amounts in a little notebook. She would need to sell a lot of pictures to make an exhibition worth the expense but she would risk that. She'd have to stay in town too, for maybe three weeks. Too long to stay with one person. She might crash for a few days with her cousin Annie, who was doing tourism in St. John's now, but Cathy suspected Annie had all kinds of people, male people, staying at her place and Cathy was not sure she could face that.

+

After that one emotional night Cathy returned to the packing with more efficiency, only moving when there was a purpose, only stopping a task when it was finished. She'd gone from a mom style to a dad style. No, that wasn't fair. Mom was always organized, she just threw a lot of flap in the way so you couldn't see it. Emotion. Dad kept his emotions buttoned down so you'd hardly know he had any. Cathy was going to have to do that.

Sarah called, asked how Cathy was doing, enthusiastic as always.

"I called to congratulate you," she said. "Paul's mother, Lena, told me you painted a wonderful portrait of Hutch—"

"Oh, god."

"Oh. Shouldn't I…? I didn't mean to pry. Let's change—"

"No. No it's not that. I'm sorry. That was rude. Sorry. It's just…well, we were together for a while. Hutch and me. Then…." Silence, except for bursts of crackling on the line and a steady soft hum. "Now we're not."

"Oh. Well, I'm sorry about that. If it's made you sad, I mean." More crackles. "It's just that Paul said the portrait was amazing and everyone was saying how fantastic it was."

"It's the best thing I ever did, Sarah, because…because I understand him. A bit anyway. But Hutch didn't like it. Didn't want it on display." Better start buttoning down right now. "And I put it in anyway." Her voice thinned out to a squeak and dried up.

"Oh, Cathy. I'm so sorry. You're upset. I'll call back later."

"No. It won't be any better later. Ever. Hutch is gone. And now there's this big hole…every minute…and it's all my fault." The crackling was almost comfortable, stopped the silences being so silent.

"Well…he might come round. Give him time. It can't have been so very bad. The picture I mean."

"I painted his stump." Big silence. "And…he didn't like me painting that little smile he has—had—for just me. Said it was private."

"Oh. Yes. I see." Even the crackling was holding its breath. "He's a…a manly kind of person, isn't he? Showing…maybe showing how he feels isn't manly. To him."

"He looks wonderful. Everyone says so. But he doesn't—he won't—"

Breathe for god's sake. Don't be such a wimp.

"I can see that he mightn't like his leg on display," Sarah said.

Cathy was nodding into the phone, wanting to say how much she loved him, how she never meant to hurt him, just to tell someone.

"...wouldn't want it pub-lic." There'd been a little hitch on that last bit. "Cathy, I'm so sorry. I know you must find this difficult to talk about. Call me when you can. I want to know how you're doing. I'll be thinking of you." And the phone went dead.

Sarah had started to say *published*, like this was a case study. A visual, in-your-face case study. It was. Just like Sarah. Hutch had said that. *You've done the same to me.* And had Cathy forgiven Sarah?

Proceed With Caution

✱

Sarah stood with the phone in her hand. She hoped Cathy hadn't noticed her slip of the tongue. She knew that tearing feeling of trying to balance one's own needs with those of others and having to choose. Poor Cathy—to finally be close to someone only to lose him. How amazing it was that Hutch and Cathy had been together at all. Athlete and artist, like opposite sides of the brain. And maybe she should have stayed on the phone longer. Cathy wanted to unload some of her troubles but Sarah had not felt up to carrying that load and really she was not the appropriate person—although who else did Cathy have? She drifted over to the portrait Cathy had given her and gazed at it.

Sarah had hung Cathy's farewell painting across from her Tunis picture in the living room because they were both so full of life. They balanced each other somehow. And now on the short wall by the door she hung the other picture, just with thumbtacks, unframed. Nothing permanent.

She and Tim had been on the adoption list forever. Tim had agreed to it back in Mariners Cove because there was plenty of time to consider. Sarah would call each year to reaffirm. Yes, Mrs. Brooks, you're on the list but there's nothing yet. It will be at least seven years, six, five…do you still wish to proceed, proceed, proceed?

Finally, a year ago, they met with the adoption people for long interviews, once together and once each separately. And then the Home Study. The adoption people asked about everything under the sun, and not just Sarah's and Tim's opinions on bringing up children but what their parents' views had been on punishment and education and, and....

"Forgot to ask how often I floss my teeth," Sarah said, growled.

"Thorough. Have to give 'em that."

It was an important hurdle out of the way and made Sarah more hopeful, but it sensitized her again to diaper commercials, to the boys shooting baskets up the street and the little pink bike with training wheels sprawled in next door's driveway.

Tim was more confident in the process after that—confident they would take just as much care with the baby selection. He was more committed to being on the list for a baby, although they'd still have to wait two years, maybe more. He even agreed to be on a second list for siblings, older kids, probably with adjustment problems. But in a far corner of Sarah's mind, pushed back but never quite out of sight, was that little question of whether Tim would back out when the time came. It was a question she didn't dare force, didn't want to face, and it was never quite the right moment to ask. It had always been a decision for the future—the danger tree on the horizon.

But now there were two little boys. She and Tim were taking their time, following the advice of the social worker—a visit every other week to a park or out for an ice cream and lately to their own house. The three year old was a delight but the older one could be difficult and Tim was being cautious. Could he handle stressful nights with these boys and still face a clinic full of complications every day? Could he love them enough? Sarah wanted both boys. Now. "We'd just need to work out how to approach each problem as it arose," she said. "Like Cathy."

"You used to say you were glad Cathy had a mother to go home to and you didn't have to have her all day."

The boys had gone through three sets of foster parents. One set had been open to adopt for a few months then backed out. Sarah could tell it worried Tim, that he was wondering why.

"And what do the children want?" said Sarah.

The social worker said, "They must be given time to decide. They must not be rushed." Sarah asked how they would know and was told, "You will know. It's different for each child but you will know."

Every visit, the three year old asked if he could stay. It hurt Sarah to say just 'til after supper. But finally the older boy drew them a picture—the picture Sarah was hanging on the wall so hopefully: two stick adults and two stick children outside a square house. *Us*, he said.

Storm Front

✦

Cathy put the phone down ages after the line had gone dead. After all the anger and hurt that case study had caused, how could she turn round and do the same to the person she loved most in the world? She needed a walk. She grabbed her jacket and keys, left her bag on the table, and charged down the street almost running. She slowed down when she hit the lunch crowd filling the sidewalks, wound through people without seeing them. They moved so slowly. She stepped on someone's heel and stumbled, said sorry but kept going, leaving the girl hunched over, rubbing her heel and cursing. Cathy sped up, sidestepped onto the road, and there was a deafening blast in her ear and she felt something brush her elbow very lightly, felt a big whoosh of air.

"Watch it, Miss," someone said. "You nearly went under that truck."

The guy looked concerned and Cathy was shrugging it off until she saw the slice out of her jacket arm and turned to see a big garbage truck close in to the curb, flying through the lights, and realized she'd stepped off without looking, without thinking. Holy...better go home.

Later she even managed a tiny smile—a garbage truck. Hutch would say she could've at least picked something with a bit of class like a Mercedes or a Jeep. But maybe he wouldn't now—wouldn't give a flying Ibrow.

✦

Back in the apartment, Hutch filled the whole silent space. She'd wasted so much time. Why did she take so long to realize his grin wasn't a trick? It was just his natural way of smiling and he was a smiley person. He did have a certain smile that said *I like you, you're cute,* but it was just that—a kind of compliment. He was never shy with compliments. And after a certain stage maybe there was a question in it, *waddya think?* Hopeful maybe. Cathy remembered the first time he'd looked at her that way, at the art dance. The first time he'd really seen her.

The phone rang—her supervisor. Her picture had been chosen to represent the college. He sounded so excited, telling her, and she'd been such a damp squib. She felt sorry about that afterwards, but it took a while for the information to sink through all the Hutch feelings. Minutes passed before the excitement started to bubble up and then she wanted to fly out of her building and tell every passerby—*they picked it, they picked it.* What if she won the contest? There was a chance now. She could learn so much and she'd practice and practice....

Then her thoughts circled round to Hutch again. Oh god, she was exposing his picture to even more people and her insides sank and sank. She would split in the middle. Hutch's face was in front of her, eyes serious, staring into hers with that soft look she loved, coming closer, blurring. She could feel his breath and the gentlest touch on her lips and the bristles, grown long enough to lie flat, warmth, pressure. Then he faded away to nothing and it was like a chill.

If she had her time back would Cathy send in that picture? Noooooooooo. Then she saw herself in this tiny apartment with Hutch, moping about because she couldn't display her best work, no chance at that competition—all because of him. She'd be blaming him. Scowling and doing her black cloud act, as Hutch called it. She didn't think she'd be able to hide the resentment—not all the time, not enough. He'd hate that, wouldn't want to be with her anymore. No matter what, she'd have driven him away in the end.

But where did that leave Hutch? She remembered how she felt when he took off with her sketches of Paul, waving her book around and laughing, how they'd all huddled around for a look. She'd felt so helpless, nowhere to run, nothing to do to stop it. She'd hated him then. Did Hutch hate her now?

Her stomach sank. She felt it. Why did scientists say everything was in your head? And romance writers said everything was in your heart. It was Cathy's stomach that called the shots—up in her throat when she was scared, down by her knees when…when the bottom had dropped out of her world. The way she'd felt that day up on the cliffs when she'd thought about jumping. She tried to think back clearly, to really see. When she'd been lying in bed the night after school finished, she'd thought of jumping, but maybe even then it was a little bit in the future, at a distance. She'd never thought of doing something immediate, like going straight down to the kitchen and cutting her wrists. Cathy shivered. There'd been a space between the thought and the action which had grown wider as she'd walked up to the lighthouse. And yet she hadn't taken her painting bag, so she'd meant business. What held her back?

She put herself on that cliff, tried to feel the wind on her face, the freshness, the ozone-spruce-saltiness. And the sunrise, so beautiful even though she had tried to ignore it that day. Imagine jumping out of a plane in a parachute and dropping through that sunrise. Would it be like going through a rainbow? As you floated down would you say to yourself, *that purple just changed to magenta*? That day Cathy had tried to focus on her problems, and the sky was a distraction—beauty maybe? Possibilties? A future?

Things had been black but not completely. They were black now, or the absence of Hutch left big dark shadows. But Sarah had learned to live without children. Hutch had learned to live without his leg. Mom got along without being able to read. Everyone was missing something. She'd just have to manage without Hutch. Her mouth said the words out loud but the rest of her wasn't listening.

Arrivals and Departures

✦

After Hutch walked out he was back to filling every minute and leaving no spaces. He knew the routine, he'd had plenty of practice.

The weekend he left had been easy enough: clearing out the mess so he could settle in, studying, and always someone around for a quick joke. He hated going back to the apartment but he'd left his stuff in a pile by the front door so he just scooped it out fast, threw his two keys on the table, and left. No sign of Cathy. And on Sunday Paul arrived.

They went to Sailors because Sean's place was blocked with people. Paul bought a round and they settled into a table near the back.

"How long are you staying in Halifax?" Hutch asked.

"Home a week Tuesday," said Paul. "Then I'm going to Mariners Cove with the folks."

He hadn't been back since just before the crash. Almost six years. Hutch nodded, kept nodding, smiled a big smile and raised his glass to Paul and they downed their beers together. Paul looked good. The sag was gone. He said art history was fantastic and he was looking into working with archives and museums in Montreal. Loved that stuff.

They chatted about the crowd from Mariners Cove: Hutch's brother Brian and his wife, Lori, were expecting their second; Jack was bringing a girl home for his brother Joe's wedding; Bud was still trying to get into med school; and had anybody heard from Andy?

They sat back without talking for a while then Hutch said, "So. Any interesting girls up at Concordia?"

"Well I've been dating someone for a few months now."

"Yeah?" Hutch stopped in mid-swig, sat up straighter. "Tell me more."

"You might remember her. Laura? That friend of my cousin Amy's."

Hutch grinned and said of course he remembered her and he was jealous. "Thought at the time she was just your style. Cathy said the same thing." And they chatted about Laura for a while.

"So what happened to you and Cathy?"

"Oh, had a fight about art and art won." Then he changed the subject to basketball and had Paul watched any games in Montreal?

Flying Colours

✦

Was Hutch hurting like this? Cathy may have painted him as he truly was in all innocence, thinking only of the how and the what, but she took the portrait into school knowing that Hutch did not want her to. It was a wonder he hadn't thrown the painting out the window.

Cathy wanted to make it up to him in some way. She could never undo the damage but perhaps she could make him feel better somehow. She racked her brains for an idea and finally settled in to paint two small portraits of Jenny and Eugene, about eight by ten inches, on two scraps of board. She had less trouble painting Jenny this time because she was less emotional, at least about Jenny, and she had more technique to fall back on when instinct didn't work. Eugene was easy.

She took them to Sean's house when she thought Hutch might be at school. Sean opened the door, said go on through, Hutch was in his room, but Cathy just passed him the package and fled.

A few days later, in the Internet cafe, she found an email from him. *Thank you. Great pictures. H.* Her heart sped up when she saw it. He'd written. She was afraid he might not. Then she was disappointed at how little he'd written. You could almost see it all without opening it. She read and reread the message but she couldn't stretch it into anything more.

✦

Cathy's parents arrived and she put on a good show. They did all the Halifax tourist sites—Citadel Hill, Pier 21, the historic waterfront, and some galleries of course, and they drove out to Peggys Cove to see the lighthouse. Mom and Dad wanted to see Hutch's portrait but it had been sent off for judging and Cathy found herself wishing they could see it so she could watch their reactions—Hutch's take on it or hers?

"Hutch didn't like that I painted his stump."

"Well, of course he wouldn't," said Mom. "What did you expect?" Silence.

"It's a compliment." Cathy's voice was a bit sharp. "He looks great even with a piece missing."

"Well, girls all have a soft spot for Hutch, so maybe he'll get away with it."

"Why didn't he stop you from painting it in the first place?" said Dad. Cathy didn't answer, couldn't answer. Because it hadn't crossed his mind. Because he'd trusted her.

+

She wore her best pants and the pretty shirt with the scoop neck Sarah had sent her, then the graduation gown. She almost had to nail the board part of the cap to her head because it was so windy on Graduation Day. Mom said it was quite like home. Cathy received her degree, her bachelor of fine arts, up on the stage and they announced her picture would be representing NSCAD at the national competition this year. Cathy couldn't keep the smile off her face then and Mom said she'd clapped until her hands were sore.

A big card was waiting for her when they went back to her building—*Congratulations from Sarah and Tim.* There was a note in it from Sarah saying she would rather have sent flowers but Cathy must be packing up now so she hadn't. And Dad said Sarah deserved congratulations too and that Cathy should send her a card and a thank-you or flowers. Cathy wouldn't be standing here without Sarah. And Mom said yes, do it.

Mom said she'd heard Sarah might be adopting two brothers aged three and five. No, not adopting—fostering. The adoption people made you foster children for a full year before they let you adopt. Nancy Stuckless's cousin lived down the road from Dr. Brooks and had been seeing them with these boys off and on for months, very dark hair and eyes, almost Sarah's colouring. The younger one looked sweet but the older boy threw a tantrum once, right there in the street. He looked like a handful.

"Nancy said she hoped Sarah Brooks knows what she's doing." Mom sounded thoughtful, sad maybe. "But nobody knows ahead of time, do they?"

Setting a Course

✶

Her father was in the departure lounge waiting for his plane to Goose Bay. Cathy and her mother sat in the airport parking lot, all set to drive back to North Sydney, loaded up with Cathy's things. Mom was in the driver's seat. Cathy was ready to read road signs and navigate but Mom said no need, Mel had explained and it was all quite straightforward.

All the way home they talked, adult to adult, about Mom growing up and Dad's parents, and how they'd had to wait years for Cathy to come along and how proud of her they were. Mom talked about working in the fish plant, the cold, wet misery of it, how so many in the community worked there and the being-together and the laughing and joking helped them get through.

It was different from before. Cathy didn't have to force herself to listen, didn't say a private thank god when Mom turned on the news. She enjoyed that whole drive, almost told her about Hutch but held back. Mom might have guessed already about…everything, but as long as it was just a guess she wouldn't give Cathy the big lecture and Cathy didn't want to spoil the day.

But there was more to her mother than Cathy had thought. Mom was like a little junco: keeping her nest cozy year after year, feeding and caring and sheltering. She should have had a nest full of babies.

At home, Cathy sat in the midst of all the mess of unpacking and drew a picture. She drew her mother sitting on the edge of her chair, ready to jump up and get someone a cup of tea. She drew her face looking a little bit excited, like she thought something good was about to happen, ready to join in: eyes wide open, lips on the edge of speech, wanting to be part of it all. Cathy would try to paint her later.

Vivid: adjective: *producing powerful feelings or strong, clear images in the mind.*

Cathy had never thought of her mother as vivid until now. Juncos were just there—all-year-round birds, grey and plump and, yes, a bit drab. But there was that flash of pretty white tail feathers as they flitted around in a group in the snow and there was always one on the top of a spruce tree, singing its heart out on a nice day.

Juncos were Mariners Cove birds: tough, full of life and bustle and song, family birds with sisters and babies. Her mother deserved more than just one awkward misfit like Cathy in her nest.

+

Mom had painted the bench and patio chairs a dark red and had a new quilt on Cathy's bed in a pretty blue and green rolling-waves design that she had just finished. Otherwise the house was the same. The poor cat was gone, but she'd lived to be seventeen. Mom called her latest cat Sir because he thought a lot of himself. Cathy called him The Blob. He had no personality at all. He spent his life sitting between the geraniums on the table in the window washing himself, and if anything startling happened he just slid under Mom's chair. He would never be a flying Ibrow.

What Next?

*

Between time spent with Paul and time finishing off projects and the push and shove of living in an apartment with two other guys, there were no spaces during the day. It was the nights. Hutch would wear himself out, body and brain, so he'd fall asleep easy enough but if he woke in the night.... Sometimes it was a bathroom break from all the beer. Once it was a car alarm that could have doubled for an air raid siren and lasted fifteen minutes. He heard thumps and curses through walls that time, which was comforting in a weird way. But once he was awake with the edge off his sleep, thoughts marched round in army boots.

The hip weakness and back pain were invisible so people didn't see them as a problem—didn't even believe in them sometimes—and Hutch found that harder to deal with than his lost leg. He hated having to stop in the middle of things to change position or be choosey about what he did and how long he did it. Hated not being able to do stuff on the spur of the moment.

But his stump could be seen and measured. And Cathy made a picture of it for all to see. Then she put a stupid wimpy expression on his face to finish him off. Jesus. Hutch sat on the edge of the bed and put the light on, reached for the latest *Popular Mechanics*.

If he just had to deal with the stump alone it would be okay. People danced and skied and skated with one leg—he'd seen pictures of amputees in canoes and kayaks. But they were all in calm water. Yes, he could probably manage his kayak in calm water. He could sit with his legs out in front now, for a short time, but he couldn't lean forwards much beyond ninety degrees, and his balance and trunk strength were only middling. He could never tackle anything challenging and he just wasn't a Sunday driver. If he couldn't handle the wild conditions he loved he wasn't about to paddle round lily pads on bathwater ponds.

But things were getting better over time. He could do more, and more often, and he'd fitted those management tricks into his life so much that he hardly needed to think about them now. And here in the city, being out on the water wasn't in his face. *Dolph* wasn't part of this life. It was when he went home.

The edge of the bed wasn't a comfortable place to sit and he didn't see himself building that sawhorse on page fifteen any time soon. He dumped the magazine back on top of his backpack, flicked off the light, lay down on his back, and twiddled his thumbs.

He rolled over and grunted sorry to the wall when he elbowed it, punched his pillow when he realized. He couldn't believe how much he missed Cathy. He'd been used to living on his own, should have been able to go back to that, no problem. Frigging picture. He'd told her and *told* her and she just went ahead anyway.

He hadn't been serious really when he said that to Paul—about art winning—just said it to shut him up. But now he realized he'd hit the exact truth. Art was part of Cathy, and every time it came down to a choice between art and Hutch Parsons, Parsons would lose. What if she was offered a year's post at something artistic in some faraway place? She'd go. She might think about it for a bit because of him but she'd go.

So if he was offered some interesting computer job somewhere she didn't fancy, would she come? She might. She would if she could take all her art stuff with her. Was he being sexist? Would he take his laptop to her exotic place? What if there was no Internet? No Internet and no leg? Shit, no.

Then he saw her paintings of Jenny and Eugene. Just how he remembered them. Laughing. Fun. It was amazing how Cathy could see into people and show it in paint. Whether you wanted her to or not.

+

Hutch met Paul again on Saturday. They strolled down Spring Garden Road and sat on a bench.

"Saw your portrait in the gallery at NSCAD," Paul said.

"How d'you know about that?"

"Cathy was at the door when I was having a look round our building so we caught up for a few minutes. Told me she'd painted your picture and it was in the gallery 'til the end of the week so I went to see it. She said you hated it."

"Don't hate it. Just don't want it on public display."

"No. I can understand that. But I have to say it's a fantastic piece of work. I can see why she would want to use it for her project."

Hutch folded his arms, looked away.

"And you look great," Paul said. "Should have heard the comments from people at the exhibition. All compliments. Couple of girls saying what a great guy you looked like."

"Go on."

Paul shook his head. "Gospel truth. 'Why is it I never meet a guy with a cute smile like that?' That's what one said. Almost gave them your number."

Hutch grinned and said he wouldn't mind if he had. Then Paul was gone, and time stretched into light years.

Staying on Course

✳

Cathy was home a week and every day she waited to hear about the contest, the internship, wondering about where the winner would stay, what they would do. Then she heard some girl in Edmonton with a Chinese-sounding name had won. There was only one winner, no second place, no honourable mentions, so she would never know if her work had even come close.

She had tried not to think about winning but something inside her had hoped—more than hoped, almost expected—to win. Why else had she felt like she was falling off the cliffs when she heard she hadn't: the pressure in her head, the fast-elevator drop in her stomach? Here you go again, a failure. Cathy sat and stared straight ahead and the tears balled up in her chest but her eyes stayed dry. She'd lost Hutch because she'd sent in that picture and now she'd lost the contest anyway.

Sarah had been so encouraging always. "You can do it! You can do anything you set your mind to." Then she'd been treated like a genius by everyone in her year at NSCAD, and she wasn't. Nobody had been surprised when her painting was picked to represent the school. People even said she was sure to win. She'd let it all go to her head.

After an hour or so Cathy walked through the woods to the light and back by the road and the action made her feel better, the sun on her face, even the gulls jeering, *thought you could win didn't you*? Go ahead and jeer, stupid gulls. This was not the same as failing grade seven. The manager of the gallery in St. John's had agreed to an exhibition whether she won or not. So maybe she wasn't the best in the country, but she was still good. And she was going to be better. Cathy was almost marching by the time she was back at the house.

Never mind the internship. There was going to be an exhibition of her very own work and the whole upstairs at that gallery in St. John's would be filled with Cathy Russell's paintings. This was beyond all her dreams growing up—graduating from art school was beyond them, actually going to art school was her grandest dream back then and even that was something she never really expected. Still, it would have been nice to win that internship…she wondered what the winning entry was like. Was it all that much better than Cathy's? It was called *Far and Away* so it could be a view of mountains or something from outer space. Anything.

+

Cathy called the gallery manager and told him about losing the contest. He just said something in an encouraging voice about stiff competition and plans for the exhibition were still going ahead, just make sure she had that portrait there as the centrepiece, and they discussed the number of paintings and sizes and other mechanical details, and when to bring in all the exhibits.

Then he started talking about an Official Opening and Cathy could picture half the town there—that's what Mariners Cove did for one of its own. They'd see Hutch's stump and this was home, worse than Halifax or Toronto. People *gawping at it.* Here was Cathy, trying to think up ways to make Hutch feel better, and she was about to betray him again in an even bigger way. It was way worse than Sarah. Cathy could not show his portrait.

"Does there have to be an opening?"

"Yes, of course." he said, sounding shocked. What was she thinking? "And you have to be there. People always want to meet the artist. You have to be there for that whole first event. Absolutely."

"Well, I'll be there but I'm not showing Hutch's portrait."

The custodian went ballistic, said he'd started the planning, sent out preliminary publicity announcements *featuring the portrait chosen to represent the NSCAD graduating class….*

He went on and on, finishing with saying, "Don't expect me to do anything for you in future if you let me down now."

Ultimatum: noun: *a final demand or statement of terms, the rejection of which will result in retaliation or a breakdown in relations.*

Oh, god. Cathy needed that manager. And she had to have that exhibition. Oh, god, god, god. So when he finally stopped for breath Cathy said well, all right. She'd loan the portrait to the gallery but she wasn't selling it. He didn't like that either but he accepted it.

"Some artists do that. As long as it's here on opening night."

Cathy spent the next five weeks wondering if she'd made the wrong decision, if she could still change her mind at the last minute. The exhibition was the middle two weeks in August and she prayed the portrait would be too late arriving from the mainland: that the truck would break down, that winds would be too high for the ferry crossing, that they'd have a hurricane, a blizzard, an earthquake…. But as she finished framing and preparing the other exhibits ready for the road, excitement and pride drowned out the worries. Her very own show. The first big step towards being an artist—first independent step.

+

Dot's daughter and family were coming to stay in Mariners Cove with Dot again for a month. Would Cathy like to house-sit in St. John's? In the end Mom came too for a little holiday and they drove to Marianne's together. The portrait was still in transit. Be late, be late, be too late.

They went shopping for an outfit. They went everywhere: big stores, little stores, fancy ones and plain. They were about to give up when Cathy saw it, just like the time she bought the slinky bronze dress. They were passing an unlikely window, full of embroidered denim hats, and at the back was a long jacket, almost a coat. It was every colour in the yellow half of the colour wheel: all the way from purple through orange and round to the edge of green—colours you would never think of putting together except in a flower bed. It was a painter's palette. It was Cathy.

They bought soft beige shoes with a pattern cut out of them, like stencils, and a tiny heel. They were beautiful. Elegant. When she went back to Marianne's house, Cathy hung her jacket over a picture in the living room and arranged the shoes in the middle of the floor where she could see them. She wouldn't have bought them because of the price but Mom said they made a perfect graduation present—walking into the future and best foot forward and all that kind of stuff.

"That outfit will work in any weather. Your coat of many colours." Mom laughed, rubbing her hands together and giving a little shiver. "My daughter the artist."

Choices

Sarah and Tim had those two little boys staying with them. *For a little while.* Cathy didn't want them around, wanted Sarah all to herself so she could explain how she understood about the case study, maybe ask what to do about Hutch's portrait. But when Cathy called, Sarah was all enthused about her meeting them.

When she arrived, Sarah gave her a hug and said, "Never mind about the contest. Those decisions are totally subjective. Maybe the judge just prefers landscapes to portraits. Who knows? And you don't need it. You have this big exhibition coming up. That's so exciting." Another hug and then she was introducing the boys. Yes, but Cathy could have learned so much from that internship....

Now here she was, folded up on the floor with the three year old, Sam, playing with his Duplo. This involved admiring whatever he made, and having whatever Cathy made taken out of her hands and pulled apart. Over and over. The other boy, Craig, was almost six, going into grade one but small for his age. He was out at the front door now, playing with the deadbolt: *click, click, click*. "Craig come and talk to Cathy." *Click click, click*. "Craig come in here please." More clicks then the door opening and shutting with louder bangs every time.

When Cathy first arrived he'd been running up and down the stairs madly and jumping off the second step, which seemed a bit high for a boy that size. Cathy pictured Hutch doing exactly that at the same age and smiled.

Later he disappeared upstairs and they could hear water running. Sarah said there was a damp patch on the kitchen ceiling where he'd put in the plug upstairs one day and left the tap turned on.

"Come up and see their rooms." On the way they paused outside the bathroom. Craig had been washing his hands, turning the soap over and over under the running water until soap suds dripped off his elbows and there was a mound of bubbles up over the top of the wash basin.

"Time to rinse them off now, Craig." It took a lot of cold water before the bubbles were beaten down. *Dry your hands, now. Show Cathy where you hang your towel.*

Cathy pulled out her sketch pad when she was back downstairs and drew a picture of Craig's soapy elbows and the bubbles and his profile. He was back to messing with the front door and Sarah said he often did that when Tim was due home.

Tim arrived and there was the usual confusion of greetings and then it was suppertime. He had brought home some kind of puzzle and after supper he was showing it to the boys at the kitchen table and they were all crowded around, so Cathy left them and sank back into a chair in the living room, pulled out her sketch pad, and started to draw. She'd not had much opportunity to study children this age. Craig had an interesting face. There was something in it she wanted to catch, something...empty? No. Unsatisfied? Closer, but still not right. She wasn't in the mood for dictionaries and anyway a pencil might do it better. She looked up at his face as she drew, then the profile, full face again, then inwards with her mind's eye.

Something touched her arm and when she looked up, Craig was standing so close Cathy was surprised she hadn't noticed earlier. He was gazing at the drawing, perfectly still. More still than he'd been all evening. She paused then continued drawing, but her focus was gone now so she added a final touch or two then tore out that page with great care and held it out to him. Cathy *never* tore pages out of her sketchbooks. He took it like it was something full to the brim, not taking his eyes off it for a second, then walked carefully out of the room.

+

Sarah called the next day to ask Cathy if she'd come and give Craig an art lesson—well both boys but mostly Craig. He'd fallen asleep that night, still with her picture in his hand.

"I'll pay you the going rate for art lessons, I don't expect you—"

"Sarah, after all you've done for me? I'm not taking a cent. When?"

They were not your traditional art lessons with scissors and glue and construction paper. He would get that in school or in group art classes. These were *seeing* lessons: just paper and crayon, pencil when he asked. *Look at it, Craig. See this kettle? Is it straight or round, heavy or light? Hard, soft, smooth...? Now draw it.* He didn't ask how do you draw heavy? He just did it, as a child would, not knowing any reason why he couldn't. It was nothing recognizable but maybe if he thought *heavy* or *hard* it would go into his picture one day. Maybe it was there already in a little boy way.

Cathy couldn't remember her youngest efforts at art. Her earliest memory was her father out painting the shed, giving her a little pot of his paint and a brush and saying go and paint on that rock. So after a few drawing-only lessons with Craig, she started on the paints Sarah had bought. *Now draw with your brush.*

Sarah said he was calmer after those lessons and the calmness lasted at least an hour, which was wonderful. After-school art classes were going on the menu for grade one. But all through Cathy's stay in St. John's, she gave Craig a see-and-draw class almost every afternoon, with a few minutes for Sam. Tim put up a big cork board on Craig's bedroom wall and they pinned up his pictures and Craig gave Cathy a portrait of her with huge snail-shell ears, because one day she had said don't forget ears, and they'd looked at ears in his animal books and on photographs and at Sarah's and Sam's.

Cathy sketched Craig again, but she didn't show anybody this time and kept it in her sketchbook, and maybe there was less of the emptiness, but maybe that was wishful thinking because she so wanted to repay Sarah.

She told Sarah the whole story, about the problem with Hutch's portrait, asked what she would do, but Sarah said only Cathy could make that decision. She wouldn't dream of giving advice for something so personal, so important. But she agreed it was pretty much a choice between love and career. Cathy argued and argued with herself but all the time, somewhere inside, she knew. Mom said the damage had already been done so what difference would this make? Dad was silent on the phone for a long time, so long that Cathy had to ask if he was still there. He said art was part of Cathy. How much did she want to be true to herself and how much to Hutch?

And just as you have green lights all across town when you're early and don't care, or red ones when you're late, nothing at all delayed delivery of Hutch's portrait to Mariners Cove. Mom patted her hand when they heard, made her a cup of tea, and said what did she want to do?

They went home to collect it and Cathy hardly said a word on the drive, and the manager set it up the Thursday before the opening and it did look good. It did. Hutch would arrive home on the middle weekend of the exhibition, so he wouldn't be at the opening. But Cathy wondered if he would come at all, and what he would say.

Fame

✶

The day after Paul left, Professor Barlow called Hutch back at the end of a class. Now what?

"My niece had an exhibit in the gallery at NSCAD recently and I went to see it," he said."I saw a portrait of you."

Hutch didn't know what to say. He looked away, tried not to show anything on his face.

"My wife wondered if you would speak to her class. Grade twelve. She had them over there for a school outing—social studies."

"I'd rather not," Hutch said, all stiff. There was a long silence and Hutch continued to look across the room, avoiding eye contact. "I'm not comfortable with that picture."

Paper crackling. Barlow pulled an envelope out of the top pocket in his jacket and held it out.

"You're free to say no, of course. Please don't feel obliged because of me." He flapped the letter up and down a couple of times. "But I would like you at least to read the letter she sent." More flapping. "If you would."

Hutch looked down at it, kept on looking. Finally he took it and held it by one corner, a little away from himself.

"Thank you," said Professor Barlow and waited for a moment.

Then Hutch collected himself and nodded and walked out. Two days later he had an email from Paul saying he'd heard the portrait had been chosen to go in the contest. His stump was going national.

He left the envelope unopened for a few days then decided he'd better send a polite No. He opened the letter.

...need to know that a young person can lead a satisfying life with a disability, as you obviously do...impressive...overcome...living example....

He grunted and growled about it for the rest of the day and then phoned.

More Fame

✶

So the evening of the exhibition arrived and everything looked good. *Splendid*, the manager said. And everyone Cathy thought might come did come, and they all sounded delighted and proud and there were comments about it putting Mariners Cove on the map and this would show the townies what Mariners Cove could do.

There were also comments in a different kind of voice about how the portrait was "Hutch to a T," and how many pictures Hutch was in, and "Oh, my," and "Well, well," and "Is there something you're not telling us?" How to reply to such questions had kept her awake nights and Cathy had rehearsed and rehearsed. Now she just smiled and said he was an easy person to paint, and yes they'd been seeing each other for a little while but she hadn't laid eyes on him for weeks. He'd be back in the province next week and she hoped he'd manage to come to the exhibition. The more times she said it the easier it became. She was proud of herself.

But there were a few whispers about it not being very nice, painting his stump that way, and they wondered what Hutch thought. "Well he can't have minded if he let her do it, right?" Cathy avoided looking to see who made those comments, tried not to think about them. Of course there were strangers looking around too but Cathy hardly gave them a thought, even though some of them might be actual customers.

There was no sign of Hutch's parents but his Aunt Liz was there with her family. She just said "Wonderful," as she left and Cathy couldn't read her face. The others didn't say anything at all.

Then the aunts arrived. The whole gang. "Fifteen of us for dinner at Rumplestiltskin's last night!" Up until that moment, the only men at the exhibition had been townies or visitors, because it was the middle of the season for guys in the fishery or construction or "off counting blackflies," which was how Hutch described her dad's job in Labrador. But the uncles came. She heard them puffing up the stairs after the aunts.

"Oh, my."

Silence. They'd reached Hutch's portrait.

"My lord. Cathy!" There was shock in that one.

"That's his scallywag face when you don't know whether to kiss him or smack him." That was Aunt Maisie.

Uncle Reg, her husband, chuckled and said that must have been some kiss. And Aunt Gert and Aunt Elsie said, both at the same time, "Hope it wasn't our Cathy."

Cathy's insides were up in her throat and she could feel her face turning red. Then she heard Mom's voice.

"Oh, you guys. They're all friends! There's a picture of Paul Wilson round here too, and Jenny and Eugene."

And next thing they were crowding round the corner, remembering the crash in soft voices, sad, respectful, and soon after that they came to a picture of the aunts playing cards, and that caused a riot and a half.

So by the time they reached Cathy they were full of comments about other paintings and only Uncle Reg gave her the gears. Not that he said anything. He just stood in front of her, clattering that unlit pipe from one side of his mouth to the other like he always did, gripping it in his teeth. But he had a grin and a saucy look on his face. And he winked. Panic. Cathy tried to think what Hutch would do and after a moment she winked back. He laughed out loud round his pipe and gripped her arm for a second then headed for the door. Cathy's knees felt wobbly for ages after they all left.

Sarah and Tim came with Paul's parents and Bud's parents, and Bud came with a gorgeous looking girl with really long hair. Paul was back in Montreal but he'd sent his good wishes and said he loved Hutch's portrait.

Sarah enthused of course and said Hutch should be proud of that picture, not ashamed of it. She said she would bring Craig in one day when the gallery was quiet.

Cathy was awake half that night, from excitement and fright and too much coffee, but mostly because she was wondering how she could face Hutch after this, or his parents, and knowing she'd blown any chance of them getting together again. Ever.

Home Stretch

✶

Hutch met the class in their homeroom in early June. He was not going to talk about Cathy. He was not showing anybody his stump. He wore his interview shirt, even ironed it, walked in with equal steps and all that. Every eye looked at his face and then down at his legs. So what did he expect? They were just a bunch of teenagers.

Mrs. Barlow was a bit dumpy looking and her face was all nose, but she had a beautiful voice with a sort of chime in it. Kind eyes.

"Would you mind telling us what happened to you?"

He felt on parade, stiff and formal. Make it snappy, Parsons.

"There was a bus crash and my legs were trapped under the seat in front. The doctors said the left one was a mess and I'd be better off without it."

There was total silence in the class. There were some shocked expressions but nobody twitched an eyelid and nobody said a word. So Hutch carried on.

"'Course the first thing I said was No. No way was anyone cutting off my leg. And I wasn't very polite." They relaxed a bit then, back to the normal level of fidgets, and there were a couple of nods and some grins.

A big guy in the front said, "So what made you change your mind?"

And suddenly Hutch was back in that bed, feeling like he was tied to the train tracks with a train coming, powerless to stop it, feeling the fear and the horror and that refusal to see, right up to the last second. He had to make an effort to answer.

"They made me look," he said and his heart was racing just thinking about it. "I was flat on my back but they found a big mirror so I could see the splint, opened it up so I could see inside. Then they made me look. Kept saying, *open your eyes, Hutch. Look at it, Hutch.* And finally, I did." He realized he'd had his eyes closed and his whole body was rigid, his hands balled into fists. He let them uncurl and flexed his shoulders a little.

The class seemed paralyzed. The shufflers had stopped their shuffling and the heavy breather on Hutch's right had stopped his heavy breathing. He heard a crow or something whacking a snail on the window sill, whacking and whacking. Then a girl sneaked a hand up and wiped her eyes. There were a few shiny eyes around the room. His heart slowed down and everything went back to normal.

Mrs. Barlow broke the tension. "A dreadful experience," she said. "But you've done so well since. In your final year at Dalhousie. Could you tell us how you got from that point to this?"

So Hutch hitched his rump on the side of the teacher's desk and folded his arms and started to explain. And it was easy. Because these teenagers were the same age Hutch had been and they looked like they understood, like they'd felt that fear right along with him. So he took them through all the steps, the problems he'd had to accept, changes he'd had to make.

"...but now I love computer science and there are so many different jobs in that field and I'm in control of my future again—as much as anybody is. Never thought I would be."

"Do people ask about...?"

"Often people don't realize so I don't mention it. I can usually tell if someone's noticed. Then I tell them yes, I've lost a bit of leg but this works okay."

Hutch tried to think of questions they might feel too awkward to ask. "Sometimes a guy might want to hide the fact that he's missing a leg, at a job interview or if he's dating somebody special. But sooner or later they'll find out. Best to let everyone know up front. And some girls *are* turned off so you need to make sure they're okay with it *before* you get too involved."

There were a few squirms and blushes here and a skinny guy who'd been turning his pen over and over groaned and pulled a face at the boy next to him.

"But I guess it's no worse than anything else that's a bit different: the guy's shorter than the girl or he's got bad acne or he's the wrong colour or comes from the wrong part of town or goes to the wrong church or he talks funny like me." There were a few chuckles at that. "There are all kinds of 'barriers.'"

Kids were nodding. Nobody spoke. The teacher got to her feet and said thank you and Hutch stood, waiting. She glanced round the class asking if there was anything they wanted to add, and most of them just muttered thank you but a girl's voice said his picture was fantastic and another girl asked how he liked being famous. Hutch pulled a face and said not much. The big guy said he bet Hutch hated that picture; he wouldn't want to see himself in a picture like that.

The two girls both said of course he would and other kids called out yes and no and soon everyone was arguing about it and the teacher said calm down and apologized to Hutch and told the kids they were getting too personal and they looked awkward and went quiet. Hutch said it was okay, good to get it out in the open, and he was surprised they all had such strong opinions. The big guy was hunkered down now and his voice was a bit defensive.

"I just don't think anybody should paint a picture of your...of you. Like that."

"Yes, it was hard. The...artist was making me see in the same way Dr. MacPherson made me see. *Open your eyes Hutch. Look at it.*" And Hutch realized that was exactly what she had done. "Cathy said I was a whole person, even with a piece missing, and she painted me that way. Painted me with a stump of a leg and called the picture *A Man.* I think I act like a man. Feel like one anyway." He looked at the class, shrugged his eyebrows, and bunched up his mouth for a second. "Cathy's shown that I solved the problem—or I've come to terms with it—whatever. So I lost half a leg." Another little shrug. "I'm still a man."

Some of the kids were giving the big guy dirty looks, especially the girls.

"Don't feel bad for saying that, buddy. That's how I felt too and it's taken me a long time to look right at it, straight on." And he felt a grin spreading right across his face, couldn't stop it. It stretched his ears, probably met at the back.

+

Hutch started an email to Cathy to tell her that he finally understood that portrait and he wished her well with it, hoped she won the contest. Did he want to say anything else? Was he ready to try again? Ready for the tug-of-war? If he had any sense he'd forget about her and put all his efforts into setting up his own work future.

He did have a few work feelers out. He's sent off applications. One was for the place where he had done his work term in Ottawa. Last fall they'd hinted in a no-promises way that he might want to apply after he had his degree. The other two places were in St. John's and his buddy from Ottawa was applying there too. In the meantime he would have to live on air and water.

He reread the email to Cathy. That was all he wanted to put in writing and it sounded so cold by itself, like it was waiting for the I-love-you bit and he wasn't sure if he did. Well, yes, he was quite sure he did love Cathy but the point was, he didn't want to—didn't want all the strings that went with it. He left the email in *Drafts* for a week then deleted it.

+

He drove to North Sydney at the end of a sunny Saturday in August, singing loudly on the highway with all the windows down. He boarded the ferry, not in the new black truck he'd always dreamed of but in a 2000 Honda Accord, bought with his last work term money and a loan from his dad. The car was previously owned by an old lady who didn't drive in the dark, in the snow, when it rained, and probably not on Sundays. At least it was black.

He stayed at home Sunday night. The folks had heard all about the exhibition. They'd been looking after their granddaughter while Brian and Lori went to a wedding, planned to go see the show next weekend.

"Everybody in Mariners Cove has been asking about you and Cathy," said his mom. "They're asking *us*. And we have to say we don't know a thing."

"I don't know a thing either," Hutch said. They asked a dozen questions but that was all he would say. He headed into St. John's early Monday morning to look for Cathy, made himself sandwiches for the trip and borrowed gas money from his dad. First thing he'd do was drive downtown to the gallery to see her exhibition. Then he'd go see Sarah Brooks. Had to find Cathy.

Driving in St. John's. Jesus. Newfoundlanders would give you their kidney if you asked for it but no way they'd let you out in traffic. And three times down Water Street before he could slide into a parking spot as someone edged out.

The exhibition was on the top floor of a two-storey house. Hutch wandered around the main floor first, getting a feel for the place. The paintings ranged from a still life of a bunch of dead rabbits hanging in a shed, to a nude girl back-on in a bath with claw feet, to weird but interesting green pictures of slob ice off Labrador. There were a few splashy things he didn't go for and some Andy Warhol–type ones.

Customers from a cruise ship in the harbour were asking questions about the Jellybean houses down Cochrane Street, shown in a little townscape. Were those real houses? Did people actually live in them? They sounded Texan, like actors from an American soap opera. They bought an iceberg picture and the manager started wrapping it on a long table in the back room with brown paper and lots of brown tape and hairy string, telling them all about Icebergs He Had Known. He nodded at Hutch as he started up the stairs, a slow old-fashioned nod that would go with tipping a hat.

Creaky old stairs they were, painted dark green at the edges but scuffed bald in the middle. This house looked the same age as his Gramps's old house, with much the same layout. It smelled of old wood and paint thinner with a whiff of exhaust from the street.

And when Hutch walked into the second-floor room his portrait was right smack in the middle with its own special lighting. He stood in front of it, absorbing it. It was wonderful. He looked happy. He looked comfortable with himself just the way he was.

The paintings all shouted Cathy. He could see things through her eyes now—the obvious things anyway: the source of light, the brush strokes, the way she used colours. A few smaller pictures he recognized from Halifax. The larger ones were of Mariners Cove.

He moved closer to examine one with kayaks and realized it was him paddling and Paul and Jenny and the rest. All the old crowd.

Then he noticed that one of the people busy in the harbour in the next picture looked like him too—and in the one next to that. He started looking for himself in each picture and he was in quite a few. Sometimes he was tiny, back-on in a corner or only partially seen in a group, but in most of them he was there.

Just four pictures had no people. Two were of that tree by their building and the other two were called *Catching the Light.* He'd been on the ferry to Change Islands once on that kind of day with the weird light when you couldn't tell up from down.

"Look at the signature on that one." It was the picture-wrapping guy from downstairs. Come to see why he was taking so long, probably. "You're down by the signature." And the man passed him a magnifying glass and there he was, tiny, lying on his side, up on an elbow, below Cathy's name. Without the magnification it just looked like any squiggle under a signature.

"What do the red stickers mean?"

"Sold." The man waved his hand round the room. "There are twenty-eight pictures and nineteen were sold in the first week. The yellow sticker on the portrait of you means it's not for sale. On loan from the artist. I could have sold that ten times over, any price."

"What kind of price?"

"A gentleman yesterday offered three thousand and would have gone higher. He wanted to talk to the artist, to see if he could persuade her to sell. Miss Russell refuses to talk to any of them." He talked like a bank manager, Head Office.

"Does she ever come in?"

"In the afternoons for a few minutes." Good. He'd wait.

The bell over the door clanged and feet thudded on the wooden floor below, a woman's voice saying, "That's it over there." The man excused himself and went down the stairs in an English-butler way, taking his own good time.

"May I help you?"

Voices bounced back and forth discussing whatever *It* was and Hutch went back to his portrait. Yes, he looked comfortable with himself, but it was still embarrassing to be nailed like this. Cathy said she'd just painted how he was, what everybody could see if they looked. But everybody didn't look. Cathy highlighted what she thought was important and made them look, and maybe that was what artists were supposed to do, but she'd highlighted parts of himself he'd just as soon keep hidden. Not just the stump... thoughts. Feelings.

The doorbell clanged again. There were more customers than Hutch had expected even for the tourist season, although most of them would just be window-shoppers like him. Mister was listing off countries where the gallery delivered and Missus kept interrupting, making him say everything twice.

"Very experienced. Never had anything damaged."

Cathy was not embarrassed to display her feelings and hopes. They were all round this room. What if people scoffed? It would not have stopped her. She'd been mocked growing up—he'd done his share of that—and it had never stopped her. She was one tough cookie. And yet, she had been crushed by Sarah's paper. Was life always this tangly?

There were creaking noises from the stairs—tired wood showing its age. A truck started reversing close by, beep-beep-beep, and Hutch wandered over to the window to check on his car. This room was full of Cathy's talent and he felt a rush of pride, of admiration for all that single-minded determination. This is how I see my world, she was saying. And Hutch was in the middle of that world.

A flicker of movement caught his eye and there she was at the top of the stairs, standing still now, looking at him.

Cathy.

Cathy.

Acknowledgements

For background information on multiple topics I thank: Mannie Bucheit for his long-ago life painting class and more currently George J. Casey, Tom Dawe of Teachers on Wheels, Alison Drover, Jon Drover, Susan Finn, Heather Foley, Linda Furlong, Becky Horsman, Mary Lawlor, Cy Power, Jennifer Shears, John K., John R., and Kate Sinnott and Elsie Thistle. Any errors are my own.

I have so many people to thank for inspiration and guidance in the actual craft of writing, starting with Miss N. Dixon, my high school English teacher, my mother, who was first to suggest I become a writer, and my father from whom I have stolen so many humorous sayings.

More recent inspiration starts with Ed Kavanagh and the participants in Memorial University's continuing education creative writing program, now sadly defunct, then the provincial Writers' Alliance mentorship program with Paul Butler, the Piper's Frith Retreat with the so-gifted Michael Crummy, the excellent creative writing courses at Memorial taught by Robert Finley and Lisa Moore, the many talks, seminars, and panels presented by the province's active arts community, and for the annual stimulation of the Arts and Letters Awards.

I thank Annamarie Beckel for her helpful advice and my editors at Vagrant (Nimbus) Publishing, Emily MacKinnon and Lexi Harrington for all their patience.

I salute the Newfoundland Writers Guild for initiating and promoting a cohesive writing group back when this province's writers, especially women, were dismissed and ignored, and for their fifty productive years. Happy Anniversary.

I thank my lovely, lovely family, who never rolled an eyeball when I started writing and have been supportive and encouraging throughout.

Finally I thank my wonderful writing group, the Port Authority, inspired by Lisa Moore after her creative fiction course six years ago. This group has weeded and watered every written thought twice monthly ever since and I thank them all: Sharon Bala, Melissa Barbeau, Jamie Fitzpatrick, Carrie Ivardi, Matthew Lewis, Morgan Murray, and Gary Newhook, with a toast to those who've moved on.

About the Author

Susan Sinnott was born in the UK and now lives in St. John's, Newfoundland. She was awarded the 2014 Percy Janes First Novel Award for her then-unpublished manuscript, "Just Like Always" (later *Catching the Light*), and an excerpt was adapted for inclusion in *Racket*, an anthology of short fiction by the Port Authority writing group, edited by Lisa Moore. Susan has also contributed to the *Newfoundland Quarterly Online*.